THE HONOURABLE MEMBER FOR MURDER

By David Weir

The Honourable Member for Murder
A Motion for Murder

THE HONOURABLE MEMBER FOR MURDER

David Weir

Allison & Busby Limited
11 Wardour Mews
London W1F 8AN
allisonandbusby.com

First published in Great Britain by Allison & Busby in 2026.

A CIP catalogue record for this book is available from the British Library.

First Edition

ISBN 978-0-7490-3379-8

By choosing this product, you help take care of the world's forests. Learn more: www.fsc.org.

FSC
www.fsc.org
MIX
Paper | Supporting responsible forestry
FSC® C018072

Printed and bound in Great Britain by Clays Ltd. Elcograf S.p.A

EU GPSR Authorised Representative
LOGOS EUROPE, 9 rue Nicolas Poussin, 17000, LA ROCHELLE, France
E-mail: Contact@logoseurope.eu

To Mum and Dad

Chapter One

'Chief of Staff?' said Maxwell Murray. 'You want me to call myself Chief of Staff?'

'Time we raised the tone a bit,' said Eliot Oakcroft MP. 'Congratulations, Max. A well-deserved promotion.'

Maxwell looked at the solid dark-oak Toblerone his boss had just placed on his desk. There it was, in gold lettering – *Maxell Murray, Chief of Staff*. Max hadn't the heart to tell Eliot Oakcroft that he'd got his name wrong. Nor was he surprised that Eliot hadn't noticed the spelling mistake; in fifteen years of working as the MP's researcher, Maxwell had never known Eliot Oakcroft to read anything all the way to the end.

'It's not that I'm ungrateful, Eliot—'

'You're doing a damn good impression.'

Chief of Staff, thought Max. In Eliot's head, the title might conjure images of fast-paced *West Wing*-style walks through the corridors of power. In the real world, though, an MP's staffing allowance didn't go all that far, and Max was Chief of Diana Burton. And that, if he was honest about it, more in theory than in practice.

'Just that it seems a bit, well, grand, when my staff amounts to one.'

'Matthew Jobson's got a Chief of Staff and so has Alexander Rattray,' said Eliot Oakcroft, gazing out towards Big Ben, across the street from the window of their 1 Parliament Street corner eyrie.

Ah, we're keeping up with the Jobsons again, thought Max, shifting the Toblerone nameplate quietly behind his in-tray. Rattray and Jobson were MPs whose offices were in the same corner of the same floor as Eliot's. They were younger, smarter, quicker and slicker, and if they'd called their sole assistants Chief of Staff, then he was only surprised Eliot hadn't gone for something like Supreme Commander for the Toblerone. He'd hide the thing properly as soon as Eliot was out of the tiny room the pair of them shared with Diana Burton, before she caught a glimpse of it and split her sides. He checked that Eliot Oakcroft hadn't seen him disguise the generous gift, but needn't have worried. The MP was fully occupied watching his own reflection. His butter-coloured hair was perfectly in place, the shiny lime-green tie thickly knotted at his throat. Like many politicians, Eliot Oakcroft MP always wore a tie of a single colour as that looked better on TV, or so went the theory. It was a theory unfortunately little tested in Eliot Oakcroft's case: fifteen years as Member of Parliament for Middlebury-Mid had not yet put him on the *Newsnight* speed-dial.

'Right,' said Eliot Oakcroft, breaking his gaze at himself with some regret. 'What's next?'

'You're meant to be in the public bill committee on the local government re-rating bill now,' said Maxwell, handing the boss a manila folderful of papers. 'That's Committee Room 14. It's Transport Questions in the Chamber at eleven-thirty, lunch with Sir Brian Charteris at one, and the trade reception at Victoria Street at three-thirty.'

'Busy day,' said Eliot Oakcroft. 'Busy, busy, busy.'

'If you could get back here about two to sign off the constituency correspondence—'

'Back here at two when I'm lunching with Charteris,' said Eliot Oakcroft MP, slapping his thigh in his mirth. He was still chortling, 'Back here at two, indeed,' as he left the office.

'Do I get to be Deputy Chief of Staff?' said Diana Burton, when she'd stopped laughing.

'It was nice of him to have it made for me,' said Maxwell, moving the Toblerone right to the edge of his desk, where Diana couldn't quite see it behind his computer monitor.

'I suppose we could use it as a door chock,' said Diana. 'Was there, by any chance, a pay rise along with this new title?'

'I didn't ask.'

'Max! You're hopeless.'

'I don't think there's any more salary in the budget, actually,' said Max.

'He must be paying you a fortune, then, because he isn't wasting it on me.'

'I'll see if I can get you a bonus.' Max knew that even with his own pay, the full allowance wasn't spent on Diana here at Westminster and Eliot Oakcroft's secretary, Julie, back in the constituency. 'I'll see what I can do.'

'Thanks, Chief,' said Diana, and, not managing not to splutter, sat at her desk to begin going through the morning emails.

For an hour they worked in companionable silence. The office, on the fourth floor of the building on the corner of Whitehall and Parliament Square, was small and square. Space was at a premium in the complex of buildings that provided office space for MPs and their staff in and near the Palace of Westminster. This room, cramped, overfilled and hidden up winding stairways, was nonetheless prestigious, reflective of Eliot's fifteen years' service and the fact that giving him something halfway decent would keep him out of the Whips' Office and from pestering them. The window looked out over the Palace of Westminster and Big Ben. Eliot's desk and a regulation green overstuffed armchair filled more than half the space, with a small round conference table occupying another quarter of it. Max and Diana faced each other across two more small desks. The room was, strictly, too small for three people to work in comfortably, but since Eliot Oakcroft MP rarely returned to it after his morning visit, it more or less worked for Maxwell and one researcher.

Max glanced at Diana working her way through the morning emails – invitations for Eliot Oakcroft MP to attend events or to speak, party bumf, random spam and the outpourings of lunatics. There might even be a legitimate constituency query in there somewhere, on a good day. Her little cap of red hair (not of a colour nature ever imagined) shone in the scant light of the office and her eyes were narrowed in concentration. There was a time when Maxwell Murray would have fallen a little in love with Diana, as, unspoken and usually unrequited, he had in his early years as right-hand man to Eliot Oakcroft MP fallen in love with, in turn, Fiona, Estella, Marina, Emilia and Margaretta, a steady procession of earnestly intelligent young women fresh from university who spent up to a year in Eliot's underpaid and underappreciated employment before marrying a stockbroker or becoming MPs themselves. Indeed, Estella Chamberlain had risen all the way, becoming a particularly ferocious Secretary of State for Law and Order who these days usually pretended she'd never heard of Eliot Oakcroft or Maxwell Murray. It was nothing more than the passage of time that stopped Maxwell falling for Diana: once, he had been the same age, more or less, as the women Eliot chose as his junior researcher; now, at thirty-eight, and after the full fifteen years in Eliot's service, Max minded the gap.

'Penny for them,' said Diana, smiling across at him. 'What

great thoughts is my mighty and powerful Chief of Staff thinking?'

'Coffee?' said Maxwell.

'You can make your own,' she grinned. It was an old joke, a legacy of her first fifteen minutes in the office four months before, when she'd taken Eliot Oakcroft MP by the hand and shown him where the kitchen and kettle were. Eliot had sacked her on the spot for her insolence, but either hadn't noticed she hadn't left or was too scared of her to push the sacking through.

'Let's splash out,' said Max. 'My treat downstairs.'

'Hold on. I'm just going to print something for you.'

'I really don't think this is for us,' said Max, sipping his cappuccino at a table in the Portcullis House atrium, an open space within the Houses of Parliament filled with tables and ringed by coffee stands and cafeterias for MPs, researchers, visitors and journalists. Diana, having outlined her case and handed him an email to read, was leaning eagerly across the table like an expectant puppy.

'Oh, come on, Max. Someone's got to help this poor woman.'

'She's Toby Cuthbertson's constituent. It should be him.'

'And I should be sitting by a pool in Los Angeles sipping a mojito while producers offer me millions for my next movie,' said Diana. 'But meanwhile, back here in the real world . . .'

Max sighed. Diana was right that Sir Tobias Cuthbertson

MP was a slender reed on which a constituent could hang the hope of any action. Though 'slender reed' was also as inapt a metaphor as you could find to describe 'the Brigadier' – Toby Cuthbertson had been found a safe berth in a safe rural seat with a safe 26,000 majority after twenty years of calamitous military service, simply to keep him safely occupied and away from risk of any further promotion.

'Let me read it again,' he said, picking up the email Diana had printed before they came downstairs. He still had no intention of doing anything about it but reading it would buy him time to drink his coffee and get back upstairs before she hectored him again.

Dear Mr Oakcroft, the email began.

My MP Sir Toby Cuthbertson has suggested you may be able to help me. My mother is in prison, convicted two years ago for the murder of my father. She has always denied killing Dad, and, even though the jury convicted her, I've never believed she could have done it.

I realise I may sound like a hopeless case or a crank. But some weeks ago something happened that removed any doubt I might have had about Mum having not killed Dad.

I saw him, walking down the pier at Cromer, you see. I know it was him. I was too surprised, and then too far away to speak to him. By the time I'd run down the pier he was gone. But I did take a picture, which is attached. The police won't take me seriously, though.

They say it could be anyone. My Uncle Tim, my dad's brother, looked at it, but he clearly thinks I've gone loopy.

Mum was supposed to have done it for his money – Dad was a rich man; not super-rich but he ran a successful PR agency. Wherever that money is, she has no access to it, and nor do I, so I can't afford the kind of lawyer who could mount an appeal. The Criminal Cases Review Commission isn't interested either, and Sir Toby suggested you might be able to help because of what he called your sterling work on miscarriages of justice.

Please give me a chance to come and explain all that's happened. You could help me free an innocent woman from prison. You could help me get my mum back.

Yours,
Miranda Cley

'Well?' said Diana, as Max put the printout on the table.

'Let's have a look at this photo of hers,' said Max, with a sigh.

Eliot Oakcroft MP's sterling work on miscarriages of justice had arisen out of a so far misguided hope that he might one day be made a Minister for Law and Order, or, indeed, a Minister for anything at all. After his first five years on the backbenches, he'd begun badgering the Whips about his promotion prospects, and, whether it was the case that his Whips had serious ideas for his future, or possibly just because they needed to keep him busy, they suggested he set up and chair an All-Party Parliamentary Group to make a name for himself. As it happened, the chair of the existing APPG on miscarriages of justice, an elderly MP who had once been a human rights barrister, died the next morning, and Eliot persuaded his weary regional Whip to smooth his passage into the chair as a compromise candidate between the various warring ex-lawyers and journalists who wanted it.

'Does your chap Oakcroft have any experience in the law or the justice system?' the Chief Whip had asked Max Murray after materialising alarmingly at his side in a coffee queue one morning.

'Eliot knows as much about those as he knows about anything,' Max had replied cautiously and not untruthfully.

'I suspected as much,' said the Chief. 'Sounds just the chap to keep them out of our hair.'

Ten years on, Eliot remained the chair of the APPG, frequently asking questions about miscarriage cases and making speeches whenever he could on the need for justice to be done. The APPG met every couple of weeks, attracting ministers, judges, lawyers and campaigners. It wrote reports and made recommendations and raised cases with the Minister for Law and Order. It reported on cases in the UK and, for the sake of MPs and Lords who'd joined it in the hope of a bit of travel, from around the world (the continued existence of the death penalty on certain Caribbean islands was regularly revisited). It was supported by the Bar Council, the Law Society, various campaign groups and, though it didn't always like to admit to it but the cash always came in handy, Fathers 4 Justice.

Eliot himself barely knew when it was meeting or whom it was interviewing or what it was reporting on. But it was, by the standards of these things, a successful APPG that produced serious reports and letters to ministers and sometimes helped to highlight real cases of injustice and right some wrongs. Successes included some suggested changes to the law protecting the rights of those arrested for crimes, and the highlighting of a few high-profile cases where someone had been wrongly imprisoned. Like any good APPG, it was as good as its active MPs and Lords, and like any great APPG, it was as good as the secretariat who made its meetings happen and wrote its reports. That secretariat was, of course, Maxwell Murray.

'The police are right, Diana,' said Maxwell Murray, squinting at the photograph on Diana's PC screen. 'This guy could be absolutely anyone.'

He was looking at an over-lit digital shot of Cromer Pier from a distance and from the esplanade above. By an ice cream stand, holding two cones, a slim man of maybe forty-five with dark curly hair, a tanned face, sunglasses and a white polo shirt had thrown his head back, laughing at whatever his companion, younger, blonde and slender in a summer dress, had just said. It was a full-face shot, but at that distance it blurred into pixels when zoomed up to fill the screen. Max flicked from the picture to the online news photographs Diana had found of Charlie Cley, businessman and murder victim, and could see dark curly hair and a square, serious face in some sort of official portrait. It could be the same man. It could also be any of a hundred thousand or so others.

'Eliot should meet her,' said Diana. 'A meeting can't do any harm.'

'We'll need a lot more than this to convince him,' said Max.

Diana smiled him a winning smile. She reached for her mouse and clicked to a new picture. The face of a seriously beautiful woman in her early twenties smiled out at Maxwell Murray, black hair and a knotted silk scarf framing high cheekbones, olive skin and sparkling dark eyes.

'I reckon we can talk Eliot into seeing Miranda Cley,' said Diana.

The apparent kidnapping of Charlie Cley had been headline news, not least because of the television appeals his beautifully distraught, tearful wife had made for information on his whereabouts. Charlie had disappeared while driving his Porsche home from the offices of his PR firm in Kensington to the ivy-covered, honey-stoned former Norfolk rectory where he, Rebecca and their daughter Miranda had lived for two decades. He'd been a man in the prime of a perfect life – rich, healthy, happily married, and shortly to float on the stock exchange the firm he and his brother, Tim, had set up in a Hackney attic above a newsagent's shop and turned into an international agency. He'd driven off from Kensington at 5 p.m. for a weekend's relaxation, and had never been seen again.

No one was quite sure who first suggested Charlie might have been kidnapped, but when that story broke in the tabloids, Rebecca and Miranda discovered how much appetite there was for pictures and television appearances by attractive women whose relatives had gone missing. The police, in time-honoured fashion, assumed Charlie had done a runner, especially once brother Tim, Charlie's business partner, revealed substantial holes, inexplicable to him, so he said, in the company's accounts.

Over the next few days, Miranda and Rebecca anxiously waited for a ransom demand, but none came. Then a dog-walker in Wicklewood Forest, less than twenty minutes away from the Cley family home, came across an unlocked and abandoned silver Porsche with rusty stains on its white leather seats. DNA tests revealed the blood was Charlie's, and the police in another time-honoured ritual put Rebecca Cley on TV again to appeal for information on her husband, while looking for enough evidence to arrest the wife for offing him.

And then, the bombshell. Patrick Alderton, their nearest neighbour but three, informed the police that he had been having an affair with Rebecca Cley and that she had told him she wanted to divorce Charlie but feared she might have to kill him to be rid of him without financial loss. Rebecca was arrested the same night. The jury did not believe her insistence that she'd barely ever spoken to Patrick Alderton, far less slept with him or told him any such thing. Emails from Charlie to his brother Tim suggesting that Rebecca, a qualified accountant, was dipping her fingers in the company till came to light at the trial. Irregular transactions from her bank account that seemed to suggest she was siphoning money away from her missing husband put the tin lid on it as far as the jury was concerned. They spent less than an hour unanimously finding her guilty.

'Not absolutely the sort of thing the APPG was set up to do, Maxwell,' said Tony Wenhamville. 'More a forum for discussing policy than investigating individual cases, you know.'

'I know, but there is the smell of a potential miscarriage,' said Max. The Peers Guest Room at the House of Lords overlooked the River Thames and was dotted with small round tables for quiet conversations and comfortable red leather sofas for afternoon naps. It was the hour at which the peerage of England, or at least that bit of it that still had seats in the Houses of Parliament, put its feet up over a scone and an afternoon cuppa. Maxwell Murray and Tony – Lord Wenhamville of Cheston Mortimer, to give him his official title – sat in an alcove by a window with a white china pot and two delicate cups between them.

'A great deal more than potential, I believe,' said Tony Wenhamville. 'I took the liberty of calling old Samuel, the trial judge, when you told me you were interested in this. He recalls no more than circumstantial evidence against Rebecca Cley, thinks the absence of a body meant the case should never really have been brought.'

'That's not what he said in his summing up,' said Max, who had spent the day since his coffee with Diana reading up on the Cley murder case.

'Of course not,' said Wenhamville. 'Due process, law perfectly clear. Not a thing he could do once the jury came to a verdict, either. No wriggle room on murder.'

The APPG had considered campaigning against the mandatory sentence for murder in English law – the only sentence where the judge has no discretion to keep the sentence down a bit if he thinks the jury's got it wrong or special circumstances apply. But since most of the English public took the view that anyone other than themselves should get life or permanent exile for queue-jumping, the political will simply didn't exist for making politicians and judges look even softer on crime than they were already thought to be.

'No room for an appeal on grounds of process,' Tony went on. 'But, *entre nous*, old Samuel knew the case stunk to high heaven and Mrs Cley's defence team were incompetent from the beginning.'

Tony Wenhamville had earnt his place in the House of Lords by rising through the ranks of judges until he sat on the Court of Appeal. He also happened to have been a close friend of Max's dad since they were both young barristers competing for the same pupillage in Gray's Inn Court. Now retired and aged seventy-four, Tony was as sprightly as ever, a slender man whose limbs seemed to jerk as he walked as if he were being manipulated by a puppeteer, and whose untameable white hair sprang from his head in all directions, freed at last after forty years on the bench and at the bar from the confines of a wig.

'You may very well be right that this poor woman shouldn't be anywhere near a prison cell,' he went on, sipping his Earl Grey tea, taken with lemon. Max, who preferred milk even in Earl Grey, was taking his black for fear of offending the old man's sense of propriety. Tony Wenhamville had become a dear and close colleague in the past seven years since he'd joined the APPG, but Max had never quite forgotten Wenhamville's shudder at the sight of Eliot Oakcroft MP wearing a pair of brown shoes with a blue suit. Having a former Appeal Court judge on the group gave it weight, and gave them a channel to other senior judges and lawyers and police officers. Eliot Oakcroft MP might do all the public appearances that went with the group; Lord Wenhamville of Cheston Mortimer opened doors behind the scenes. 'Old Samuel's quite unrestrained in his contempt for your Mrs Cley's barrister,' he said, 'thought the chap could have got Mother Teresa convicted of shoplifting vodka. Jury hated him, apparently. Surprised Mrs Cley couldn't afford better. Rich woman, wasn't she?'

'She thought she was, but when her husband disappeared she found all their savings had been transferred into accounts she didn't have access to. The house was mortgaged to the hilt. Legal aid wasn't available because of her theoretical wealth.'

'So she ended up with Desmond Wedge KC, and may

God have mercy on her soul,' said Wenhamville. 'I've always thought the sentencing guidelines should knock three years off any sentence for anyone defended by old Wedgey. All the same, Max, right or wrong, we're not really here to investigate individual cases, are we?'

'We've written to the Secretary of State for Law and Order and the Lord Chancellor about others.'

'Fair enough, but in this one, however unsatisfactorily, we have a perfectly fair trial and no grounds for appeal. There's no public clamour for this woman to be released. The apparently dead husband has never turned up.'

'His daughter believes he has.'

'You trust her?'

'Haven't met her yet. Eliot Oakcroft's meeting her tomorrow.'

'Is he?' said Wenhamville, steepling his fingers. 'Is he, indeed? Pretty girl, by any chance?'

Max sat back as the old man looked into space.

'Look,' said Wenhamville, 'there's no harm our asking a few questions about this, if we do it discreetly, eh? There's clearly some judicial doubt about this conviction, even if there's no legal doubt I can see. I'll have a word with George in the Attorney General's Office, see if there's any info there on this one. And if you've the time to sit here for half an hour, I'll try to have Allan West drop by.'

'Thanks, Tony,' said Max. He loved the way Tony Wenhamville could casually mention people like Allan West, as if the man weren't the recent ex-Commissioner of the

Metropolitan Police. 'If I can tell Eliot you're content with us making some enquiries?'

'You can tell Eliot Oakcroft anything you like, Max – in one ear, out the other, as you know better than anyone. Don't let him promise this girl too much, though, will you? Don't get her hopes up too high.'

Chapter Two

'I don't suppose Eliot ever came back to sign the constituency correspondence,' said Max when he returned to the office an hour and a half later. Diana was putting papers into her shoulder bag, preparing to go home. 'I did them myself,' she said, pointing to a pile of thick cream envelopes in the out-tray by the door. 'I'll drop them in the post as I go.'

'You really shouldn't forge his signature, you know,' said Max.

'Someone has to. I texted to remind him, but no reply.'

'You could have paged him.'

'Paged him?'

'Eliot still carries his pager.'

'In case someone calls him from 1986?'

'And a Nokia. And a BlackBerry, I think.'

'What? He charges all these things and carries them about with him?'

'He likes to keep in touch.'

'I think my irony-meter just melted,' said Diana. 'Now, does my Chief of Staff fancy buying the inferior orders a drink while he tells her where he's been all afternoon?'

'Yes,' said Max, surprising himself. He should do another hour or two's work to clear whatever emails had accumulated all afternoon, and prepare Eliot's schedule and papers for the morning. But it could all wait. He was tempted, often, not to bother typing Eliot a schedule and arranging the necessary papers, just to see how the MP would cope, but it was a temptation he always managed to overcome, even if it meant getting into the office around six the following morning. 'Yes,' he said. 'A drink. But let's do it off the premises.'

'Very secret squirrel,' said Diana, arching an eyebrow at him. 'You do know how to intrigue a subordinate minion.'

For a moment after they had walked out onto Whitehall, Max was at a loss where to go. The Houses of Parliament operated like a little village isolated within the greater London, with its own restaurants, coffee shops and bars. The place even had its own barbershop. Max realised with momentary horror that he'd almost entirely forgotten what pubs were nearby; he always went to one of the internal bars for the occasional end-of-day drink – Central London drinking at northern mill town prices, too. Why benchmark your prices against the local pubs when the Wetherspoons in Warley was so much cheaper?

'Come on,' said Diana, pointing across Parliament Square. 'Let me show you London.'

The Westminster Arms, across Parliament Square and down the road from Methodist Central Hall, had a small ground floor where civil servants, reporters and politicians stood gossiping at the end of the day. Its basement, though, had small booths, theoretically for serving food. Diana placed Max in a booth and fought her way back with a pint of bitter for herself and a large Chardonnay for him, with an efficiency Max would never have managed for himself. Diana had shared the office with him for four months, but he felt like he'd known her for ever, not least, but not only, because she closely resembled in so many ways the long line of Dianas who'd come and gone through Eliot Oakcroft's office in the past decade and a half.

'So, my Chief of Staff,' she said, as she slid in beside him. 'Talk turkey. Spill the beans.'

'Could we agree that you never again call me Chief of Staff or yourself a subordinate minion?'

'Nope, Chief,' she said. 'You've caught the boss's eye and you must take the consequences. Mere 'umble mortals such as myself, no better than we ought to be and knowing of our place, will be privileged to call you Chief from now until the end of time.'

'Until the end of your contract, you mean,' said Maxwell, then wished he hadn't as he saw the girl's face fall.

'You won't be renewing me?' she said.

'I'd renew you like a shot,' said Max. 'I just assumed you'd move on.'

'Why would I do that? Why would you think that?'

'None of Eliot's researchers has ever done more than the contracted nine months.'

'Does he fire them? Is he firing me?'

'No. They just leave.'

'Well, I can see how working for Eliot for ever isn't a viable career plan, no offence intended.'

'I'm not entirely sure you've grasped the full meaning of that phrase,' said Max.

'But I'm not aiming to quit in October. I love this job.'

'Great,' said Max. 'You're great at it.'

'We could really make a difference,' said Diana. 'We could achieve things in this job. So, spill. What's going on with the Rebecca Cley case?'

Max looked at the young woman beside him. Diana was twenty-eight, her curriculum vitae perhaps a shade imprecise on the period between studying politics and economics at Southampton and being the only remotely plausible applicant to fill the role as Eliot's junior researcher. Whatever it was she'd done between times, she'd immediately turned out to be quick and efficient, always ahead of him and Eliot in knowing what news was breaking. (Max had never quite mastered social media; Eliot Oakcroft often proudly announced that he had neither Twittered nor Tweeted and had no intention of ever doing so.) She was also sharp at seeing the political implications of new policies, stories or simple gossip.

'Tony Wenhamville gave me the go-ahead to make some enquiries,' he said. 'He's finding out what he can from the judges – they didn't think Rebecca should have been convicted. And he got me a chat with Lord West.'

'You should always take someone with you to chats like that,' said Diana. 'You could really do with a decent note.'

'There's nothing more likely to make Allan West clam up than a researcher with a notebook,' said Max, grinning at the unsubtlety of her attempt to get in on any important meeting. 'Anyway, he told me the police weren't entirely convinced Charlie Cley had been kidnapped, thought it was some scam to run away from debts his company was running up. Began to be suspicious that Rebecca, the wife, was in on nicking company funds from Tim, the brother. Only then the car turned up covered in Charlie's bloodstains, and they abandoned the idea he was doing a quiet runner. Then, when the neighbour, the odd-job man Alderton, told them about the affair Rebecca Cley was having with him, the local superintendent thought it was game, set and match. They stopped looking for anyone else. Corners were cut, Ts uncrossed, Is not dotted. Lord West said a few senior coppers down there are quite happy the Criminal Cases Review Commission won't touch it. Some stones to overturn, he reckons.'

'Brilliant,' said Diana. 'So what do we do next?'

'That's the weird thing,' said Max. 'After he'd told me all

that, West went off to the bathroom—'

'You don't have to give me every detail,' said Diana.

'And when he came back, he told me not to touch the case with a bargepole either. Wheels within wheels, he said. Apple carts to upset. Tread carefully in case of disturbing the undergrowth.'

'What does all that bollocks mean?'

'I think he was hinting that we should butt out, in case we interfere with some sort of investigation into what's going on.'

'Oh,' said Diana.

'He seemed to be hinting that the existence of this photo Miranda took might be making them take another quiet look locally.'

'Locally,' said Diana. 'The force that fitted Rebecca up in the first place is marking its own homework.'

'Thing is,' said Max, 'normally, I'd take a nod and a wink from the country's most senior ex-police officer as absolute word to steer clear of this one.'

'Normally?' said Diana.

'Thing is,' said Max, 'his phone pinged just before he went off to the loo. And I didn't believe a word he said when he came back.'

A quick drink had turned into three and Max had learnt more about Diana in a couple of hours than he had in the four months they'd been working together in the same small room. Inevitably, he'd asked whether she planned to be an MP herself.

'I don't know,' she'd said. 'I'd really rather do something where you can achieve stuff and change things.' She put down her pint glass and paused a moment. 'What about you?'

'Oh, no, no. No. Not me. I'd be a hopeless MP.'

'You'd be great.'

'Thank you.'

'Well, you'd be better than Eliot anyway,' she said.

'Thank you,' said Max.

'Though, since Tinky-Winky, Laa-Laa and Po would give him a run for his money, that isn't saying much for you.'

'I should formally discourage you from being rude about your boss, and mine, behind his back,' said Max.

'I'm perfectly prepared to be rude to his face,' said Diana. 'I'll get the drinks in. And you, think about being an MP.'

Max watched her make her way to the bar, finding her way confidently through the men grouped there, talking loudly at each other. She didn't know that he had once imagined himself an MP. More or less straight from university, a spell in the party's research department, a place on the candidates A-list. Shortlisting for three separate seats, in two of which he'd been the reserve candidate. In the first, he'd lost out to an Etonian who'd since exchanged his seat in Parliament for six years at Her Majesty's pleasure for tax fraud. In the second, a local councillor had proved the value of knowing everyone on the selection panel. And in the third – well, Maxwell didn't like to think about his third failure to impress a selection panel, or about Estella Chamberlain, a former colleague in Eliot's office, and, yes, a former girlfriend, who'd beaten him at the post and now seemed to find Maxwell Murray invisible. Estella's career since then had matched her name, too: two years as backbench lobby fodder, then junior ministerial posts and now Secretary of State for Law and Order. An ironic title given her attitude towards justice in competition.

'Bitter?' said Diana, pushing a pint across the table towards Max. She'd brought back a tray with two pints and two glasses of white wine on it.

'Mine was the white wine, actually,' said Max.

'Yeah, but if ever a man needed a rapid pint down him, Max, it's you. Down in one?'

'What?'

He watched Diana sink a third of her pint in one gulp and signal him to do the same. Ten seconds later both their pint glasses stood empty on the table, and she was pushing a white wine at him.

'So,' she said. 'Tell me why you're not an MP and Estella Chamberlain's in the Cabinet?'

'How do you know about Estella Chamberlain?' said Max, shocked by her directness.

'Everyone knows about you and Estella Chamberlain, Max, but no one knows what really happened. First thing the researcher's grapevine told me when I came to work for you.'

'I'm not entirely sure I like being researcher grapevine gossip.'

'Don't knock it, Max. Everyone says you're the best boss in the party.'

'How come I always find it impossible to recruit from within, then?'

'Who is it we work for again?' asked Diana. 'Everybody wants to work with you.'

'But no one wants to work with Eliot.'

'No one who wants a career,' said Diana, cheerfully. 'And everyone knows Estella done you wrong. What's the story, Max? You can tell me.'

'You and the researcher grapevine?' said Max. 'Estella and I were colleagues, we were friends, we were candidates for the same seat. She won, I lost.'

'OK, Mr Straight Bat,' said Diana. 'So how come you never stood for another seat?'

'We're not all Hamlet or Macbeth, I guess,' said Max. 'I found I like it behind the scenes. Making things happen without having to worry about every word I say, everything I wear, everything I do making it into the newspapers.'

'You trying to tell me Eliot Oakcroft is Hamlet? Or is it Estella who's Lady Macbeth?'

'Eliot's my boss, Diana, and I'm yours. Don't push it too far.'

She stopped smiling and looked away from him into the wider bar. 'You're way too good to be Eliot Oakcroft's bag carrier, Max, and you've been doing it fifteen years.'

Maxwell Murray had been Eliot Oakcroft's researcher for only three years when Estella Chamberlain arrived in the office. On equal grade and equal pay, the two of them had worked well together and begun a brief affair when the inevitable happened. A winnable seat in the West Midlands was looking for a bright young candidate, and both of them were on the A-list. They'd agreed it would be a fair fight, no hard feelings whichever of them won, commiserations if they both lost to the local candidate who joined them in the final three. They'd travelled to the constituency together but booked separate rooms in the hotel. Lunch with the local chap had been enough to tell them one of them would win, since he barely knew which end of his spoon to eat soup with. A long afternoon in Max's room seemed the ideal preparation for the evening selection meeting.

When Max woke from his post-coital doze, his first thought was the alarm clock by the bed. Only 6 p.m., the clock said – plenty of time to get to the 7 p.m. meeting. Estella had gone, back to her own room, he assumed, as he stretched and yawned and looked at the dusk beginning to settle outside the Premier Inn. He'd even, he thought, considered simply not trying too hard at the selection meeting – he was the more experienced candidate, and Estella had spent the entire day telling him so and hoping she'd have another decent chance soon. He'd even considered taking his foot off the pedal to let her win, knowing how badly she wanted to be an MP. And then he realised that it shouldn't be dusk at 6 p.m. and began to shake the clock.

It wasn't just Estella that was gone. Estella who'd turned the clock back. Estella who'd taken his overnight bag with her, and his suit and shirt and shoes. His laptop, with his speech and all the details of where the selection meeting was taking place. His wallet. His phone. The staff of the Premier Inn were well trained and efficient, but their training did not extend to getting an entirely naked man with no means of paying his bill or contacting anyone to a constituency selection meeting that had started half an hour ago.

Late that night, in the back of a mate's car and a borrowed T-shirt and jeans, Maxwell Murray realised that he simply didn't have what it took to be a Member of Parliament.

It was after nine when Max left Diana at the Westminster Arms to go home to his flat in Westbourne Park. He knew as soon as he let himself in that someone else was there.

'Ronni?' he called, steeling himself against finding some burglar barrelling out of the living room at him. Then the smell from the kitchen told him it wasn't likely a burglar was cooking something involving tomatoes and basil.

'Ronni,' he said, turning in to the galley kitchen. 'I didn't know you were coming.'

'And I didn't know you'd be reeling home from the pub at this hour, Maxwell Murray,' said Veronica Murray. 'Hot date?'

'Work stuff,' said Max, accepting the hug Ronni was offering.

'Makes Max a dull boy,' said Ronni. 'Hope you haven't eaten.'

Max had always loved how much Ronni could make a simple pasta sauce taste like food for a king. She stood five feet two in her socks, blue jeans and untucked red shirt.

Her black hair was shoulder-length, but characteristically tied back in a ponytail. As she turned back to her cooking, Max watched the quick, efficient movements, a body full of energy, and not a joule of it ever wasted. She was as unlike him as anyone could be who shared parents and an upbringing.

The Westbourne Park flat had belonged to their father, a judge, until they inherited it when both parents died in a car crash in France. Max had been seventeen, Ronni fourteen. They'd briefly shared the flat during his university years at Oxford, then hers at UCL, after they'd sold the family home in Hampshire. Max had long bought her out of the flat after she'd decided to spend most of her life abroad, but she kept a key and stopped over whenever she was passing through London. She was a journalist but no risk to Max since she worked as a freelance foreign correspondent, almost always somewhere else. In fact, she'd told him once, she'd rather die than do political journalism – gossip about people no one's ever heard of and typing up the press releases handed out by the Government's press officers, she'd called it; she wasn't always far wrong.

Max hadn't heard a word from her in weeks, but, as they ate the pasta, felt as if having supper with her was the most natural thing in the world. The round dining table in the bay window of his living room had had to be cleared of files, papers and books before they could set it. He realised he hadn't eaten a meal at home off a table since Ronni had last stopped for a couple of nights, maybe three months before.

He realised no one but he had eaten a meal in the flat since then either. Ronni, as she always did, had made enough for four and a salad, and had a bottle of red on the go. Max poured himself a glass of water, and Ronni acknowledged that as she refilled her glass.

'Don't worry, Max,' she said. 'You can have your life back in a month or so. Honduras for two months for me from then.'

'I'd get tired of all the travel and glamour.'

'I get tired sitting still. And who needs glamour when you've got Eliot Oakcroft?'

'Not tonight, please,' said Max. 'I can take a lot of ribbing about working for Eliot, but could we leave it out for tonight?'

Ronni put down her fork and put out her hand. She led Max to the sofa in the centre of the room, again clearing policy reports and papers and a newspaper to make space to sit. Max winced slightly as she stacked them on the floor nearby. To her, they may have looked like a disorganised pile lying there; to him, they did now that she'd moved them higgledy-piggledy, jumbling the order he'd left them in. They sat at either end of the sofa, using the armrests and cushions as back supports, their feet stretched out around each other.

'Sorry,' she said, 'I was only taking the piss.'

'I know, I know. I'm just tired.'

'Who were you in the pub with?'

'A colleague. Her enthusiasm and belief we can achieve something began to get me down.'

'You are sorry for yourself,' said Ronni. 'Want to tell me about it?'

'Nothing, really,' said Max. 'I've got a new researcher.'

'You've always got a new researcher, Max.'

'This one might stick around, if I don't disappoint her.'

'Max,' said Ronni, refilling her wine glass again. She offered him the bottle, but he smiled and shook his head. 'Max, they don't leave because you disappoint them. You work for an idiot.'

'He opens doors for me. He lets me get things done. We've got a case, a woman in prison for a murder she probably didn't commit. Only, Diana's so eager, so enthusiastic, so naive about how much we can do to get her out. I don't want to let her down.'

'She's young?'

'Twenty-eight.'

'You're not . . . ?'

'No, we're not, and I'm not interested in her. Not that way, anyway.'

'OK, so we'll turn to your love life later. We might need a laugh.'

'Ha, ha.'

'So why's this one under your skin?'

'She's nosy. She asks a lot of questions.'

'About what?'

'About me.'

'And you don't like the answers?'

'No,' said Max. 'No, I don't think I do.'

Chapter Three

Max felt the effects of a long night talking with his sister when he caught the Underground at six o'clock the next morning. Inevitably, there had been a second, OK a third, portion of Ronni's pasta. Inevitably, she'd opened another bottle. Almost resignedly, Max had added a few glasses of Rioja to the white wine and beer already swilling around his stomach. It was no way to mark a Tuesday night, especially when the office would be calling first thing.

He got off the Tube a stop early to walk over St James's Park to Westminster, clear the cobwebs away. He loved the park early in the morning, its peace before the tourists would disturb the ducks and squirrels, the absence of any more traffic than the odd runner or a cyclist on the way to early work. He cut across the park and down the grand street where the Foreign Office and Treasury faced each other, past the statue of Robert Clive with a carving so ornate it suggested to those with less than 20/20 vision that the nineteenth-century Indian governor was called Olive. Across Whitehall by the Cenotaph and into the complex of parliamentary buildings via what looked like an ordinary office door on the corner of Parliament Street. Once through that door, a passholder had access to the entire enclosed estate, and Max took the lift to the fourth floor, too early to drop by the Vote Office for an Order Paper or the Portcullis House café for a coffee.

He enjoyed having the office to himself, wanting to get his head down before Diana Burton or Eliot Oakcroft made their appearances. Typing up Eliot's schedule, he noticed that Diana had arranged for Miranda Cley to meet Eliot in Portcullis House at 11 a.m. Quick work. He was surprised to see that Miranda would be accompanied by Tim Cley, presumably the Uncle Tim she'd mentioned in her email, her dead father's brother and business partner. It made sense, he supposed, to have Uncle Tim along too, and it would help if the whole family was on board with raising questions about Rebecca Cley's conviction and imprisonment. He pulled together a file of documents about the case – Miranda's original email, the photo, newspaper clippings on the murder and Rebecca's trial – then typed out a half-page note of key points for Eliot to scan before the meeting. Eliot liked to carry a folder of papers to his meetings. He'd even scrawl some notes on them beforehand. Once, disposing of a folder after a meeting with a constituent about a planning dispute,

Max had checked what sort of thing his boss found it worth noting ahead of a meeting. Eliot had reminded himself to get a bet on for the St Leger and practised his signature half a dozen different ways.

When he'd finished all that had to be done, Max slipped out of the office and walked downstairs, avoiding any chance of meeting Diana or Eliot Oakcroft as the lift opened. Why it was that a fuzzy head and a bloated stomach would be improved by the grease and stodge of a full English breakfast was one of the wonders of the world, but it somehow seemed an essential thing to do. Fortunately, House of Lords catering was firmly fixed in a prelapsarian age before the invention of health food, *MasterChef* or any vegetable that wasn't a carrot or a pea. He found his way to the Lords cafeteria, less likely there to meet anyone he knew, and settled himself at a corner table with a plate piled high and a black coffee. He was absent-mindedly spearing a bit of black pudding and reading *The Telegraph* when Diana slipped into the seat opposite him.

'Morning, Chief of Staff.'

'Don't start that again.'

'Sorry! Here,' she said, pushing a bowl of yoghurt and berries at him.

'I've got breakfast, thanks.'

'That's no meal for a man your age and weight after a night on the tiles.' She pulled away his half-eaten fry-up and put the yoghurt bowl in its place. 'Think about your ventricles. Give your arteries half a chance.'

'I did not have a night on the tiles.'

'Have you looked in a mirror this morning?'

'I don't shave in the dark.'

'You shaved?'

Maxwell ran a finger along the line of his jaw. Ah! This was why he kept an emergency shaving kit in his desk.

'Eat your yoghurt, Chief,' said Diana kindly, and carried his uneaten fry-up away to the clear-up zone. Max took a spoonful and found a blackberry bursting in his mouth, filling it with sweet juice. How or when the idea that a piece of fried fatty dead pig tasted better than a blackberry had entered his head, he didn't know, but not for the first time, he realised it was wrong. He'd eat fresh fruit for breakfast every day in future, he decided on the spot. He'd start tomorrow. Or at the weekend, maybe, once he'd had a chance to get to Waitrose.

Diana returned with two white mugs of black coffee.

'Why are you here?' said Maxwell.

'Why is any of us here? What's life all about?' Diana was waving an airy hand, adopting the tone of a university professor with fifty minutes of unprepared lecture to fill.

'More specifically,' said Maxwell, 'why, when you have work to be doing in the office upstairs, have you tracked me down to the Lords canteen to interrupt my quiet and thoughtful breakfast?'

'You weren't in the office, but I knew you had been. You'd left your spoor.'

'My spoor?'

'To wit, m'lud. One Caffè Nero cup with the dregs of a cappuccino – honestly, you're as fuddy-duddy as Eliot when it comes to coffee choices – one copy of *The Times*, crossword half completed, and folded open to the Opinion page, and one laptop you'd yet again forgotten to security-lock before you left your desk.'

'Ah,' said Maxwell. 'Which I assume you kindly locked for me without reading anything?'

'Only after I emailed the security department to tell them you've been ignoring their reminders and essentials training.'

'Which you absolutely did not do.'

'Which I absolutely did not do,' grinned Diana. 'I did tidy up my annual report a bit, though.'

'I haven't written you an annual report.'

'You have now,' said Diana. 'I'm very, very good and well worth a serious pay rise.'

'Very funny,' said Max. Maybe it was the fruit, or maybe it was the distraction of Diana's youthful exuberance, but he was beginning to feel like a human being again. 'So, why did you need to track me down?'

'Oh, just thought you'd want to know the Secretary of State for Law and Order has asked Eliot to come see her this afternoon, before Eliot asks you what sort of trouble you've got him into now.'

'Estella Chamberlain?'

'Unless they've had a reshuffle since yesterday, she's the one.'

'Estella wants to see Eliot?'

'Morbid, I call it,' said Diana. 'I mean I see him every day because I have to, but imagine doing it if you had a choice?'

'Why?'

'Exactly what I ask myself.'

'No,' said Maxwell. 'Why does she want to see him? What is the subject of this meeting?'

'Unspecified,' said Diana, 'but urgent. Three p.m. this afternoon at Queen Anne's Gate. Interesting thing is,' she added, 'her private secretary suggested Eliot Oakcroft MP might want to bring one Maxwell Murray with him.'

Chapter Four

When he met Eliot Oakcroft in Portcullis House to brief him on their upcoming meeting with Miranda Cley and her Uncle Tim, Maxwell Murray was still pondering over why the Law and Order Secretary – a woman who had shown a marked aversion to his company on the rare occasions they'd run across each other since the night of the great Premier Inn betrayal – might urgently want to see him now. Portcullis House was the village green of Parliament, a modern building (well, in comparison with the rest of the place, anyway) above Westminster Tube Station with an attractive, light atrium beneath a glass ceiling surrounded by cafeterias and coffee bars. Max would have preferred a private room for a sensitive meeting, but Diana hadn't been able to book one at such short notice. Diana herself was at security, waiting to usher their guests into the building once they'd cleared the airport-style scanners and been issued with visitor badges. Max found a table large enough to seat five on the edge of a block of tables, reducing the possibilities of being overheard, at least in one direction. He seated himself facing back into the atrium, with a stairwell and the gents' toilets behind him, so that their guests would be facing away from the other tables. He placed a slim manila folder at the chair next to his, containing Eliot Oakcroft's briefing note and a copy of the photograph of the alleged sighting of Miranda Cley's dead father on Cromer Pier.

Max, with a view right across the atrium, watched Eliot Oakcroft MP arrive at the opposite diagonal, coming up the escalator that led back into the Palace of Westminster and the Chamber of the House of Commons. Eliot worked his way through the rows of tables as he crossed the hundred metres or so to Max's table – slapping a back here, nodding a recognition there. He was dressed in one of his many regulation dark blue suits, jacket buttoned, the suit perfectly tailored, beautifully pressed. He wore a pale lilac shirt and today a purple tie. Say what you like about the man, Max had to admit that Eliot looked the part – a casting director seeking an extra to play a backbench MP would grab him without a second thought. It was only when he began to speak his lines that his limitations became apparent.

Eliot hailed Max from about twenty feet away and flung himself into the chair, as if he were tackling a speedy winger at Twickenham. 'Let me tell you, Maximilian,' he said, 'about the night I had last night.'

Max sometimes wondered whether his employer of the last fifteen years really knew just how much calling him Maximilian got on his wick. He'd long given up correcting Eliot and could no longer tell whether the MP really didn't know his name or just called him Maximilian to annoy him. Nor did Maxwell really listen as his master rattled off some anecdote involving a Pall Mall club, the daughter of a countess and some red wine of the kind Max could never pay for. Not that Eliot was likely to have paid for it either, mind you. There would have been or would be in future some favour sought for his glimpse of how the rich lived, and the less Max knew of it, the better and more deniable it would be. Eliot often began their daily chats with tales of his life – sometimes even Eliot's wife, a chilly and imperious figure Max had fleetingly been patronised by but twice, featured in the stories – and he had never once, Max thought, shown a smidgeon of interest in whatever it was Max did when he wasn't at work.

When the flow stopped, Max opened the manila folder and handed Eliot his half-page summary of the Rebecca Cley murder conviction. 'So, what is this?' said Eliot. 'Meet and greet, tea and sympathy, thanks very much and goodbye?'

'We thought it might be worth asking some questions around this one,' said Max. 'Seems some genuine possibility the mother may have been wrongly convicted.'

'You'll draft some questions for me,' said Eliot.

'May not have to,' said Max, 'at least not at first. Since we started discussing this quietly yesterday, Estella Chamberlain's been in touch. You're meeting her at three this afternoon.'

'About this?'

'Don't know. Her office got in touch this morning looking for an urgent meeting.'

'They're short a junior minister at Law and Order,' said Eliot, gazing into a future he'd been imagining since he was elected fifteen years ago.

'I doubt this meeting's political,' said Max, bursting the dream bubble. 'They've asked me to come along, too.'

Eliot took a moment to return from the land of red boxes and ministerial cars, sadness clouding the blue eyes in his square, open, slightly ruddy face. Then the eyes narrowed. 'Estella Chamberlain asked for this meeting after you started poking around in this murder case,' he said.

'Might be coincidence.'

'Are you getting me into trouble, Maxwell?'

'I can't see how,' said Max. He was relieved to see Diana coming through the security pods a hundred yards or so away, followed by a tall, balding but fit-looking man in a suit that looked even more expensive than Eliot's and a petite brunette woman in a dark suit jacket, trousers and flat-heeled shoes. Even from this distance, he could see that the photograph he'd seen of Miranda Cley yesterday had been seriously misleading. In that she'd looked like a million-dollar film star. In person, she was worth at least five million. He pointed Eliot towards Miranda. The heads of others at tables nearby, less self-absorbed, had already turned that way.

'Our guests,' said Max.

'Blimey,' said Eliot, rising and brushing any imaginary crumbs from his suit jacket. 'You don't get many of them to the pound.'

Hands were shaken, guests were seated and Diana was despatched to fill orders from the nearby coffee stand. Max noted her blink of surprise when Eliot handed her a £20 note rather than expecting her to claim it back later from petty cash. These were guests he intended to impress. He also made sure that Miranda Cley was next to him, with Tim Cley opposite and next to Maxwell Murray.

'First visit to Parliament?' Eliot asked Miranda, but it was her uncle who answered.

'Been in a few times before, know some people in your party, know my way around,' he said. Max thought the cufflinks in Uncle Tim's double-cuffed shirt might be worth more than his own car. Tim Cley had also taken a black leather conference folder from his slim attaché case and a Montblanc rollerball from his inner pocket. Max was trying to read what the relationship was between Miranda Cley and her uncle but Miranda's face was unreadable, her attention entirely focused on Eliot. Watching her lean forward eagerly towards the MP she thought could help her, Max felt a lurking unease about the endless risk of implying something could be done and then disappointing. It was easy to do in a speech about a big issue or an email back to a campaign group, but the physical presence of a young woman focused on getting her mother out of prison was a different kettle of fish. Over-promising and under-delivering on this one would hurt.

'I've never been before,' she said, gazing at Eliot. 'I thought we'd be in the Big Ben bit. I didn't know there was more than the Big Ben bit.'

'Dozens of buildings,' said Eliot, patting her hand. 'Huge estate, as it happens. Perhaps I could take you on a little tour,' he added, half-rising. 'Get you a quick whizz round the Palace before you go?'

'We don't want to waste your valuable time,' said Tim Cley. 'We should get down to business.'

'Well, perhaps afterwards, my dear,' said Eliot, favouring Miranda with the smile he practised for TV interviews. This time, Max didn't have much trouble reading the young woman's reaction. She was still smiling brightly but with the tiniest furrow on her brow. 'Now then,' went on Eliot, picking up his manila folder and riffling its fairly thin contents. 'As you can see, I'm fully briefed, but I always find it helpful to hear, in your own words, what it is I can do for you.'

He'd addressed every word straight at Miranda, but it was again her uncle who answered.

'My niece believes her mother, my sister-in-law, was wrongly convicted, Mr Oakcroft. She wants you to get Rebecca out of jail.'

'My group doesn't have the power to do that,' said Eliot, and Max was glad he wasn't so dazzled by Miranda that he'd forgotten he wasn't the Lord Chancellor and Lord Chief Justice rolled into one. 'But we'll do what we can.'

‘That’s all she wants,’ said Tim Cley, placing his Montblanc on the yet unmarked page of his folder. ‘Justice for Rebecca’s all she’s after.’

‘Remind me of the details of the case?’ said Eliot, taking the half-page summary Max had prepared for him from his own folder. ‘Why, in your own words, should we try to get your mother out of jail?’

‘My father’s still alive,’ said Miranda Cley. ‘So my mum can’t have murdered him.’

‘It’s possible Charlie’s still alive,’ said Uncle Tim, taking her hand by reaching across the table. ‘But even if he isn’t, and I have to be frank, I have my doubts, we need to know how he managed to shift three million quid out of the business before he vanished.’

‘I understand you were Charlie Cley’s business partner,’ said Max. ‘And the firm’s financial director.’

‘What you’re insinuating, son,’ said Tim, glaring at Max, ‘is nothing I haven’t heard ever since Charlie got himself killed.’

‘He wasn’t killed,’ said Miranda, and Max was now sure that whatever the relationship was with her uncle, she didn’t like him. ‘He’s alive and he didn’t have the brains to steal that money, and you know it.’

‘Only other person could have stolen it was your mother,’ said Tim Cley. He turned back to Max. ‘Sure, I was the finance director, and that was fine when we started out, but Rebecca’s a qualified accountant and Charlie had full access to the accounts.’

'My mother didn't steal that money,' said Miranda Cley, sitting back in her chair with her arms crossed. Anyone watching from across Portcullis House (and Max was conscious that a steady stream of glances and open stares were coming their way) might have read the reaction as petulance, but to Max she seemed tightly coiled.

'And neither did I, so it must have been your dad,' said Tim. 'Look, let's just calm down and remember why we're here, shall we? I think Charlie's dead, and this, whatever it is, is probably a wild goose chase. But Miranda thinks her dad's alive, and if there's even a gnat's crotch's chance of getting Rebecca out of the hellhole, then that's got to be worth investigating, right?'

Both Cleys and Max turned towards Eliot, expecting some sort of summing up. Eliot had sat back in his chair with his fingers steepled under his chin, his blond head gleaming, his blue eyes gazing at the sky above the transparent roof of Portcullis House. A man deep in thought. Max recognised the signs and quietly prayed that whatever came out of his mouth would be at least tangentially relevant to what he was supposed to have been listening to.

'Very interesting,' said Eliot, returning to earth. 'Very interesting, indeed. Tell me, what was the nature of your business?'

'We started that firm in an attic above a shop,' said Tim Cley, as Max breathed a sigh of relief. Four years ago he'd sent Eliot on a 'Small Talk with Your Constituents' course run by someone who'd once coached the Queen on engaging with her subjects. Four grand that had appeared in the IPSA accounts as 'Training: miscellaneous', but which a grateful nation would surely accept had been well spent. Max suspected that Tim Cley suspected that Eliot hadn't listened to a word he'd said and had very little interest in listening to another one, but he watched as Tim gave the MP the benefit of the doubt.

'We built that business up from nothing into an international brand before Charlie vanished,' he said. 'Public Relations, PR, you know. We've done a bit for your party, *pro bono* as well, I should mention, not that that puts any obligation on you to help, of course. Charlie was the frontman, the geezer – he could talk the talk, hind legs off a donkey, all that. I was the back-room boy, admin, personnel, contracts, finance.'

'One of the first rumours was that Charlie was kidnapped,' said Max. 'Was there ever a ransom demand?'

'How about we just talk you through it from the start,' said Tim Cley. 'No point getting it all out of order.'

'Quite right,' said Eliot Oakcroft, 'keep it tight, keep it orderly. But above all, keep it brief. Essential details. Broad brush.'

'Mum and Dad loved each other,' said Miranda Cley, quietly. 'I know she can't have killed him.'

'We'd got the business built up,' said Tim Cley, as if he hadn't heard her. 'Great client list, fully capitalised, seventy-eight staff in four European countries. We were getting it ready for the stock exchange launch, you know, when he disappeared. Charlie was in great form. If there was trouble at home, I knew nothing about it, and we'd always been close, so I would have done.'

'They were great at home,' said Miranda. 'There's no way Mum was having an affair.'

'An affair?' said Eliot Oakcroft. Max was glad the woman had mentioned that; Eliot's attention had begun to wander again.

'We're getting ahead of ourselves,' said Tim Cley. 'So, day he vanished. Nothing out of the ordinary. About four in the afternoon, off he went, on his way back out to Norfolk. About ten that night I get a call from Rebecca asking if I know where he is. Out of the ordinary, that. Alarm bells ringing right off. I mean, Charlie, bit of a lad when he was younger, but all that's behind him since he met Becks. We raised the alarm about midnight after calling round his mates in case he'd stopped off somewhere for a quick drink, lost track, all that. Nothing we can do, the coppers said, grown man, no reports of traffic accidents, bet he turns up in the morning.

'Morning comes, no Charlie. His mobile's off, he's not answering texts, emails. Rebecca's on the phone every ten minutes, going frantic with worry. Then we get a call from a newspaper asking us if Charlie's been kidnapped. Kidnapped? First we've heard of it. Last we should have heard of it, too. Never a ransom demand. Never any indication of that. But once a tabloid's got a story, all the others pile in and the coppers wasted four days chasing a tale that was never there.'

'You can't trust a thing the papers say,' said Eliot. 'One time, they reported I'd been bribed to lobby the Foreign Secretary about letting an ex-prime minister of Berenardine – do you know it? Lovely little island in the Pacific, you really ought to visit – have an amnesty on his corruption charges. Nothing at all in it, of course, and, I ask you, how was I supposed to examine prison conditions in Berenardaville if I didn't spend a couple of weeks there fact-finding for myself?'

Tim Cley was blank-faced and Miranda Cley's brow had furrowed as she tried to figure out what relevance Eliot found in what he was saying. Max was merely glad the boss hadn't mentioned that he'd spent his two weeks in the Prime Minister of Berenardine's personal villa, the one impounded by the local Inland Revenue the day the man was finally arrested.

'And then they found Charlie Cley's car,' Max said. Tim Cley gave him a look that said he'd realised who he needed to talk to. That, like his brother and himself, Eliot was the frontman and Max the one who got things done.

'Charlie's Porsche,' he said. 'Hidden in scrubland in Wicklewood Forest. Only twenty miles from where he and Rebecca lived. White leather seats, bloodstains on them. Not enough to suggest a bloodbath, but plenty enough to be worried about.'

'It was Dad's blood,' said Miranda. 'They tested it, and it matched.'

'So,' said Max. 'We know he got close to home, and we know something happened to him.'

'Police assumed he was dead,' said Tim Cley. 'Started investigating Rebecca, started investigating Miranda, started investigating me. Right bloody pain in the arse, and wasting time they could have spent trying to find his body and who killed him. But they would have it that since Charlie was a wealthy man – who stood to get his money if he was dead?'

'He'd split it all between Mum and me,' said Miranda. 'She got the house, and I got a lot of cash.'

'Only you didn't, darling, did you?' said Tim Cley. 'Because the second we took a look into the books, we found that three million or near enough had gone walkies and we are, right now, up a creek without a paddle.'

'There's still the house, and what else my mother could pass on to me,' said Miranda. 'But she's under an injunction not to do anything with it, and I can't claim it without accepting that she murdered him, which I won't, because she didn't. But unless we have proof that he's dead, I can't touch a penny.'

'Wait a minute,' said Eliot Oakcroft. 'Wait a darned minute. Are you telling me there's been a murder trial and your mother's been convicted, but you can't get the money because there's no proof he's dead?'

'That's the system,' said Miranda. 'But this isn't about the money.'

Max noticed Tim Cley glancing at his niece as she said that. It might not be about the money for her, but it was definitely the money that was bothering him.

'Wait a minute,' said Eliot, again. 'I'm still thinking through this thing about your dad being murdered but not dead. Is that seriously the law? Something should be done about that.'

'Well, Mr Oakcroft,' said Tim Cley, 'that was one of the things we were hoping you might say, what with you being an MP and a lawmaker.'

'I didn't make that law,' said Eliot. 'I didn't vote for that, did I, Max?'

'I think it was the law long before you were here, Eliot,' said Max.

'Well, you can draft me a question, draft me a ten-minute bill, see if we can get that changed.'

'And how about investigating my mother's case?' said Miranda Cley. She pushed a photograph across the table, a professionally taken black and white shot of a woman who looked just like Miranda would in twenty years or so, if she didn't eat much and went to the gym and the hairdresser a lot. Eliot's pupils dilated at the sight of Rebecca Cley before some vestige of professional sense kicked in.

'I'm sure my all-party group can make some enquiries, get some balls rolling, look at the wheels within wheels and all that sort of thing,' said Eliot, rising to his feet. 'Tell you what, how about I leave your uncle with Maxwell here for twenty minutes or so while I show you around this great Parliament building of ours. Sort out some details with Max, we'll fix up a session, write some letters, have a chat with ministers, that sort of thing, see what we can do, eh?'

A glance exchanged between Miranda and Tim Cley,

and she got to her feet to walk away with Eliot Oakcroft.

'Can you give me a second?' said Max to Tim, and wrote a quick text to Diana to follow the MP and the visitor and act as a chaperone. As he sent it, he realised that Tim Cley had unscrewed his Montblanc pen again and laid it on the blank surface of his notepad.

'I'm a straight-talking man, Mr . . .' he said.

'Murray. Maxwell Murray.'

'I'm a straight-talking man, Mr Murray, and I'm not entirely without a bit of clout around your party. I know when my chain's being jerked, and I know when I'm talking to the organ grinder. What, exactly, is your boss able to do for us?'

'What he said,' said Max. 'Ask some questions of ministers, put on some pressure to have the case reviewed. We don't have the power to reopen the case or get your sister-in-law out of prison but we do have influence, we can open some doors.'

'And it'll be you doing that, not Mr Eliot Oakcroft MP?'

'Mr Oakcroft will oversee everything that's done.'

'I call a spade a spade, Mr Murray. But have it your way. What else do you need to know?'

'Why was Rebecca Cley convicted of killing her husband? What was the evidence that convinced a jury she was guilty?'

'You've read the trial transcript?'

'I've read the press coverage. We've ordered the transcript.'

'I could say dodgy judge and biased jury, but I won't, Mr Murray. It was Patrick Alderton got her sent down. Without him, there wouldn't have been a shred of evidence against her.'

'The next-door neighbour?'

'Neighbour implies he was on the same level as Charlie and Becks. He lived in the village. Charlie, Becks and Miranda have a six-bed stone ex-rectory with a few acres. Alderton had a bungalow some cowboy built out of brick and pebbledash about twenty years ago, a scrubby old field out the back of his place. There is no way on earth that Rebecca had an affair with that man.'

'Why did he say they did?'

'Fantasist,' said Tim Cley. 'Complete and utter liar. He told me about it first, before he went to the papers. Asked me for money to keep the story to himself. I took one look at the scruffy little git and knew he was talking utter shit. Told him to go put his head in a blender. Sometimes, since, I wish I hadn't. Little bastard went straight to *The Sun*.'

'He had pictures of himself and Rebecca,' said Max, slipping a newspaper cutting out of the manila folder Eliot Oakcroft had left behind. The cutting showed a curly-haired, skinny but muscular man and there were two pictures of him with Rebecca Cley. In both, she wore a bikini by the swimming pool at the home she shared with Charlie and Miranda. In the first, Alderton had clearly taken a selfie with himself bare-chested, apart from the mass of thick black hair on it, in the foreground while Rebecca prepared to dive into the pool. In the other, Patrick Alderton had his arm around her as they both raised glasses of champagne.

'He did some work at their house,' said Tim Cley. 'Man's a handyman, a navvy. Those pictures are entirely innocent – for God's sake, Miranda took the one with the champagne.

They were celebrating his finishing work on a new hot tub.'

'He's got no shirt on.'

'It was hot.'

'You can see how it looks.'

'You can make anything look like anything if you know how,' said Tim Cley.

'How much money have you got tied up in the accounts you can't access?' said Max, then watched Tim Cley give him a long, cool stare.

'The sixty-four million dollar question,' he said. 'How come Oakcroft's the MP and you're the bag carrier?'

Max waited for Cley to say something else.

'It's a lot of money,' said Tim Cley eventually. 'I've got enough elsewhere to keep the business afloat, but I won't pretend it isn't affecting us, won't deny I'd like it freed up. As Miranda said, though, this isn't all about the money – she just wants Rebecca released.'

'She?' said Max. 'And you?'

'And me,' said Tim Cley. 'I don't know if Rebecca had anything to do with Charlie being killed. I can't figure out why she'd want him dead. As I said, the only two people who could have been shifting money out of the company account are Rebecca Cley and me. And since it wasn't me . . .'

'You think Rebecca stole your money.'

'I wonder if she and Charlie had cooked up some scam, some scheme to get themselves out of something. Kind of nonsense he might have got himself into, stupid flash bastard that he was. But if they did, I don't know what it was, and I have no idea where that money is right now. What I do know, I think, is that she wouldn't have killed him, and it's a crying shame she's been in jail for two years now for something I just can't think she did.'

'It's hard for us to tell,' said Max, 'whether you're supporting Miranda in searching for her dad or would rather we didn't find him.'

'I don't like to see Rebecca in prison,' said Tim. 'Leaves a bad taste, that. And Miranda's a good kid who deserves none of this. If she thinks Charlie's still up and walking about, we should give it a look. Me, personally, I think he's dead and gone and she saw a ghost on Cromer Pier. Saw what she wants to see. If Charlie was alive, he'd have been in touch. All that stuff about him doing a runner with my millions, that's just not on. Charlie was a great frontman, a great PR, but he didn't have the financial nous, didn't have the brains to be embezzling from the firm or squirrelling cash away behind my back. I don't know if Rebecca killed him or not, but I do know Miranda's wasting her life away trying to get her mother out of jail. If we can sort this out one way or another, Mr Murray, if we can get to the truth about what happened to Charlie, I'll be satisfied. And even if Becks did kill my brother, and it shatters Miranda's dreams and breaks her heart, at least she'll be able to get on with her life.'

'I'll see what we can do, Mr Cley,' said Maxwell Murray.

The Ministry of Law and Order sounded more imposing than it looked. The courts, like the Old Bailey or the Royal

Court of Justice on the Strand, were based in ornately historic buildings full of wood panelling and stone sculptures. The civil service department that administered those courts, the police forces that sent them customers and prisons to deal with them later was in a nondescript 1960s glass-fronted office block not too far from Victoria Station. Having presented himself at the front desk and been handed a visitor's pass, Max sat on an acrylic orange sofa in a waiting area that felt much like the reception of a particularly large budget hotel. He'd been there twenty minutes when Eliot Oakcroft MP turned up at the front desk, went through the rigmarole of suggesting the receptionist should know who he was and then, with a good deal of huffing, dug out his parliamentary ID to prove it. And then he performed a pantomime of outrage at having to hand over his mobile phone, one of Estella's requirements being that anyone who met her should do without anything that could record the conversation or photograph her. Eventually, stuffing his reluctantly issued visitor pass in his pocket, Eliot walked over to join Max.

'I thought Estella Chamberlain was seeing us at three o'clock?'

'It's only quarter past now,' said Max. 'You know they always overrun.' *Which is why*, he added silently, *you're never on time yourself.*

'Disgraceful,' said Eliot, sitting himself down. 'I'm a busy man. Next time, make sure she comes to us.'

'I gather your tour with Miss Cley went well,' said Max.

Actually, he'd gathered nothing of the sort from Diana, who'd caught up with the pair in Central Lobby. According to Diana's account, Miranda had deftly avoided all attempts to guide her by arm, elbow or waist, raced through the House of Commons Chamber and politely explained that she couldn't stay to lunch as she had to be back in Norfolk by early afternoon. 'Learn anything useful from her?'

'Not a chatty girl,' said Eliot Oakcroft. 'Bit stand-offish. Do make sure we keep in touch with her, though. I'd like to see her again.'

Max's hopes hadn't been high. Even if Miranda Cley had tried to tell him something, Eliot Oakcroft wasn't the kind of man programmed to take it in. Eliot's two operating modes were speaking or waiting to speak. His idea of listening was nodding his head and saying 'Indeed' at random intervals.

A young man, mid-twenties, suit, neatly trimmed black beard, appeared at their side, asking, 'Mr Oakcroft?'

'About time,' said Eliot Oakcroft, standing.

'The minister apologises for keeping you waiting, sir,' said the young man, with all the sincerity of a phone message saying *your call is important to us*. 'If you'd follow me.' The lad must have been about twenty-four but somehow conveyed the air both of owning the place and of being the kind of superior servant who takes no responsibility for the quality of the house guests.

Max followed Eliot as Eliot followed the young civil servant towards security pods and scanners.

'Did you hand over all your mobiles?' Max whispered to

Eliot as a security guard held out a small square tray.

'Certainly not,' said Eliot.

'OK,' said Max. And waited for the klaxons to go off the second Eliot set foot in the security pod.

'Might I trouble you for your mobile phone,' murmured the civil servant once Eliot had been released back into the public atrium.

'This is ridiculous. I'm a Member of Parliament.'

'I can't imagine why the Secretary of State doesn't trust you.' The words were as soft as a scalpel through a pat of butter.

Eliot dropped his BlackBerry into the oblong grey tray. A civil service lip curled.

'And the rest,' muttered Max. A civil service eyebrow soared as the Nokia landed. A civil service brow furrowed as the pager came out of Eliot's pocket.

'What on earth is that?' said the young man.

Max smiled weakly at him as Eliot re-entered the security pod. Through the security barriers, into a lift, and along a carpeted corridor they went, and into an anteroom where three equally young, equally bearded men sat working at computer monitors. Each looked up at their companion and the intruders, as the young man gave the kind of barely perceptible shrug that says, *Don't blame me!*

'If you'd wait here just a moment,' he said smoothly, then disappeared discreetly through a door hidden in the wall panelling.

Eliot took a look around the minister's outer office

and paced to and fro. Over the fifteen years they'd worked together, Max and he had made this walk to ministerial offices often enough for the routine to be entirely familiar, but Eliot seemed to find it newly insulting every time. The MP's eye, and then hand, had fallen on a ministerial red box stowed on a shelf. Eliot's fingers flicked across the embossed crown that symbolised His Majesty's Government, his eyes greedily moving over the gold lettering that said *Rt Hon. Estella Chamberlain MP*.

Max himself stood quietly by the unoccupied desk in the room, presumably belonging to the young man who'd led them in here. In earlier times, it had often been possible to read, upside down, whatever interesting document sat in the wooden out-tray. Now, the tray was still there but purely decoratively, since Estella's office appeared to have abandoned the use of paper. Max wasn't sure what he regretted more: the switch to digital or the uselessness of having trained himself to read upside down, a skill that had gone, for young people today, the way of fletching or using a landline. The discreet door in the wall panelling opened, and the young man himself stepped out to usher Max and Eliot into the presence of the Secretary of State for Law and Order.

Estella Chamberlain was standing in front of her desk as they travelled the acre or so of carpet separating it from the door. She walked towards them, smiling. Not yet forty, Estella was slim and slight in a cream trouser suit, with short dark hair cut to emphasise her elfin features. She could walk into any pantomime as a gamine principal boy; it would be only when the curtain went up they'd find she was Queen Rat.

'Eliot,' she said, leaning forward to kiss the air eighteen inches or so either side of his face. Some people who had once been employed by someone ten years older than them and now their inferior would be shamefaced about it. Estella was not among their number. 'Too long, too long. We must get together more often,' she said. 'Hello, Maxwell,' she added, without favouring him with a look. 'Come, come, Eliot. Coffee?'

She led them to a comfortable white sofa by a low coffee table and seated Eliot next to herself on it. Max was left with an armchair, facing his boss and the back of Estella Chamberlain's head. He was simultaneously, and not for the first time, fascinated and horrified that he and this woman had spent eighteen months in a relationship twelve years before. He found he could barely remember what had brought them together, what they had done with their time. It was like a fact reported to him about someone else, another person altogether. Anyway, since Estella clearly had no intention of mentioning they so much as knew each other, he set himself to concentrate on what she was about to unleash on Eliot Oakcroft.

'I can't tell you how grateful we were for your group's work on the Unduly Lenient Sentence Scheme, Eliot,' she said, leaning forward to demonstrate the copy sitting on the coffee table of the Miscarriages of Justice APPG's recent report on the same. Eliot graciously accepted the compliment with a wave of his hand. Max knew Eliot hadn't read a word of the report that he and Tony Wenhamville had jointly drafted. He wondered, looking at the neatly printed copy on the coffee table, whether Estella Chamberlain had either. There was a telltale few millimetres of an A4 sheet tucked inside the front cover: the one-page summary produced by one of the bearded wonders outside in the private office.

'Of course, we can't possibly put all your recommendations into practice,' she said, tapping Eliot Oakcroft on his beautifully tailored knee. 'But I can assure you they're at the forefront of our mind as we develop new areas for tougher sentences.'

'That's our job,' said Eliot. 'I like to think of us as critical friends, helping to guide you in the right direction.'

'I think the APPG recommended the opposite,' said Max, surprising himself. 'Doesn't the report argue for shorter, fewer and better-targeted sentences to relieve pressure on the prisons?'

'Let's not quibble about the details,' said Eliot smoothly. 'It's good to hear a positive response, Secretary of State.'

'Yes, that would be lovely,' said Max. 'Is one coming?'

'The Government's policy is entirely clear,' said Estella without missing a beat or looking behind her. 'But we do so admire the quality of your thinking, Eliot. Please, do keep up the good work. It's vital that you are out there, holding us to account.'

'Glad to hear we've had some influence,' said Eliot. 'And, as you know, my interest in justice and law and order is my absolutely driving passion.'

'Oh, absolutely,' said Estella, pouring Eliot some coffee. 'No question of your commitment to the cause, or the Government.'

'I gather, by the way, the department's looking for a new Minister for Sentencing Policy,' said Eliot.

'And I'd love to hear your thoughts on who that should be,' said Estella Chamberlain. 'Milk, sugar?'

'One's own hat would, one hopes, be in the ring,' said Eliot, flinching a little.

'Oh,' said Estella, entirely failing to disguise her surprise, at least from Max. 'I see. Well, of course. Above my pay grade, I'm afraid,' she added, pouring milk. 'PM and Chief Whip arrange all appointments, as you know, but I'm sure your name's been mentioned.'

'A word in the Chief's ear, perhaps,' murmured Eliot.

'Consider it done.'

'Ten years on the Law and Order APPG now,' Eliot went on, 'and there's not a subject in Parliament on which I'm more knowledgeable.'

'I'll be sure to say something after Cabinet tomorrow,' said Estella. 'Now, I mustn't keep you too long. I understand you're looking into the conviction of Rebecca Cley.'

'You're well informed,' said Max, surprising himself again, and earning a glare from Eliot Oakcroft but once again the back of Estella Chamberlain's beautifully coiffed head. The pixie cut around her ears couldn't hide their twitching, though.

'Bit specific for your group, isn't it?' said Estella. 'I mean the

Government is fully supportive of your work on identifying areas where miscarriage of justice might happen in principle, or mechanisms for correcting general errors in the law, but you're not really the right body to investigate whether a perfectly proper individual conviction is sound, are you?'

'The family have been to the police, the Crown Prosecution Service and the Criminal Cases Review Commission,' said Max. For the first time, Estella turned away from Eliot towards him, giving Eliot the chance to fish out from his inner jacket pocket Max's half-page summary of the Cley case.

'And all of them have said that the conviction is entirely sound, Mr Murray,' she said in a voice that would chill Tabasco. 'As you know, Mrs Cley had no grounds for appeal.'

'Why, exactly, does the Government care about this case?' asked Max, looking Estella in the eye. Eliot Oakcroft, having skimmed his note, would be ready to pick up the ball again in a second. 'Why does it matter to you?'

'His Majesty's Government's only concern, Mr Murray, is that justice be done,' said Estella, glaring through him. 'It would be regrettable if a sentimental sympathy for a daughter deprived of both her parents led you down a blind, and potentially dangerous, alley.'

'Dangerous?' said Max, holding her stare.

'Dangerous to the soundness of the principles of justice,' said Estella, holding right back.

'We've promised the girl we'll ask a question or two,' said Eliot. 'Seems unfair she can't lay her hands on her father's loot.'

Estella held Max's eye for a moment longer, before

turning back to Eliot Oakcroft and softening her shoulders. 'The girl's suffering some hardship?' she asked.

'Dad's been murdered but isn't officially dead, it appears,' said Eliot. 'Girl can't have his money until seven years have passed.'

'I see,' said Estella. 'Well, if that's the nature of your concern, I'll see whether there's something we can do to free up the funds. Obviously, a law change would take some time, drafting, consultation, then finding a slot in the parliamentary timetable.'

'But we have your assurance you'll look into it,' said Eliot.

'Absolutely,' said Estella, getting to her feet and beginning to walk the two men towards the door of her office, which silently opened as they approached. Max assumed one of the private secretaries outside was listening in, probably, in the absence of a note-taker, recording the meeting. 'So there'll be no question of your pursuing this one too vigorously, I understand. And do remember I'll have that word with the Chief Whip when I see him next.'

Eliot Oakcroft remained silent until they were back out on Victoria Street and walking towards Westminster. 'Well,' he said. 'Well, well, well. Result, I think?'

'Result?' said Max.

'That was a very definite promise, Maxwell. A very definite promise.'

'She only said she'd look into changing the law on inheritance from a murder suspect.'

'Oh, yes,' said Eliot. 'That was a good result, too.'

* * *

'What I can't figure out is why she bothered having me there,' said Max. He was back in the office and Eliot had been safely packed off for the evening to make a speech at a charity dinner. 'She could have flattered Eliot out of doing anything more without involving me at all.'

'Obvious, isn't it?' said Diana.

'You couldn't make it a bit more obvious, I suppose,' said Max.

'Estella Chamberlain could talk Eliot out of doing anything, but she needed you so that she could find out if we knew anything or were taking this case seriously.'

Max sat back in his chair and looked at Diana, telling him this while typing. He'd spent the last two hours trying to figure out what Estella Chamberlain was up to. Diana had cracked it in ninety seconds, while still clearing constituency emails at the end of a long day. His own political antennae weren't usually this defunct; it was Estella befogging and befuddling him again. He was over her, he knew he was over her. He was sure he was over her.

'I've got confirmation of the prison visit day after tomorrow,' said Diana. 'I assumed Eliot wouldn't want to come so I've put my own name down with you.'

'Didn't you hear what I've been telling you?' said Max. 'Eliot's calling us off this one. Letter telling them the Secretary of State's promised to look into the financial point. Promise to keep in touch with further developments.'

'He didn't actually say we shouldn't do anything else, though, did he?'

'Well, not as such, I suppose, but we both know what he means.'

'Yeah, but I've arranged the prison visit now, and there'd be no harm in hearing what Rebecca Cley has to say, would there?'

'Eliot could just sack us, you know.'

'Yeah,' said Diana, 'but if he tried, he'd have to find someone to fill out the redundancy forms for IPSA for him. Come on, Max. We don't have to be on the train until eleven o'clock. It's a Friday. He won't be here. He'll never know we went.'

'You don't think Estella Chamberlain might get a hint from the director of the prison service?'

'You scared of Estella Chamberlain, Max?'

'Yes.'

'Oh, well, the adrenalin and terror'll be good for your liver,' said Diana, shutting down her computer. 'I'll pick up the train tickets from the travel office on my way down to the Tube.'

'Cancel them,' said Max. 'I'll drive.'

'You've got a car?' Diana stopped in her tracks. Max had never seen her look so shocked. 'You live in Central London on what Eliot pays you and you've got a car?'

Chapter Five

'You've got a car,' said Diana, settling herself once he'd picked her up at her Crouch End flat. She handed him a flask of coffee as she got in, and two bagged croissants from Pret a Manger. 'And quite some car,' she added. 'If I'd have known, I'd have got something less flaky for breakfast.'

'It's not really practical around town,' said Max, heading for the North Circular and the M11 out to Cambridge. 'And I can't really afford the petrol. Bit of a gas guzzler I'm afraid.'

'It's brilliant,' said Diana, 'and who needs an environment or air quality, anyway?' She ran a hand across the walnut facing of the dashboard, fiddled with the handle on the glove compartment. 'I didn't really peg you as a car man at all, Maxwell. If forced, I'd have guessed a Ford Fiesta.'

'Thanks very much.'

'But this? I'm seeing a whole new Maxwell Murray. Stick on a pair of goggles, a boiler suit and a white silk scarf and you'd walk into Formula 1 at Silverstone 1953. Can we put the top down?'

'Only if you want hair like Bridget Jones.'

'Bridget who?' said Diana, who was twenty-eight.

'It was my father's car,' said Max, a few moments later. 'I can't quite bring myself to get rid of it.'

'He can't be too old to drive it himself?'

'He wouldn't be, no. He'd have been sixty-three, sixty-four next month. He died. My mother and he died when I was seventeen.'

'Oh, shit, Max. I'm so sorry. I didn't know.'

'No reason you should. You were barely alive.'

'I'm so sorry. I just open my big mouth.'

'It's not a problem,' said Max, smiling across at her. 'It's just something that happened.'

'Both of them?'

'Car accident. On holiday in the south of France. My sister hadn't gone out to dinner with them, thank God. She was in the cottage alone when the police came to tell her.'

'God. I can't imagine,' said Diana. 'Where were you?'

'I was seventeen that year. First time I refused to go on holiday with them. Stayed home, alone. My dad didn't mind. My mum was upset with me.'

'Max. I'm so sorry.'

'It's a long time ago,' said Max, finding the turn for the M11 out to Cambridgeshire and Norfolk.

Rebecca Cley was not in prison in Norfolk. But HMP Norton St Meald happened to be the closest women's prison to her home, as well as being one of the few to house both men and women. Their appointment to see her was for late afternoon. They'd agreed to visit the Cley home on the way, just south of Wymondham, and to take Miranda Cley to the prison with them. As they passed Wicklewood Forest on the A11, Diana pointed out that was where Charlie Cley's Porsche had been discovered by a dog-walker, undamaged but with Charlie's bloodstains on its seats.

'We're early, aren't we,' Diana said. 'We could stop and have a look.'

'At what?'

'Where it happened,' said Diana, fishing a sheaf of newsprint out of her bag. 'Where they found Charlie's car.'

'We'll never find the spot where that was,' said Max.

'Want a bet?' said Diana, waving her phone at him. Max could see a map of Wicklewood Forest with a large blue dot on it.

'X marks the spot? How did you find that?'

'Real crime website,' said Diana. 'If you ever go missing, the cops will just love my browsing history.'

Max pulled off the road into a lay-by when Diana told him they were close to the spot.

'The papers said the Porsche was in a thicket of trees,' she said as they got out of the car.

'Only about twenty thousand to choose from, then,' said Max. 'Any haystacks on your map so we can search for a needle?'

'Give me a second,' said Diana, checking her phone. 'According to *Blood in the Woods*, there should be a clearing about seventy metres down that path.'

'Police really are going to love your search history,' said Max as he followed her down a track into the forest. 'How did you find these sites?'

'Everyone's allowed a hobby,' said Diana, striding ahead into the woods, her nose glued to her phone. Max wasn't entirely sure he wanted to follow her. But, stretching after the drive, he found the scent of the trees and the fresh air lifting his mood. Even a wild goose chase had its benefits, it turned out.

Or a wild dog chase, which was what Diana was suddenly on as a springer spaniel lived up to its billing by leaping out of the undergrowth and capering around her in circles, while she bent to her haunches to pretend to catch him.

'To heel, Scamper,' said a stentorian voice from the wood as the dog jumped towards and evaded Diana's laughing hands. 'To heel, sir, to heel.'

'Not sure he heard you,' said Max as a man emerged from the woods, scowling at his scampering dog.

'She,' said the man, shortly.

'Sorry, you called her sir.'

'Force of habit. Forty years a dog man. Never had a female before. Uncontrollable, you see, much like the rest of the species, eh?' The man barked what might have been a try at a laugh, and Max could feel himself being metaphorically poked in the ribs at the nineteenth hole of a particularly unreconstructed golf club. The man looked in his sixties or early seventies and might have dressed for a photoshoot for a walk in the woods with the dog – sleeveless Barbour, checked shirt on which the binoculars around his neck sat, mustard corduroys, brown brogues. Max was conscious, even tieless, that his suit and black slip-ons were raising white bushy eyebrows on a face the colour of Heinz Ketchup.

'Not entirely dressed for a ramble in the undergrowth, are we, now?' foghorned the man. 'Are you ghouls or are you journalists?'

'I beg your pardon?'

'You're one or the other,' said the man, easily. 'I recognise both sorts now. Shoes like yours, journalist. Girl your snapper, is she?'

'Snapper?'

'I've learnt all your chaps' jargon now, you know. And your prices. What's my info worth, then?'

'I'm sorry,' said Max. 'I haven't the first idea what you're talking about.'

'No, no, of course you haven't,' said the man. 'Only I've been taken for a free ride too often to fall for that one this time. You're not from the *Daily Post*, are you?' he added, taking a menacing step closer.

'No,' said Max. 'We're not journalists at all.'

'Oh,' said the man. 'Ghouls then. Better dressed than the average specimen. To be honest, I prefer the ghouls to the journalists. At least they're honestly despicable. I expect you want to see the site, do you? Satisfy your morbid curiosity.'

Diana was still playing with the dog, and Max desperately wanted her attention so that they could get away from this madman. Finally, she looked up and said, 'Aren't you Rodney Ferrars?'

'I have that honour,' said the man, turning back to a mystified Max. 'How does she know that? Are you sure you're not journalists?'

'We're investigators,' said Diana. 'We can't pay you—'

'Then I have nothing to say to you.'

'But we'd be happy to mention you in our book.'

'A book,' said the man Max now knew as Rodney Ferrars. 'A book, you say? Well that puts a different stamp on matters, that's a fish of a different flavour.'

'And if the TV series comes off . . .'

'Diana,' said Max, warningly. An interest in real crime websites. A willingness, apparently, to make up stories to obtain information. Diana's CV had contained nothing of such qualifications for the life political, and Max was uncomfortably aware that his new status as her Chief of Staff wasn't going to help him if she dropped Eliot Oakcroft's name any time soon.

'Television,' said Rodney Ferrars, and Diana might as well have named this week's Lottery numbers to put that light of desire into his eyes. 'Are you telling me that I might be on television?'

'Now, where exactly was it you found the silver Porsche, Rodney?' said Diana, taking the misty-eyed man by the checked-shirted arm protruding from his sleeveless Barbour.

'We could, maybe, do a picture of you, with Scamper here, if you took us to where you found the car.'

'It wasn't Scamper who was with me when I came across the car, you know,' said Rodney Ferrars. 'General sniffed it out, you see. Splendid old boy. Stood guard until the police arrived, you know. Immovable. Eating from the great dinner pail in the heavens, these days, sadly. Miss him, you know. Not afraid to say so.'

'You and your good lady wife must miss him enormously,' said Diana.

'I have never had the honour to have a good lady wife,' said Rodney.

'You stun and astound me,' said Diana, 'and I'm so sorry to hear General's gone on ahead.' Rodney Ferrars walked arm in arm with her down the track, beaming and pointing the way while Max, wondering at just what he'd unleashed on the poor old man, trailed behind, with Scamper vanishing into and reappearing from the wood until they came to a small clearing.

'Here it was,' said Rodney Ferrars. 'I was walking with General, as we did every evening about that hour, when I caught a glimpse of the silver through the trees. How did that hooligan get his sports car down here, I thought to myself, and what manner of no good is he up to. I came down to give the driver a piece of my mind, only driver was there none, and I thought to myself, well, that's a bit fishy, a flash car like that with its doors open, probably joyriders abandoned the thing, and then I saw the blood smeared on the seats.'

'All over the seats,' said Diana.

'Well, not exactly all over,' said Rodney Ferrars. 'Drops here and there. You know how the newspapers like to exaggerate everything.'

'Which way round was the car?' said Max.

'Ah, now that was interesting,' said Rodney Ferrars. 'It was pointing back towards the pathway, as if the fellow had reversed it in.'

'Driven in carefully, then,' said Max. 'Not like it had been stolen and abandoned.'

'I thought he might have been expecting some sort of assignation,' said Rodney Ferrars, raising his binoculars. 'Lot of that sort of thing goes on in these woods, you see.'

'Romantic?' said Diana.

'Drugs,' said Rodney Ferrars. 'Band of Travellers over that ridge there, dealing who knows what, you know. There's some funny types about these woods.'

'You're telling me,' said Diana.

'Drug deal gone wrong was my first thought. Fallen out with the scurf merchants in the caravans, got a bit of a hiding. But then I realised there was no sight of the fellow, so I called the police, and in they came, and the press came with them, and there we were, me and the General being interviewed and photographed all night about what might have happened to this fellow, Charlie whatsisname. Murder everyone thought, but no body. All sorts of nonsense spoken after that.'

'Like the kidnapping story,' said Max.

'Ah,' said Rodney Ferrars, his ketchup face going more HP Sauce. 'Now that, sir, is the bone of contention I have with the *Daily Post* people. That kidnapping angle was my idea, you see.'

'Yours?'

'"Keep that one under your hat," said the reptile from the *Daily Post*, when I mentioned it to him. "If I can have that exclusive there'll be a pretty penny in it for you." So I told it to him and to none of the others, you see.'

'What made you think Charlie was kidnapped?' said Max.

'Chap must have been kidnapped. I said as much to the *Daily Post*. You don't leave a car like that behind voluntarily, I said. If they murdered him, where's the body? Stands to reason he was taken.'

'There wasn't any evidence of that.'

'I had the evidence of my own eyes, sir,' said Rodney Ferrars, 'and the benefit of stout common sense. Not enough attention paid to good old common sense, these days, you know, what with all this "evidence" and "statistics" people keep throwing about. The *Daily Post* sold millions of papers on the back of that exclusive story and not a penny piece of it did I ever see. I've written, you know, several times. Most offensive replies.'

'No wonder the police discounted kidnapping,' said Max to Diana.

'Well what do you expect of the police,' said Rodney Ferrars. 'I could tell you a thing or two about the police, you know, harassing law-abiding citizens just because they express a sturdy commonsensical view about the Travellers littering the woods and flogging who knows what to all and sundry. They ought to be out arresting real criminals.'

'I see,' said Max, suffering flashbacks to Eliot Oakcroft MP's last constituency surgery, when the MP had said much the same thing to a bemused constituent with a council tax query.

'Put that in your television programme and smoke it,' said Rodney Ferrars.

'Mad as a snake,' said Max as they drove on towards Norfolk. 'Democracy always seems such a brilliant idea until you meet The People.'

'Useful, though, don't you think?' said Diana. 'I mean, the kidnap story's absolute nonsense, and it's interesting that it wasn't the bloodbath the papers were implying.'

'If he's to be believed.'

'I doubt he's capable of telling an untruth about a fact. He hasn't the imagination.'

Max glanced across at Diana, sitting with her stockinged feet up on his dashboard. He knew he should tell her off for holding out the prospect of a television show to Rodney Ferrars, knew how much trouble they could be in if anyone ever discovered they'd basically lied to a lonely elderly man to make him tell them his story. On the other hand, it had worked, and Rodney had filled them in with much detail on the two briefcases full of company documents left behind in the car, and which Rodney had had half an hour to thoroughly rifle before the police made it up from Diss to take charge of the crime scene. He'd had time to tell them, too, what the jackanapes in office of a custody sergeant at Diss had said to him once his fingerprints had been found all over them. Charlie Cley, it was clear, had been carrying papers that demonstrated how much trouble the PR company he and his brother had founded was in, and how desperately they needed a loan to tide them over until the next rental payment on their expensive London offices fell due in six months' time. The image of Charlie and his brother Tim as successful businessmen had taken a quick knock in Rodney Ferrars' version of how their finances looked.

'It's really weird that none of that financial stuff came out at Rebecca's trial,' said Max. 'If the company's in the state it's in, that surely would have been a bigger motive for her to get rid of him than the affair with the next-door neighbour. I mean, it was her money he'd ploughed into the firm.'

'I notice Tim didn't mention it either, when we met him the other day.'

'Perhaps the Cleys are less wealthy than we think.'

'Or than Miranda Cley thinks they are,' said Diana.

It was after 2 p.m. when they turned off the A11 at Wymondham.

'You'll find a map book in the glove compartment,' Max said. 'It's just south of Wymondham down some narrow lanes.'

'Got it,' said Diana, showing him her phone, the blue

dot of their car following a blue line to their destination. They came off the A11 at Wymondham College, through Morley St Botolph.

'If we get to Wicklewood, we've gone too far,' said Max.

'Next left,' said Diana.

It was a narrow lane, with barely enough room for two cars to pass each other, and currently made no easier by two skips parked outside the first house along the lane, full of soil and gravel deposits.

The Cley house stood at the end of a short row of substantial low white homes, all in their own grounds behind high hedges. When the single-lane road ran out, Max simply drove straight through an open five-barred gate onto a gravel driveway and found plenty of room to park even though a Range Rover, an Alfa Romeo sports car and a mildly incongruous white Lada were already there. The house itself was a square three-storey former rectory in golden stone, which had been extended with single-storey wings to east and west. The nearest neighbour was about a quarter of a mile away back down the narrow road. This house was the end of the line.

'How the other half live,' muttered Max.

'Says the man driving the bottle-green Bentley,' said Diana. 'How the top one per cent live, I reckon. I thought they couldn't afford a lawyer.'

'Asset-rich, cash-poor, I'd guess,' said Max. 'Can't access Rebecca's and Charlie's bank accounts, anything they sold would presumably be tied up the same way.'

Miranda Cley was at the door waiting for them. She looked, if anything, even more breathtaking out here in the open country air than she had at their Westminster meeting. Max noted the simple red and black check shirt, black jeans and trainers, and that there were women who'd spend a million at the Queen's couturier to achieve about half the dazzle of straightforward bone structure and a clear-skinned smile.

'I've just made coffee,' she said, putting out her hand to shake Max's in a gesture that seemed more practised than natural. 'Come on round the back.'

They walked through the hallway of the central cottage, a square room with three doors off either side and two symmetrical curving staircases that led to an upper gallery running all the way round the hallway. Ahead of them was a set of French windows leading out to a back garden that might have hosted Wimbledon.

'This hallway's about the size of my flat,' Diana whispered to Max.

Max noticed that this central hallway was filled with photographs of Rebecca Cley, many in collages on pinboards, many more in individual frames on sideboards and occasional tables. A large black and white one, portrait size, looked down from the right-hand wall. Rebecca's dark hair had fallen, or been placed, over the right side of her face and she looked out from beneath the curtain it formed, with a clear-eyed, unsmiling gaze. Her face looked free of make-up, in the way only a very expensively posed studio portrait could achieve. She looked beautiful but over-posed, and the prominence of the picture seemed odd to Max. In the dozen or more snapshots that had been placed in a collage on the opposite wall, Rebecca alone, Rebecca with Charlie, and Rebecca with Charlie and their daughter looked unforced and natural as she laughed and her hair tossed in the wind. Looked happy.

Miranda led them through the French windows to a patio. On a rustic wooden table halfway down it, a silver coffee pot sat on a silver tray beside silver cream and milk jugs and sugar bowl. Three white cups sat in saucers, each with a teaspoon and a napkin in a silver ring.

'Do you live here on your own?' Diana asked.

'Since Mum went to prison, yes,' said Miranda, pouring coffee and passing the silver tray of cream, milk and sugar. 'We had a housekeeper live in before, but I'm doing without now. Uncle Tim stays over sometimes.'

'Must get lonely. Miles to the nearest neighbour, never mind a town.'

'I suppose so. But I've always lived here. Guess I'm just used to it.'

'Have you got someone nearby if you needed them?' said Max.

'Eight houses in the village,' said Miranda. 'Known most of them all my life, too. I can call on anyone, except Patrick Alderton, obviously.'

'Alderton still lives here?'

'Other end of the lane you came down, first house you passed as you came in.'

'He's the one having building work done?'

'Swimming pool, or so he claims. Looks like a hole in the ground to me. He's been digging it out for years now. Sometimes I think he'll never finish it. Do we have to talk about him?'

'We should talk to him,' said Diana. 'Really. If we're going to find out what really happened.'

'He's lying about my mum,' said Miranda. 'He did some work for us but she barely knew him.'

'In a place this size?'

'You'd be surprised how little we all see each other,' said Miranda. 'Basically, we're all in our houses or gardens or driving somewhere else.'

'No dinner party circuit locally, then?'

'Yes, but not with people from this village,' said Miranda. 'Apart from Alderton, they've all lived here for ever. Daily exodus to Norwich and London any time from 5.30 a.m., daily return any time up to midnight. Whoever they spend their weekends socialising with, it isn't each other. Nice people, but we keep ourselves to ourselves around here.'

'So,' said Max slowly, 'if anyone was having an affair, it would probably go unnoticed?'

Miranda flushed and the line of her lips set. 'My mother was not having an affair. With Patrick Alderton or anyone else. We were completely flabbergasted when he suddenly turned up in the papers claiming he was her lover. Lies, total lies. We assumed the papers must have paid for his story, and Patrick's not a man to turn away an easy few hundred quid.'

'There were those photos, though. By the pool with his shirt off, arm around your mum.'

Miranda flushed again and looked down at the table in front of her. Diana shot Max a glance that suggested he should back off a bit. 'We know he did a bit of work around here, Miranda,' she said. 'We know those pictures are completely innocent if you look at them just in that light.'

'He hung round here a lot for a time,' said Miranda, still staring at the wooden table. 'He's somehow become the local handyman – if you need a bit of plumbing or electrics or gardening done, he's your man. Cash in hand, nothing through the books, cheap. We had him round a lot when we were fitting the hot tub and Dad asked him to do it. That's when the pictures were taken. Mum never gave him a second glance, honestly. He always swaggered around with his shirt off. He thinks he's God's gift. But he's just not her type.'

Max wondered whether Miranda was accidentally suggesting that her mother had another type of man in the village or local area. But he left the conversation to Diana, more or less the same age as Miranda, even if the former did, right in this moment, seem years older than the clearly upset young woman biting her lip and toying with her coffee cup. They could have been sisters, almost.

'Did he ever behave inappropriately with your mum?' Diana said. 'Come on to her or anything?'

'No, he wasn't interested in her.'

'Did he ever try anything on with you?'

Miranda looked up at Diana with the answer to that one

written on her face. 'He's a horrible, horrible man,' she said. 'He never had an affair with Mum. He only said that to get some attention, get some money out of the newspapers. It just didn't happen. Shouldn't we be on our way to Norton St Meald?'

'It won't take us two hours to get there,' said Max, but Miranda had disappeared back into the house with the coffee tray before he'd finished.

'Guess we'll be hanging about there rather than hanging about here, then,' said Diana. 'Reckon she's still got the hots for Patrick the handyman?'

'Don't mention that again, will you?'

'Interesting, though, don't you think? Patrick's diddling Charlie's daughter but something makes him tell the police he was seeing Charlie's wife. We need to talk to him.'

'Diana,' said Max. 'We are MPs' researchers, not private eyes or police officers.'

'I know,' said Diana. 'Fun, though, isn't it?'

As they walked back into the hall, Miranda was visible through the doorway of a long kitchen-cum-breakfast room that looked out on the back lawns, washing up the coffee cups.

'Is there a loo I can use?' yelled Diana, and Miranda came towards them. 'This is going to take me a while,' Diana muttered to Max. 'Have a look around while you've got the chance.'

'Don't you dare,' muttered Max. Miranda walked across the hallway and showed Diana into a cloakroom. Before

Diana closed the door, she gave Max a thumbs up behind Miranda's back.

'I'll just fetch my coat,' said Miranda, going up the circular staircase.

Alone, Max stood in the centre of the hallway. That large portrait of Rebecca Cley dominated. He realised what it was that made him think he wouldn't have chosen it. She looked uncomfortable, something in her eyes that the photographer, no matter how skilful, couldn't erase. He picked up a cabinet photo in a silver frame from a sideboard beneath it – Rebecca, head back laughing, arms around Miranda, smiling carefree back at the camera; and Charlie, bronzed in an open-neck shirt, looking sideways at his wife and his daughter with a broad grin on his handsome face. They were in front of the Pavilion Theatre, and Max realised that the picture had been taken on Cromer Pier, the same place where Miranda had so recently snapped the man she thought was her apparently dead father. There was an ice cream stand over Charlie's shoulder, and it occurred to Max that there had been an ice cream stand, too, in the new photograph, possibly even the same one, given its position. There was no indication of when this picture had been taken, but from the age Miranda looked, it must have been not long before Charlie Cley vanished from the face of the earth. He didn't have the look of a man who was about to die.

Cautiously, Max pushed the door in front of him and found himself inside a comfortable lounge looking out on the garden behind the house. Deep sofas and book-lined walls suggested a library; a desk discreetly tucked in a corner contained a laptop with a printer behind, hinting that this might be where Charlie, or perhaps Rebecca, busied themselves when working from home. The shelves were filled with books that looked as if they had been read. Max couldn't imagine a better place to live and to work than this. If one of the theories was that Charlie Cley had chosen to run away from all of this, then either the theory or Charlie himself was mad. A tray on a small table by the desk contained drinks – whisky, vodka, gin, all expensive brands. Max picked up the bottle of red wine on the tray and, though no connoisseur, recognised that a Chassagne-Montrachet wouldn't have come off the cheap shelf at Lidl. He took a picture on his mobile of the label; he'd ask Tony Wenhamville later exactly how much a bottle of that one cost.

'My father's favourite drink,' said Miranda Cley behind him, causing Max to spin around. 'We've crates of it in the cellar, waiting for him to come home to drink them. Would you like to keep that one?'

'I'm sorry,' said Max, putting the bottle back, 'I didn't mean to disturb.'

'No, of course,' she said. 'We've plenty of it though, and we're not paying you for all the trouble you're taking.'

'No payment required,' said Max. 'We're here to help.' And, though it was hardly worth explaining, no payment was desired since any gift Eliot Oakcroft or his staff received worth more than £25 had to be declared. And declaring bottles of wine was more trouble than it was worth once the lists were published and diary columnists were looking for comedy items to fill their pages.

Miranda had changed into a dark trouser suit that somehow made her look even younger and more fragile than the check shirt and jeans had done, like a teenager trying to be a grown-up. It seemed a patronising thought to have about a woman he knew to be twenty-five, but Max realised that from the start Miranda had seemed to him younger than she was and trying not to be, as if she'd stalled at the point when her parents were both taken out of her home and her life. He remembered feeling the same way himself when he'd been told about his own parents dying in the car crash. When he'd met Ronni at Dover after she'd been driven back from France, and when she, his fourteen-year-old sister, had suddenly seemed old and wise and mature while his seventeen-year-old self had regressed into adolescence.

'You must miss them both very much,' he said.

'Hardly anyone ever says that,' said Miranda. 'People think I must miss Dad. They don't always realise I lost them both.'

They walked into the hallway to find Diana looking intently at the photographs around the walls. 'I'm looking forward to meeting your mum,' she said. 'She looks fun.'

'Hardly anyone ever says that any more, either,' said Miranda, walking out of the front door. Diana raised an eyebrow at Max, who shrugged back.

'Cool car,' said Miranda, looking at the Bentley sitting in her driveway.

'Yours aren't bad, either,' said Diana, pointing at the

Range Rover, Alfa Romeo and Lada on the gravel driveway. Miranda laughed. The first time, thought Max, she'd looked relaxed since they arrived.

'The Lada's mine,' said Miranda, with a shrug. 'The cool ones are Mum's and Dad's.'

'You take the front seat,' said Diana, holding the Bentley door open for Miranda. 'I'll get some work done in the back.'

Max drove out onto the lane and back towards the village. The two skips outside the first house on the lane had been joined by a white flatbed truck that was blocking his way. He touched his horn to let the driver know he was there.

'Patrick Alderton,' said Miranda, as the flatbed's door opened, and a tall, slender but muscular man in a white singlet and blue jeans sauntered back towards them. Country music guitars were twanging on the flatbed's radio, audible with the door left open. In London, Alderton's arms would have spoken of time in a gym. Out here, they might mean hard labour.

'On your travels, Miranda,' he drawled. His accent announced he'd been born in Norfolk. 'Apologies for the hold-up. Be out your way in a moment or two.'

'No rush,' said Max, feeling the tension in Miranda.

'Be sure to give my regards to your lovely mother when you see her,' said Alderton. 'We all miss her round here. I was saying to the boys only the other night in the pub what a shame it is Rebecca Cley's not around to have her odd jobs done.'

'And you're just the man to do them,' said Diana, leaning

out of the car for a better look at him. Max wasn't sure how good the man was at reading sarcasm. Nor was he sure how they'd get out of this if Alderton turned nasty, although he had quietly engaged reverse.

'Haven't seen you round here before,' said Alderton. 'Friends of the family, are we?'

'Something like that,' said Max. 'Can we help you shift whatever the obstruction is?'

Alderton appraised Max for a moment, then smiled and held his hands by his side, palms outwards. Max wouldn't have been surprised if he'd spat out of the side of his mouth. He turned slowly and sauntered back to his flatbed, climbed in and rolled it forward and to the side of the road, leaving just enough room for Max to squeeze by. As they passed him, he honked his horn and flashed his lights at them. Max raised an arm in a wave, but without looking back to see what gesture Alderton might be giving him.

'What a creep,' said Diana. 'Has he been watching us since we got here?'

Miranda stared straight ahead of her at the road.

Chapter Six

Diana was busy in the back of the car with a laptop perched on her knees and under headphones. Max assumed she'd be clearing Eliot's constituency email correspondence the way she did most mornings. It wasn't something he could have done himself sitting in the back of a swaying car, but all he saw of her in the rear-view mirror suggested she was concentrating as efficiently as always. Miranda, beside him, seemed content just to watch the Norfolk countryside, or as much of it as one could see from the A47, as they drove around King's Lynn and south into Cambridgeshire.

'Lucky your mum's so close,' said Max, as they approached Norton St Meald. 'Must make visiting easier.'

'It should,' said Miranda. 'Makes it all the worse I've hardly been.'

'Visiting's difficult?'

'Mum doesn't want me to come.'

'I'm not sure I'd want my children to see me in prison,' said Max.

'How many have you got?'

'No. None. Not married,' said Max. 'I mean if I had kids.'

'I don't know why she doesn't want to see me,' said Miranda. 'It's like she's given up. Sometimes I hope she did kill him.'

'You can't mean that.'

'I don't. Not exactly. Only, if he is alive, and he's left her and run away, that'll kill her even more than him being dead.'

Max had visited a lot of England's prisons in the last ten years as part of his work with Eliot Oakcroft's miscarriages of justice working group. Norton St Meald wasn't typical, he realised as he drove into the car park. From here, in spite of the fencing around the whole site, it looked like a low-rise former polytechnic or the kind of quick-build apartment block springing up all around London. Yellow and red facing, wide rectangular windows. It had been intended as a flagship prison when it opened in 2005, an experiment in putting men and women on the same site instead of in different prisons, even if it still kept them strictly segregated in separate accommodation blocks. Like many prisons, it also felt, from the car park, as much like a hospital or school as anything else – signposts and boards showing the way to reception and the various blocks.

Reception was more typical, though – a small room with a prison officer behind a glass screen to examine passports or driving licences, a post-office-style hatch for the surrender of mobile phones, keys, pens and wallets, and lockers for handbags or briefcases.

The formalities completed, a door opened and Max, Diana and Miranda stepped into an airlock. When the door had closed, there was a few seconds' wait, and then the door on the other side opened to let them step into a corridor that might have been in any modern secondary school, bar the posters advertising drugs counselling, informing on how to make a complaint about prison office behaviour, and listing rules. Max's personal shudder was due to the one barring prisoners from walking about with their hands down their trousers, a rule that more than anything else told him how alien life in a prison must be from any normal form of social interaction. Waiting for them as the airlock closed behind were two prison officers in regulation blue jumpers and a dark-haired woman of about forty in a grey trouser suit.

'Sarah Marshall,' she said, extending her hand to Max, apparently automatically identifying the older man as the leader of this group of visitors. 'Deputy Director. I gather you're here representing Eliot Oakcroft MP.'

'This is a personal visit to Rebecca Cley, actually,' said Max. 'But, yes, Diana and I do work for Mr Oakcroft. Miranda, of course, is Rebecca Cley's daughter.'

'Yes, we've met,' said Sarah Marshall, not looking at Miranda, 'and I'm aware of Miranda's work on her mother's case. Do I take it Eliot Oakcroft is supporting the campaign for Rebecca's freedom?'

'Mrs Cley,' said Miranda. Her voice echoed even in the corkboard-lined corridor. 'She's Mrs Cley.'

'We aim for an inclusive and collaborative environment here at Norton St Meald,' said Sarah Marshall smoothly. 'Naturally, I'm keen to facilitate the use of whatever terminology our prison users prefer, but we do aim to keep things relatively informal. As you're a little early for your appointment, might I discuss some aspects of Rebecca's regime with you, Mr Murray?'

'Sure,' said Max. 'Be helpful to know something about how she's doing.'

'Perhaps Miss Cley and your assistant might wait in the recreation area?'

'Anything you tell Diana and me is entirely in confidence,' said Max. 'And I'm sure Miss Cley can be trusted, too.'

'I'm afraid it's not policy to allow civilian visitors access to any part of the prison other than the recreation room and visiting area,' said Sarah Marshall. 'I thought your assistant might want to wait with Miss Cley rather than leave her alone?'

'It's fine, Max,' said Diana, taking Miranda's arm. 'See you later.'

Miranda and Diana were led away by one of the two blue-jumpered prison officers as Sarah Marshall and the other marched off down the corridor into the centre of the prison. Max followed, noting that the pastel walls of the reception area soon became dusty brick painted institutional green and white, although still acned with posters about mental health, HM Prison Inspectorate visits and prison rules. Sarah Marshall turned into an alcove that opened out into a more pleasingly decorated administrative block where two staff sat at desktops typing. Her office was just behind, and the prison officer showed Max into it and closed the door behind him.

Sarah Marshall sat behind her desk and indicated the upright chair in front of it for Max. She punched a number into the telephone on her desk. She had a window behind her, looking out on a patch of green surrounded by flowers. The desk was bare, bar a laptop and an empty plastic in-tray. The office contained no sign of anything personal, just functional modern equipment in a blandly painted space.

'Mr Oakcroft,' she said.

'At your service,' said Eliot Oakcroft via the speakerphone.

'We spoke this morning about your assistant, Mr Murray, and his unauthorised visit to my prison.'

'It's not unauthorised,' said Max. 'Rebecca Cley authorised it yesterday.'

'I think the governor means not authorised by me,' drawled Eliot.

'Deputy Director,' said Sarah Marshall.

'I thought I was speaking to the governor,' said Eliot.

'We don't have a governor,' said Sarah Marshall. 'Norton St Meald's management hub sits outside the civil service.' Which might, thought Max, explain the smartness of Sarah Marshall's suit. 'We have a director.'

'And you're not him?'

'He's a her,' said Sarah Marshall. 'I mean she's a woman. I'm the deputy. I run the women's side of the prison.'

'Ah,' said Eliot. 'I appear to have been misled.'

'Not by me,' said Sarah Marshall. 'Look, we spoke this morning and you agreed to tell Mr Murray that a visit to Rebecca Cley would be highly inappropriate at this time.'

'You told me you were the governor.'

'No, I didn't, and that's beside the point.'

'Are you suggesting I'm mistaken?' said Eliot. Max sat back and smiled at the increasingly confused Sarah Marshall. She probably didn't realise it yet, but she'd just played the losing card.

'No, of course not, but I fully explained who I was,' she said. Max winced on her behalf.

'Well let me explain,' said Eliot Oakcroft MP, and Max could see him standing up at whatever table he'd been sitting at and drawing himself to his full height, 'that if my representative, Mr Maxwell Murray, my Chief of Staff, in fact, requires your co-operation and assistance, Deputy Director, then you should do all in your power to provide it.'

'This isn't what we agreed,' said Sarah Marshall, looking in disbelief at the speakerphone. Max felt sorry for her. She clearly had no idea how politics worked.

'So I trust you'll let Mr Murray see, on my behalf, whatever he wants to see, in my name, and next time HMP Neston Heath—'

'Norton St Meald,' said Max. Correcting Eliot was an automatic reflex.

'Norton St Meald,' said Eliot. 'Next time HMP Norton St Meald wishes to communicate with me, I am sure the governor will have the courtesy to do it himself.'

'Director,' said Sarah Marshall, looking as if she'd just been coshed with a sandbag. 'And it's herself,' she added, but the burr on the speakerphone told her Eliot Oakcroft had hung up on her.

'Was there anything else?' asked Max, pushing his chair back. 'Perhaps we could see Mrs Cley now?' Under other circumstances he'd have sympathised with Sarah Marshall. He'd seen too many civil servants run the irresistible logic of a perfectly sensible policy into the immovable force of Eliot Oakcroft's self-regard. But after the warning-off from Lord West and the veiled threats from Estella Chamberlain, he was beginning to wonder why officialdom was so keen to prevent any investigation of Rebecca Cley's potential innocence. Sarah Marshall was looking at him with ill-concealed – no, let's face it, absolutely unconcealed – dislike, but she rose from her desk and wordlessly led him back down the corridor to the recreation area. Having handed him back to the prison officer watching Diana and Miranda Cley, she stalked back down the corridor without a word of goodbye or a backward glance.

'I doubt she'll be sending you a valentine,' said Diana as the prison officer led them down another corridor and into a cafeteria space. 'Did you kill her hamster, or what?'

'Tell you later,' said Max.

The shutters were down on the serving area, and the symmetrically spaced tables and chairs were bolted to the floor. The prison officer pointed out a coffee vending machine as he led them to a table for six and tactfully withdrew beyond hearing distance. More or less.

Rebecca Cley, as she walked towards them, looked familiar from her photographs, except that in all of those she was smiling. Her chestnut hair was shorter but still falling to her shoulders and, without make-up, her high-cheekboned features and clear skin made her resemblance to Miranda even clearer. If Estella Chamberlain ever needed a poster girl to show that life in prison wasn't Dickensian, then Rebecca Cley would be her ideal; on the other hand, Estella would probably want to send the opposite message. The watching warder, stout, avuncular, not one you'd want to meet down a dark alley, allowed Miranda to hug her mother while Diana and Max sat quietly, noting the clear affection the pair had for each other. When Rebecca sat, she faced Diana and Max across the table, with Miranda on the end, close enough to hold her hand, until the discreet coughs of the warder told her not to.

'Mrs Cley,' said Max, 'we're grateful to you for seeing us. Is there anything you'd like us to take back about how things are for you here?'

'Things are fine, thanks,' said Rebecca. 'As fine as they can be, anyway, given where I am. Got my own cell, a chair, plenty of books.'

'We're going to get you out, Mum,' said Miranda.

'We'll see,' said Rebecca. 'I'm just keeping my head down, biding my time. There's far worse off than me in here.'

'I've never been inside a prison before,' said Diana. 'Wasn't what I was expecting.'

'Me neither,' said Rebecca. 'Most of these women shouldn't be in here.'

'Lots of you didn't do it?'

'No, no,' said Rebecca, 'I mean, I shouldn't be here because I didn't murder Charlie, how could I have? But most of the women in here did the crimes they're supposed to have done, but they shouldn't be in prison – what's the use? Drug addicts and little benefit fiddles and beaten up by their pimps and their minders and their boyfriends.'

'We've done reports on this,' said Max. 'We've recommended getting rid of short-term sentences and not putting women in prison except for really violent crimes.'

'Reports,' said Rebecca, 'recommendations. They're all still in here, though, aren't they? And even if they weren't, they're in here because their lives were crap outside and their lives'll still be crap when they get out, so reports and recommendations aren't going to fix things.'

'We'll get you out soon, Mum,' said Miranda. 'Get you away from these people.'

'They're not bad people,' said Rebecca. 'They might have done bad things but they're not bad people.'

'And they know you're innocent,' said Miranda.

'I keep that to myself more now,' said Rebecca. 'Realised

after the first couple of months I get a lot more respect if they think I killed my husband. Lot of them wish they'd done that themselves. Lot of them should have done that themselves, save them the trouble that got them in here.'

She stared at her hands in front of the table and took some deep breaths. Miranda's hand crept towards her mother's, but a cough from the warder at the door sent it back again to Miranda's lap. Max glanced at Diana, who nodded to him to start talking, but Rebecca beat him to it.

'But you're not here to get my views on the state of the prison system, are you? What can I tell you that I haven't told everyone else already?'

'Who do you think killed your husband?' said Diana. Max and Rebecca both raised their heads to gaze at her, surprised by the directness of the question. Miranda thumped the table with both her hands.

'He isn't dead,' she hissed, taking the photo of Cromer Pier out of her pocket. 'No one killed him.'

'We're not sure that's him,' said Max. 'Do you think it's him, Rebecca?'

'Can't be,' said Rebecca, not looking at the photo. 'If he wasn't dead, he'd have been in touch. If he wasn't dead, he wouldn't let them keep me in here.'

'Look at the picture, Mum. Look at him. Two months ago on Cromer Pier having an ice cream. He's alive.'

'He can't be.'

'It's him, it's definitely him.'

The warder from the door had drifted closer to see what

it was they were looking at. Apparently, a photograph in the middle of the table wasn't enough to make him intervene, and he strolled back to his post as nonchalantly as a very large man being watched by four unhappy people can.

'If,' said Max, 'if we assume for the moment that that isn't Charlie Cley in the picture and that he has been murdered, who do you think would have done it, Rebecca?'

'Everybody loved Charlie.'

'Someone mustn't have.'

'Have you spoken to Tim?'

'He came to see us with Miranda. Told us Charlie's disappearance was causing you all trouble. Told us he was convinced you didn't kill him.'

'Well, he would be convinced of that, wouldn't he?' said Rebecca.

'Because Dad's alive,' said Miranda.

'He isn't alive, Miranda. I wish he was and I know you miss him, but even if he'd leave me in here, which he wouldn't, you'd have heard from him by now.'

'You've got such a wrong picture of him, Mum.'

'Don't start that.'

'He's selfish and stupid and out for himself.'

'He's your father and he's my husband and you can leave him alone, OK, or I go back to my cell right now.'

Miranda slumped back in her chair, turned away from her mother. Max could see tears in the corner of her eyes, though whether tears of frustration or tears of love, it was hard to tell. Rebecca studied the table, or at least the part of the table to the side of the photograph, which Max had noticed she had still not once looked at directly.

'Did Miranda show you this picture last time she was here?' he said.

'I tried,' sulked Miranda. 'She won't look at it.'

'He's dead so it can't be him,' said Rebecca. 'And he'd hardly be laughing with some woman Miranda's age if he was alive and free and able to get me out of here.'

So she'd looked enough at the picture to clock the blonde woman in the sunglasses laughing at whatever the man who might be Charlie was saying, noted Max.

'Can I ask you about your relationship with Patrick Alderton?' he said. Miranda glared at Max.

'It wasn't me who had a relationship with Patrick Alderton,' said Rebecca. 'He did work on the house. I paid him. I have no idea why he claimed we were having a relationship.'

'You reckon someone paid him off to do that,' said Diana.

'I don't know,' said Rebecca. 'I don't know why he lied to the police, lied to the court, lied to the newspapers, but I do know he'd pretty much do anything if someone was willing to pay him.'

The warder at the door coughed and, when Max caught his eye, signalled his watch. Max mouthed 'five more minutes' at him, and got a nod.

'Do you know who could have paid him to drop you in it?' he said to Rebecca.

'Could be anyone,' said Rebecca. 'Have you spoken to Tim about all this?'

'It wasn't Uncle Tim,' said Miranda. 'He doesn't even know Patrick. And he's as broke as we are since Dad did his vanishing act.'

'So he tells us,' said Rebecca.

'Come on, Mum,' said Miranda. 'Tim mortgaged his house to pay for your lawyers. He's as stuffed as we are.'

Max had a flashback to watching Tim Cley in his Savile Row suit, taking notes with his Montblanc pen in his Smythson leather folder. Perhaps the very rich had a different definition of stony broke than his own.

'Tim Cley paid for your lawyers?' he said. 'I thought you weren't able to afford legal advice.'

'I wasn't,' said Rebecca. 'Tim fixed it all up. Some friend of his who'd done work for the firm in the past.'

'I thought Desmond Wedge was an old school friend of his,' said Miranda. 'At least, that's what he told me.'

'Well, maybe,' said Rebecca. 'I was a bit confused at the time, what with Charlie being missing and then being accused of killing him. Tim dealt with all the legal stuff and Mr Wedge, whoever he was and however Tim knows him, was my brief.'

'Was he any good?' said Max. He could see Diana looking sharply at him, and remembered that he hadn't told her Tony Wenhamville had said Desmond Wedge KC was more hindrance than help to any of his unfortunate clients.

'I'm sure he did his best,' said Rebecca. 'To be honest, the whole trial was a bit of a blur.'

'The point is,' said Miranda, 'Uncle Tim paid for the best defence counsel money could buy.'

'He can afford to, can't he,' said Rebecca. 'After all, someone's got the company's money and whether your father's alive or he's dead, we know it can't be him. He wouldn't have known how to cover his tracks. That leaves me or Tim, and it wasn't me.'

There was a pregnant silence as Max and Diana looked at each other, unsure what to say, and Miranda Cley looked daggers at her mother who gazed mildly back at her with her hands meekly in her lap.

'Are you saying,' said Diana, 'that Tim Cley killed your husband to hide his own embezzlement?'

Rebecca's gaze came into focus as she looked curiously at Diana. 'I was wondering when you were going to say something,' she said. 'That's not quite how I'd put it, but I can't think how else it could be.'

'Oh, this is ridiculous,' said Miranda, slamming her hands on the table. 'We've been over and over and over this, Mum. Dad is not dead and wherever this bloody money is, he has it. Uncle Tim couldn't have killed him any more than you could. Uncle Tim loved Dad, maybe more than you did.'

'I loved Charlie,' said Rebecca, 'I loved him to bits and he loved me, but he couldn't half be annoying when he wanted to be. Your Uncle Tim loved Charlie too, but Charlie could drive him bonkers. You know what he was like, love, always late for meetings, never prepared, always thinking he could talk anyone into giving him anything he wanted just because he was charming and funny and handsome.'

'He fooled you,' said Miranda.

'No, he didn't,' said Rebecca. 'I knew what he was like. I just loved him whatever his flaws. But Tim could get really mad with him when he nearly screwed up an account by being late or making mistakes or just getting overfamiliar with the clients. And he was hopeless with money, you have to admit that.'

'That's why we're in the mess we're in. That's why Tim's broke.'

'You think Tim would let Charlie have that much control over the money?' said Rebecca. 'You think Charlie would even know how to withdraw it all and hide it away where Tim can't find it? He barely knew how to use a cash machine, Miranda. If he was trying to embezzle the firm like they said he was, he'd have cocked it up and Tim would know all about it.'

'Are you saying you think Tim had a motive to kill him?' said Diana, and once more Rebecca and Max looked up at the directness of her question.

'If anyone did, it was Tim,' said Rebecca.

'Tim didn't do it,' said Miranda. 'If Tim had killed Charlie, it would be a fit of rage, a moment of anger, not a plan to hide his car a hundred miles out of London and make it look like he'd vanished.'

'Maybe you should talk to Tim,' said Rebecca, rising and signalling to the warder.

'We'll do what we can to get you out of here,' said Max, also rising.

'I'd like that,' said Rebecca. 'I'd like that very much.'

For a second, as she stretched her hand out, Max thought she was going to shake his. But she picked up the photograph from the table and tore it into four, then eight pieces and scattered it on the floor, before she turned to let the warder take her back to her cell.

'She's completely deluded,' said Miranda. 'He's my dad and I love him and he's brilliant, but she can't see what a selfish, philandering bastard he could be. You saw her with that photograph, refusing to look at it, refusing to see him with that woman in Cromer. It's how she dealt with all his little affairs, all his little bits on the side, just pretend they never happened and they don't exist.'

The Bentley cruised easily along the A47 back into Norfolk; Miranda sat in the back talking constantly while Max and Diana in front exchanged significant glances.

'She doesn't seem to like your Uncle Tim much,' said Max. 'Were they ever close?'

'I don't know, but they've always been wary of each other since I've been old enough to notice. Mum always thought Tim took advantage of Dad, always thought it was Dad who got the business for the firm, even if it was Tim who did the paperwork. She's always said Dad's percentage of the profits wasn't enough when pretty much every client signed up because he charmed them into it.'

'So she's always had a grudge against him.'

'That wasn't how it was, though,' said Miranda. 'Tim's not flash like Dad but clients trust him and stay with the firm because he puts the work in. Almost everyone figures out Dad's a bit of a rogue pretty soon after they meet him. Everyone except my mum, that is.'

'Can I ask you something personal?' said Diana. Max was surprised by the question. Well, not by the question so much as the fact that Diana was asking permission to ask something obviously direct, when she'd been doing that all day to Rodney Ferrars and Rebecca Cley.

'OK,' said Miranda, doubtfully.

'Did you have an affair with Patrick Alderton?'

'What? No. No, of course not.'

'Only I noticed your mum said it wasn't her he was having a relationship with, and then she sort of gave you this look and you sort of blushed a bit and got busy with your hair, and I just wondered.'

'He did a couple of favours for me, and then he tried it on a bit,' said Miranda. 'Mum misinterpreted a situation, that's all.'

'I don't think we really need to know about this,' said Max, who could see Diana was going to ask more, and switched on the car radio with the volume set high.

'Could we have some music from this century?' shouted Miranda from the back.

'Even the twentieth century would do,' yelled Diana.

'The car's so old the dial's stuck on Radio 3,' bellowed Max. 'And the volume control's broken.'

Saint-Saëns' Organ Symphony blasted them all the

way back to Wymondham. And Max's rear-mirror view of Miranda Cley told him not to turn it off. Diana had struck a raw nerve, a very raw nerve indeed.

Once they'd dropped Miranda at home, Max and Diana drove into Norwich for dinner before her train back to London.

'I could just come to Cromer with you tomorrow,' she said, once they'd ordered their pizzas and a bottle of Valpolicella.

'You can't. You're on constituency duty with Eliot.'

'I'm pretty sure I've read something about constitutional bars on cruel and unusual punishments,' said Diana.

'That's America,' said Max. 'They've written their constitution down. We make ours up as we go along. And Eliot's constitutional responsibility is, once a month, to go to the constituency of the people who elected him, even if they have absolutely no idea who he is, so that he can sit in a draughty village hall while they present him with problems he has no power to solve – and you sit there taking notes of which councillor, quango, debt collection agency or police force needs to know about them.'

'He's got Julie to do that,' said Diana. 'He won't care if I'm not there. He won't even know.'

'Julie panics,' said Max. Julie was Eliot's long-term constituency secretary, inherited from the previous MP and capable of hiring the village hall and typing out a list of appointments. The trouble with Julie was that Eliot would promise people he could sort out their rent arrears, settle conflict in the Middle East, get their terminally dim son into Oxford or whatever else they asked, and Julie would then try to do it.

'One of us needs to be there, Diana,' he said. 'Remember when we left them to it and Julie rang the United Nations to get an appointment for Eliot with the Secretary-General so that he could give his advice on Nagorno-Karabakh?'

'I remember,' said Diana. 'Does he have to do constituency surgeries? He hates them. You hate them. I hate them.'

'But his constituents love them,' said Max. 'And if they've taken the trouble to elect him, they ought to get to see him sometimes.'

'They do love him, don't they?' said Diana. 'You really can fool some of the people all of the time.'

A silence fell for a moment, each of them alone with their thoughts. Max's had turned, as they often did, to the enigma of Eliot Oakcroft MP. To anyone who'd worked or spent more than five minutes in conversation with him, he might as well have been a mannequin in a well-tailored suit and tie. But his constituents, or at least the couple of hundred of them who knew who he was and took the opportunity to bring their problems to his monthly surgeries, seemed genuinely fond of him. 'He tells it like it is,' they said to each other. 'He gives them what for.' Someone had once defined politics as the art of the possible; Max had discovered from his years of watching Eliot in action that it was, for an alarming number of Eliot's voters, the art of the promise. Telling people you'd solve their problems seemed more effective than actually doing so. 'He's a gent,' they'd say as they queued to meet him, and Eliot would smile, and shake hands and clap backs, and make jokes, and they'd go away happy that the Member of Parliament was on their cases and exploring avenues and turning wheels and whatever else it was they did down there in that London all week.

Max glanced across at Diana, wondering if she too was musing on the wonder of their boss. 'Still thinking about Eliot?' he said.

'God, no,' said Diana, pulling a face. 'I was wondering if there'd be a bar on the train or I should grab some gin and tonic tins at the station. So, that Miranda Cley – bit of a dark horse, eh?'

'I'm not sure what you're getting at.'

'Oh, come on, Max,' said Diana as the waiter arrived with their wine. The lad didn't look old enough to drink it, never mind serve it. 'I mean, seriously, is she shagging the handyman or what?' said Diana, and the waiter's face went roughly the same colour as the Valpolicella.

'Do you think we could keep this conversation on a civilised level?' said Max. The boy with the wine bottle was hovering uncertainly. His struggles with the screw top made Max grateful they hadn't let the boy loose on a corkscrew.

'Do you want to try it?' the waiter said.

'Sure,' said Max, wondering why they still went through the whole wine-smelling and sniffing ritual in the Norwich

Pizza Express, and wondering what the boy would do if he sent the opened bottle back. He sniffed the slightly shakily poured centimetre that went into his glass while noticing the lad was gazing at Diana like a cow who'd spotted a full trough.

'Fine, fine,' said Diana, offering the boy her glass and signalling him to keep pouring. 'Tell me, Max,' she said, once he'd filled them both up and she'd sent him on his way with a smile that would leave him not minding if he didn't get a tip later. 'Have you got a girlfriend?'

'Yes, no, yes, well, I can't quite see how that's germane to the issue or any business of yours.'

'Thought so,' said Diana. 'Tell me, have you had a girlfriend in the last five years?'

'Look,' said Max, 'let's get one thing quite clear—'

'Because my Aunt Susan, that's my mum's sister, she's just got divorced, and she'd be great for you, really, and I think she's not after anything serious right now, and if you, you know, you wanted, I could set you up so easily.'

Max was glad to see his American Hot arriving along with the chance to sit back and take his time.

'Thank you,' he said. 'Thank you for that kind offer. If I want to take it up, I'll let you know.'

'Oh, don't be such a stuffed shirt. You really, really need a bit of fun, honest you do.'

'Could we talk about something else, please?' said Max.

'Please yourself,' said Diana, 'but it's a good offer – she's a laugh, you know. Don't forget it.'

'I'll bear it in mind,' said Max. 'Now, how about we focus on the case for five minutes?'

'Fair enough,' said Diana. 'Well, first, Rebecca Cley didn't kill anyone, and Charlie Cley's alive out there and hiding with all the money. What we need to know is whether Tim Cley knows he's still alive and wants to kill him for nicking all his money, or knows he's still alive and is helping him hide out.'

'And why would he do that?'

'We haven't really dug into how well their business was doing. If Tim's fronting for a dodgy firm and Charlie's lying low for a while gets them over a hump, then there's a plan.'

'A plan that involves Charlie, and Tim, letting Rebecca rot in prison.'

'Does seem a stretch,' said Diana.

'We need to see Tim,' said Max. 'We need to find out more about what was going on between the brothers.'

'So, I get on to that tomorrow while you go touring Cromer Pier?'

'That's about the size of it,' said Max.

'Right,' said Diana. 'Better get me to the train station then.'

Chapter Seven

Max had happy memories of Cromer. At least he thought he did. They'd gone there, the family, when he was a boy, on a long weekend break in a caravan, and he still possessed a souvenir. There had been a fair in the park on top of a small cliff out west of the town centre, a grander affair than might be expected, including a flyover by the Red Arrows. *All necks craned skyward for a glimpse of the precision flyers*, read the caption in the *North Norfolk News*, beneath a photograph of Maxwell Murray, aged nine, and his sister Veronica, aged six, he not quite craning his neck away from an ice cream cone the size of his head while Ronni waved excitedly at the sky with hers. Did he remember that day, that weekend? he thought as he drove down Prince of Wales Road to the seafront the morning after his dinner with

Diana. Or did he just remember the photo and his sister's incredible excitement the next morning when his father spotted it in the local paper? Although Ronni had probably long forgotten both the excitement and the photo, Max still had it in a box somewhere and came across it from time to time. The tricks that memory played.

Max drove to a car park facing out over the seafront, not far from where those precision flyers had done their work three decades ago. For all he knew, the Red Arrows still treated Cromer to a display for their annual fair. From the edge of the car park he could see the pier running out from the beachfront into the sea, with its small Cromer Theatre out there on the end of it. And in the middle of it, an ice cream stand that featured in another photograph, the one Miranda Cley had taken of the man she insisted was her father. Max put that photo back in his wallet and strolled along the promenade towards the steps down to the pier.

There are few things in life that tell you that you need a haircut as much as a breeze off the North Sea. Max swept flyaway strands out of his eyes as he approached the ice cream stand. It was an old-fashioned bike with a freezer box from the days when vanilla, strawberry and chocolate were as exotic as ices got. The lad wielding the scoop, dressed in black trousers and waistcoat over a white shirt with armbands, looked, fortunately, very much like the one in Miranda Cley's photograph. He'd also found a solution to the breeze off the North Sea. Thick black hair, backcombed above his forehead, glittered in the sunlight. Add a white scarf and a Spitfire and he'd stroll into a Brylcreem Boys movie.

Getting his attention was going to be a problem. The sunshine had brought hundreds of people onto the pier and it seemed every one of them wanted an ice cream. Max contemplated joining the queue but doubted he'd have much chance to ask about the photograph. He stood watching, unable to make up his mind on how to make contact, until he realised the boy had noticed him. He strolled off down the pier, inspected the theatre at the end of it, and then took a bench where he could watch the ice cream operation until the queue died down or the boy, as he surely must, took a break or ran out of the stuff.

He'd dealt with a few emails and read some messages from Diana telling him a meeting with Tim Cley was set up for next week, when he realised a bulky man in a black suit had sat next to him on his left. And another, nearly identical, was joining him on the right. Instinctively, he tried to rise, but found a hand on each arm pressing him back into place. He looked around the busy pier at the dozens of people who had entirely failed to notice anything odd going on. And even if they were looking, what would they see? Two men, a bit pudgy, in black suits, black shirts and black shoes with a slimmer, better-dressed man sitting between them, in a navy jacket, white shirt and fawn chinos.

'And what's your game, then?' said the one on Max's left. Nothing threatening in his tone, just a gentle spirit of enquiry.

'Only we heard from young Stanley over there that you've been taking an interest,' said the one on his right. Ah, this was the one that would beat Max up and throw his body over the pier.

'So, as I said, what's the game?'

'I only want to ask him some questions,' said Max.

'Questions, is it?' said Lefty, reaching across to finger the lapel of Max's Hackett jacket. 'Questions, you want to ask him. Lovely bit of fabric, this, by the way, my friend, lovely bit of schmutter.'

'Look, I don't know who you are or what you want, but if you think you're intimidating me, you're absolutely right,' said Max.

'We don't want any trouble,' said Lefty. 'Questions. What would be the nature of these questions, then?'

'He's in a photograph someone gave me and I wanted to ask him about it.'

'Ah, photographs, is it,' said Lefty. 'I get the picture.'

'You get the picture,' said Righty, a meaty hand slapping his meaty thigh, packing quite a punch. 'That's a good one, that is. Getting the picture.'

'I'd say, jacket like this, shoes from Church's if I'm not mistaken, I'd say our gentleman might have a bit of money if he's interested in pictures,' said Lefty.

'You've got the wrong end of the stick,' said Max, reaching for his inside pocket, and finding his arm sharply clamped by his side.

'Best not make sudden movements like that,' said Lefty.

'I was going to show you the picture,' said Max.

'What, here?' said Righty. 'With all these kiddies about?'

'It's not that sort of picture, is it?' said Lefty, signalling his oppo to let Max's arm alone. 'I'm beginning to get a feeling there's more to this than meets the eye. Getting back to where we started, chum, what exactly is your game?'

'I'm investigating a murder,' said Max, getting his wallet from his jacket pocket. 'Or possibly not a murder. Look.'

The two men leant in to examine the picture in Max's hands, and he had a brief fantasy that he could just bang their heads together and escape. Then a briefer thought that Diana would have done just that if he hadn't had the sense to send her back to London.

'So what?' said Lefty. 'Geezer and a bird buying an ice cream and our Stanley in the background. What's he got to do with a murder?'

'The geezer shouldn't be in the photograph because he's supposed to be dead,' said Max. 'I was hoping your Stanley could tell me more about meeting him.'

'Well, then,' said Lefty, getting to his feet. 'That all seems fair enough and on the level. Why don't you just ask him?'

Max, helped to his feet by Righty, looked down the pier to where Stanley was still serving endless cones and tubs to a queue of young mums and innumerable toddlers. 'When does he get a break?' he asked.

Fifteen minutes later, Stanley and Max were sat in a café up the stairway from the pier on a narrow back street. Stanley had been more than happy to leave his ice cream bike with Lefty and Righty, and promised he'd be back in half an hour.

'Are you sure you're OK leaving it with those two?' Max said, as he brought a caramel iced latte with whipped cream to the table, and a black espresso for himself. Behind the boy, the wall was decorated with lurid representations of Cromer landmarks done in purples and oranges. A particularly virulent Pier at Sunset even had a brown smudge that might have been Stanley and his ice cream bike.

'Course I am,' said Stanley. 'Trust that pair with my life. My cousins. They keep an eye on the business.'

'Two of them for an ice cream cart?'

'Thirty-eight ice cream carts between Sheringham and Hemsby,' said Stanley, with an air of wonder that Max could possibly not appreciate that he was the representative of a catering empire. 'Seventeen burger vans and fourteen fish and chip shops and all. Oh, and the Thai place in East Runton, but that's just for Lawrence now he's back from his gap year, won't last a year my Uncle Ferdie reckons, then Lawry'll be back on the Happisburgh campsite candy floss 'til he's repaid his flights.'

'Sorry,' said Max. 'I hadn't realised it was quite so complicated. No wonder you've got people patrolling.'

'I'm sorry if they came on a bit rough,' said Stanley, sitting back in his chair and spooning whipped cream into his mouth. 'Only I wasn't sure what you were up to, and you get some funny types down the pier.'

'Talking of which,' said Max, sliding the photograph across the table, 'do you remember this guy?'

'Flash Harry,' said Stanley instantly. 'Paid me with a twenty, told me to keep the change. Asked me where I got my hair done.'

'Your hair?'

'He needed his hair cutting, wanted to know where in town he could get something as good as mine.' The boy swept a hand across his luxuriantly gelled barnet. The whipped cream he hadn't realised was on his hand wasn't improving it any, but Max could tell it had been cut and shaped with care.

'Do you know if he got his hair cut in town?'

'I wasn't following him, but if he did, it's Short Cuts up Pinner Lane, and you have to ask for Mark. But he's got a waiting list so if the guy did go there, it probably wasn't that day.'

Worth a try, though, thought Max. And if he'd paid with a credit card, there might be a way to find out if he was Charlie Cley.

'Did he tell you anything else about himself?'

'He went on and on about himself all the time, but no, not really. I only remember him because of the tip, really.'

'OK,' said Max. 'Listen, thanks for your time and thanks for the hairdressing tip.'

'I'd like to be a private detective,' said Stanley. 'How'd you get into that game, then?'

'Well, I didn't, exactly,' said Max.

'That explains a lot,' said Stanley, happily draining the

last of his iced caramel latte. Max could almost see the enamel stripping from the boy's teeth. 'I'm not sure you're very good at it, anyway.'

'I'm sorry?' said Max.

'Well, all that hanging about on the pier for one thing,' said Stanley. 'And you've missed something really obvious in that photograph.'

'What?'

'If you really want to know about this guy, why don't you just ask Lulu?'

'Lulu?'

'I think she's worth another iced caramel latte, don't you?' said Stanley. 'By the way,' he added, pointing at the Pier at Sunset on the wall behind him, 'do you like her work?'

Lulu Marchbanks, twenty-six, slim, blonde and an artist who struggled by on sales of her jagged landscapes and a £2 million trust fund, turned out to be the woman in the photograph that might contain Charlie Cley. She also turned out to be not at home when Stanley took Max round to her house twenty minutes after ingesting his second iced caramel latte. After thanking Stanley for all his help, Max took a walk through the town to Short Cuts up Pinner Lane. It turned out to be a red herring. Mark, the salon's maestro, said he'd never seen the man in the photograph and would remember if he'd cut his hair, since he remembered every head he'd ever sculpted. And, to kill the time until he tried Lulu again, Max had a quick trim from the salon's trainee, Belle, who differed strongly from him in her interpretation of the word 'trim' and the phrase 'keeping a fair bit on top'.

Running a hand across the stubble as he rang Lulu's doorbell ten minutes later, he was surprised that the door simply buzzed open. He walked into a hallway stacked with canvases, used and unused, and followed a call of 'through here' into a huge room with three glass walls and a glass ceiling providing almost dazzling light. At the centre of the room was an easel with a canvas on it, and in front of it, barefoot and in a long T-shirt spattered with orange and purple paint, a smiling blonde woman with sunglasses on her hair.

'You must be Stanley's private dick,' she said, and Max realised she was not looking at his face. 'He said you were a looker.'

'Thank you,' said Max, uncertainly. 'Did he tell you what I was looking for?'

'Let's have a look at this photo,' said Lulu, bouncing across the room and looking right into Max's face. 'I'm not sure about the haircut, by the way, but he's right about the rest of you.'

'How well do you know Charlie Cley?' said Max, taking a step backward.

'Never heard of him,' said Lulu, taking the photograph and studying it. 'Oh, I remember this guy – Lamborghini, took me over to Burnham Market for dinner, ordered the most expensive red on their wine list, don't think he even knew what it was.'

Max took a few more photographs from his wallet, the ones Miranda Cley had printed out of her dad. Lulu looked at four of a man in a suit without recognition, but when she got to the one of him by the swimming pool wearing nothing but a pair of trunks, she raised her eyebrows and whistled. 'Yup, that's him,' she said. 'Very hairy chest, very hairy back.'

'His daughter thinks he's Charlie Cley,' said Max. 'What name do you know him by?'

'Might have been Charlie,' said Lulu. 'Though I'm thinking something else, Toby maybe, or Zac.'

'Right,' said Max. 'So you don't know him well.'

'Don't know him at all,' said Lulu. 'He picked me up on the pier about ten minutes before we got the ice creams, then he came back here for the afternoon, then he drove me over to Burnham Market and we stayed there for the night, and that was the last I saw of him.'

'He has a house at Burnham Market?'

'Hotel. At Holt. Very nice if you're looking for somewhere for tonight. After dinner, maybe?'

'Not his hotel, I'm guessing.'

'Nope. I've no idea where he lives, if that's what you're asking.'

'It is. I need to find him.'

'Then you'd probably appreciate his phone number?'

'You've got it?'

'Where did you say you were taking me for dinner?'

Chapter Eight

'Wow,' said Ronni when Max arrived back at their Westbourne Park flat on Sunday afternoon. 'I know you said you were visiting a prison, but did you have to let them cut your hair?'

'Remind me never to use a small-town barber again,' said Max, throwing his arms around her. She was wearing one of his old rugby shirts that made her seem even tinier than usual.

'You're disgustingly cheerful,' she said, grinning. 'Baldness really isn't going to suit you, by the way. I'd resist it as long as you can.'

'Not everyone finds it unattractive,' said Max, running his hand across the stubble and flushing a little at the memory of Lulu Marchbanks doing the same in the restaurant at Holt last night. He disengaged from Ronni's hug and flung himself onto the sofa. There were cushions at either end of it, and space for the two of them to sit there comfortably. The coffee table had been cleared of his spray of books and papers. There was a smell in the air, a clean smell. 'Have you been tidying the place? Have you even left the flat since I've been out?'

'I wasn't going to let a guest see the tip you live in. I tell people my brother's a high-flying political consultant, not an overgrown student.'

'It's not a tip. It might look a bit untidy but I've got a system. I know where everything is.'

'I know you do, Max. I've put all your books back on the right shelves, honest.'

'You had a guest?' said Max, catching up with the point. Was Ronni wearing perfume, or was that just air freshener up his nostrils? 'Tell me more.'

'None of your business,' she grinned, and sat opposite him on the sofa, the armrest behind her back, her knees pulled up to her chin inside Max's rugby shirt. 'And weren't you due home last night, Maxwell Murray?'

'Something came up,' he said.

'For once you weren't missed,' said Ronni. 'Your dressing gown needs a wash, by the way, and you're almost out of shaving foam.'

Max looked at his smiling sister. He knew next to nothing about a romantic life she kept strictly to herself. 'Anyone I know?' he said.

'And what was it that kept you out in Norfolk all the livelong night?' said Ronni. 'Did you find anything out?'

Max smiled. The main thing he'd found out was that he could scare the bejesus out of himself by seeing a shorn-haired ruffian in the mirror of a hotel in Holt before realising he was looking at his own reflection.

'I did pretty well for myself,' he said. 'I might just have a positive identification of Charlie Cley, alive and well and possibly living somewhere in Norfolk. And, even better, I have what might very well be his phone number.'

'Might be?'

'The witness who gave me it wasn't entirely sure it was his or what his name was, but she recognised his photo.'

'And was more than happy to give you his phone number.'

'She took a bit of persuading,' said Max, stretching like a cat and putting his arms behind his head.

'Tough work, this detective business,' grinned Ronni.

'Someone has to do it,' said Max.

'Well, you're not the only one,' said Ronni, shifting Max's feet off the sofa and onto the floor, and reaching across him for a spiral-bound notebook on the coffee table. 'I got to wondering why the Secretary of State for Law and Order might want you to keep your nose out of all this. So I made a few calls, did a bit of digging. I assume you're a regular reader of the Register of Members' Interests?'

'More a regular writer,' said Max, sitting up. 'I fill in Eliot's declarations every month.'

'Truth or fiction?'

'Truth,' said Max, 'although a certain amount of creative writing might sometimes be required.'

'It's a work of genius,' said Ronni, turning her laptop towards him. 'Publish as much incredibly boring incidental detail as you can to make sure no one's ever going to think of trying to read it, and you can hide pretty much anything.'

'What have you got?'

Ronni opened her notebook. 'Six hours' solid work, this, Maxwell – have you any idea what I should be charging you?'

'More than Eliot pays me for a week, less than he asks for a speech.'

'People pay Eliot Oakcroft large fees to listen to him make speeches?' said Ronni, a look of genuine surprise on her face.

'No,' said Max, 'but he still asks for a gigantic fee. Says people have to realise what he's worth.'

'I think they do,' said Ronni. 'If they've heard of him at all, I think they know exactly what he's worth.'

'Whatever,' said Max. 'But what do I owe you? Sunday roast and a bottle of Valpolicella at the pub on the corner cover it?'

'Done,' said Ronni. 'Anyway, your old friend Estella Chamberlain – I think she'd love your new haircut, by the way, she's fond of a short back and sides – had two donations of £10,000 for her constituency office from a company called Parallel Parking. Companies House records its sole director as one Anthony Green.'

'So what? Who's he?'

'I don't know, since I can't find any info anywhere on any Anthony Green.'

'Can't be an unusual name,' said Max.

'No,' said Ronni, 'and that's the problem. There are a couple of dozen Anthony Greens out there, but I can't find a thing about the one who's registered as the sole director of Parallel Parking. None of the other Anthony Greens lists Parallel Parking as belonging to them. And I turned up not a news story, not a LinkedIn or a Facebook account, not a trace. This particular one isn't listed as a director or trader for any other company. And the company doesn't seem to trade or file accounts. The address registered at Companies House for Parallel Parking turns out to be a storage block in Wandsworth.'

'Should we go out there and have a look?' said Max.

'Number 28 bus, takes about an hour,' said Ronni. 'Like I said, I've been doing my research.'

Somewhere just off the South Circular Road, down towards the railway lines going out west from London, sat a set of small industrial estates, wire fences around them, with a single entrance for cars and a barrier operated by some unseen operative. They were also about ten minutes' walk from the bus stop where Ronni and Max had alighted on Wandsworth High Street. And on one of those estates stood the premises of Parallel Parking.

'There'll be no one here on a Sunday,' said Max as Ronni's phone guided them towards the right security booth.

'I'm pretty much betting there's no one at Parallel Parking most of the time,' said Ronni.

'They can't all be working from home.'

'I doubt it employs anyone,' said Ronni. 'Couldn't find anything about what it does, what it makes or what services it provides; annual accounts are more or less dormant. Single director, Anthony Green. No online presence.'

'What's the point of a company like that? Why have a premises at all? It must cost them to rent.'

'Depends what they've got,' said Ronni. 'If it's basically just a plate on a wall and a storage box, then it won't cost much, and you've got a shell company you can use to transfer any money you don't want anyone looking at too closely.'

'That's got to be criminal.'

'Probably. But if you're properly incorporated, file your accounts on time and pay your rent and your rates and your corporation tax, nobody's going to be too bothered what you're actually doing. Units on estates like this rent out little spaces all the time.'

'How do you know all this?'

'I had a bit of help with the research,' said Ronni. 'Told you I had a guest over the weekend.'

'Who?'

'Do we discuss these things, Max?'

'No, we don't.'

'He's a business reporter. Nice guy. Owed me a favour.'

'And?'

'And I'll be invoicing you for the two large cod and chips, with mushy peas, and four cups of tea it took to get him to cough up all that lot.'

'I'll pay for his fish and chips. You can buy your own.'

'Who says I had any?'

'Ah,' said Max, grinning. 'Geoffrey Sunderland? Still on the *FT*, is he? Still single?'

'Still unattached,' said Ronni, 'though still double, or even triple the size he should be . . . Anyway, as I say, he owed me a favour.'

They'd reached the edge of the industrial estate. A small, empty security booth stood beside the barrier across the entrance. A metal noticeboard behind it listed the occupants of the estate, metal nameplates that could be slid in and out of grooves as companies came and went, among them Parallel Parking. Ronni walked up to the car barrier and touched it, causing a buzzing noise in the security booth.

'Watch what you're doing,' said Max. 'Do we want them to know we're here?'

'Of course we do,' said Ronni. 'What was the point in coming if we're not going to try for a look around.'

She ducked under the barrier and motioned Max to follow her. He could see a man coming from the building ahead of them, a man in a blue shirt and a peaked cap. He could also see his five-foot-tall sister striding towards the man, and ducked himself beneath the barrier to follow.

'This is private property, miss,' said the man, who Max could now see was older and frailer than he'd expected of a security guard.

'I'm looking for Mr Green,' said Ronni. 'He said he'd be here today.'

'Be a first time if he was,' said the security guard. 'There's no one here, miss. It's Sunday, you know.'

'Sorry to disturb,' said Ronni. 'Expect you were watching the match back there.'

'To be honest with you, I was,' said the man. 'Wouldn't mind getting back to it, too, if you wouldn't mind stepping back beyond the barrier, there.'

'Of course,' said Ronni. 'Only you wouldn't need to watch us if we just went over to the Parallel Parking office to have a look through the window and see if Mr Green's in, like he said he would be.'

'He did, did he?' said the man.

'He did, didn't he, Max?' said Ronni.

'Yes,' said Max, wondering if a single syllable had ever been less convincingly delivered in the Wandsworth district of London, and that even with a prison just up the road.

'How many times did he say it?' the security guard asked, putting his hand out, palm up.

'About forty times,' said Ronni, 'or maybe it was a round fifty.'

'Well, if it was fifty, I expect I could let you have a look just to check,' said the guard.

'What's in your wallet, Max?' said Ronni.

'My wallet?'

'You know I don't carry cash.'

'What makes you think I do?'

'I've known you all my life, Max. You carry Lemsip, aspirin, sixteen pens, a stapler and a roll-up shopping bag. If you've come out the house without at least a hundred quid in your pocket, I'm not your sister.'

'Did Mr Green say it a hundred times?' said the security guard.

'Let's call it sixty,' said Ronni, and Max reluctantly counted out two twenties and two tens. The guard pointed them in the direction of a single-storey prefab towards the back of the compound and walked happily back towards his office.

'What match is on?' said Max.

'No idea.'

'How did you know there was one he'd be watching?'

'Isn't there always?' said Ronni.

The prefab building had a small plate on the door reading *Parallel Parking*. The door handle turned but the door was locked. The single window was curtained, but the curtains didn't quite meet, enough for Max to see a table with nothing on it, a chair behind it and a metal filing cabinet in the corner. On the wall was a whiteboard. It was as white as a whiteboard can be, without even the smudge of something written before and not quite wiped off.

'Looks to me like the mysterious Mr Green hasn't been here for a while,' said Ronni. 'And if the guard's never seen him, maybe he doesn't exist.'

'Not much more we can learn here, is there?' said Max.

'We can learn where there's a pub, so you can spend that forty quid you've still got on that dinner you owe me,' said Ronni.

* * *

Across the road from Wandsworth Town Rail Station, they found a bar with all they needed – drinks and little tables where two people could sit and talk quietly. Fish and chips or burger and chips on the menu. Any ambition of covering those plus the promised bottle of Valpolicella out of the forty quid in his wallet dashed to ribbons. At least the food was good though, and Max, not for the first time, wondered how it was that someone as small as his sister could motor through her chips and then get started on his without the embarrassment of asking and without becoming the size of a house. He was happy to sit back and let her do it, though. Even as the plates were put down in front of them, the voice of Diana, like some hyperactive Jiminy Cricket, had been muttering imprecations in his head about arteries and saturated fats.

'I'm really not sure where you're going with all this,' said Max, refilling Ronni's half-empty glass and his own entirely empty one. 'So, Estella's getting some iffy contributions from a dodgy businessman. Why would that make her stop us getting Rebecca Cley out of jail?'

'Doesn't that depend on who the dodgy businessman is?'

'You said he didn't exist. What we've just seen makes that seem pretty likely.'

'Looking that way,' said Ronni. 'Although by one gigantic coincidence, he shares his date of birth with one Charles Anthony MacAllister Cley.'

Max sat back and watched her finishing the last of his chips. Information, he thought, that could have been shared at any time in the last three hours. Ronni, even as a kid, had loved to keep little nuggets of gossip to herself, to drop at the time of maximum impact. While the love of gossip went a long way to explaining why she'd chosen to become a journalist, he couldn't help feeling her unwillingness to share it must sometimes be a drawback.

'Charlie Cley?' he said. 'You think this Anthony Green guy is Charlie Cley.'

'I don't know,' said Ronni. 'It's a working theory, though. I'm going to keep digging.'

'If he is Charlie, and if Charlie's still alive, and if he was giving money to Estella . . .' said Max, tailing off into thought. Which Ronni completed for him.

'Then the Secretary of State for Law and Order would be helping out a criminal to keep her own nose clean,' said Ronni. 'And that, big brother, would begin to be the kind of story I would be interested in.'

'I don't believe it,' said Max. 'Estella wouldn't do anything this dodgy.'

'She's as bent as a banana.'

'She's too careful to get caught at it, though.'

'Come off it, Max. Remember what she did to you.'

'Yeah, but that was just me and her, and her word against mine, and who was I going to tell anyway without looking like a complete idiot?'

'You told me,' said Ronni, 'but, yeah, to be fair, you did look like a total turnip.'

'Thanks, sis,' said Max. 'And it was all your kindness and sympathy got me through the crisis.'

'Tough love,' said Ronni. 'Being laughed at for a week did you the world of good.'

Max leant back, putting his hands behind his head, and flinching slightly at the still-unfamiliar prickles. The shock of seeing a bullet-headed thug in a mirror in the hotel last night when he'd got up for a pee had taught him to hope his hair would grow back quickly. It was his worst moment in a hotel since he'd woken to find Estella Chamberlain had stolen all his clothes. He smiled across at his sister, sadly. Ronni was right; she had simply got him through the humiliation of being double-crossed by the woman he'd thought he loved by making him see how ridiculously funny it all was.

'Estella's a piece of work all right,' he said, 'and I don't doubt she'd do anything she could get away with. But I don't believe she'd be so dumb as to cover up for a crook, not if there was an obvious connection and she could be found out.'

'Neither do I,' said Ronni. 'Not yet, anyway. I'd need a lot more of a link than a coincidental birthday. But can you find out if Charlie ever ran another company, if he did set up Parallel Parking?'

'I can ask Tim Cley,' said Max. 'I need to meet him this week.'

'Are you sure you can trust him?'

'I don't know. Rebecca Cley's convinced Uncle Tim's up to no good, but Miranda seems to trust him. At least, she's keeping him in the loop on what we're doing. And, although he doesn't believe Charlie's alive, he's supporting Miranda in calling us in to investigate. He needs to find Charlie to get his money back.'

'Not unless he already knows where Charlie is,' said Ronni. 'Not unless they're in it together.'

'Why?'

'If you have limited income and lots of people you owe money to, emptying the till and vanishing to start a new life somewhere else might be an attractive option.'

Max whistled. 'That's brilliant. But it makes no sense. If Tim was up to his neck in this, he wouldn't really want an investigation.'

'And he's done all he could to avoid one,' said Ronni. 'He couldn't stop Miranda Cley coming to you, but he could get himself inside to find out what you knew. And persuading her to approach someone as dim and useless as Eliot Oakcroft kind of suggests he didn't really want much done.'

'Eliot's not as bad as you paint him,' said Max. 'He has hidden depths.'

'He doesn't even have hidden shallows,' said Ronni. 'Seriously, if you wanted to persuade your niece you were getting something investigated but you wanted it left well alone, who'd be a better bet than Eliot Oakcroft?'

Max got up and stretched his arms, feeling a little defensive. He knew, God knows he knew, that Eliot wasn't the ideal MP or perfect boss. But Max had worked for the man for fifteen years and had a sort of affection for him. And he had his good qualities, didn't he? It might take Max half an hour and a lot of doodling with a pencil to figure out what they were, but there must be some.

The street outside the pub was quiet, a Sunday afternoon greying gently into evening. What Ronni was suggesting would mean Charlie Cley had conspired to put Rebecca Cley in prison and leave her there. He took the phone number out of his pocket, the one Lulu Marchbanks had given him that might be Charlie Cley's.

'So, what do you say? Shall we try this phone number, then?' he said. He typed the number into his phone and hit ring. It rang. Until he stopped it.

'No answer, and it doesn't go to message,' said Ronni. 'But we're sure it's his?'

'Lulu Marchbanks insisted it was his, but she wasn't entirely sure what his name was, so she might have got the wrong number.'

'Lulu Marchbanks, is it?' said Ronni. 'Nice of Lulu Marchbanks to give it up to you, all the same. I assume you got Lulu's number, too?'

'I'm pretty sure she got mine,' said Max, fearing that he might be blushing. 'I'll pass it on to Tony Wenhamville. He might know someone who could do something to track it down.'

Chapter Nine

Max arrived at work on Monday morning to the unprecedented sight of Eliot Oakcroft MP sitting at his desk in his office, furiously typing on his phone. The shock was so great he checked his watch to see it hadn't stopped and misled him.

'What time do you call this to start work of a morning?' said Eliot, glancing up from his phone. 'The early bird catches the worm, you know.'

'It's eight twenty-five, Eliot,' said Max. 'I'm always here for eight-thirty.'

'Not today, it would appear,' said Eliot. Max chose not to point to the clock on the wall as he took off his coat and fired up his laptop. 'We need to run a tight ship around here, Max. A tight ship. We have caught the Chief Whip's eye, you know, and if he happens to drop by, I want him to see an operation that's shipshape and Bristol fashion.'

'What's he said exactly?' said Max. 'Does he want something?'

'Here you go,' said Eliot, handing over his phone. A WhatsApp message: *We've got our eye on you, Oakcroft. Steady the Buffs. Keep your nose clean. Call off the dogs.*

'Ah,' said Max. He doubted Eliot had twigged that his dogs were named Maxwell Murray and Diana Burton, and thought it might be best to keep it that way for as long as possible. In fact, based on past Eliot form, a question suggested itself: 'Did you read the whole message, Eliot?'

'So, what do you think about that, then?' said Eliot. 'Got his eye on me, eh. That's a sign, isn't it, that's a sign?'

'Ah,' said Max. 'I see. And it is, of course it is.' He handed Eliot back his phone, in spite of the temptation to scan whatever else it was Eliot was getting through his WhatsApp groups. Diana had offered to steal Eliot's phone and surreptitiously add herself and Max to the juicier ones, but Max's better angels had resisted the temptation so far. 'Does this mean you're going to be in the office at this time every morning?'

'Well,' said Eliot, rising with a cheerful smile on his face, 'now that I know you're here, and can rely on you being here at this ungodly hour every day, apparently, perhaps I can take myself off for a bit of breakfast and leave you to it.'

'OK,' said Max. 'No need to rush back.'

'Is there anywhere a chap can get a bite of breakfast on the estate at this hour?'

'The Portcullis and Terrace canteens have been open since half seven.'

'Good Lord,' said Eliot Oakcroft. 'The things one learns every day. Why don't the House authorities tell us these things? Why won't they communicate properly?'

Both those cafeterias have gigantic signs outside them detailing their opening hours, thought Max. *They're on the intranet with opening hours and menus fully displayed. And the fact that you, Eliot Oakcroft, don't know that doesn't mean it's a secret.*

With the office to himself, he skimmed the morning post, a copy of the Order Paper for the House of Commons business that day, some internal circulars to be filed in the bin. The Chief Whip had his eye on Eliot Oakcroft. Wanted him to keep his nose clean. Wanted him to call off the dogs.

'Morning, Chief,' said Diana Burton, entering the room like a bouncing ball that had been eating a lot of sugar. 'Did my eyes deceive me, or was our lord and master actually here before 10 a.m.? Woah, no, wait, there's something wrong with my eyes this morning. Did they use shears for that haircut or did they just put you in a mincing machine?'

'I'm just trying a new look,' said Max disconsolately.

'Try again,' said Diana, 'and try soon. Try very soon. What did Eliot make of that?'

'Don't think he noticed.'

'Well, he's only known you fifteen years,' said Diana. 'You can't expect him to notice everything. Though anything would be nice.'

'Why are we upsetting the powers that be so much with this Rebecca Cley investigation, do you think?' said Max.

'I'd a lovely sleep, thank you, Chief,' said Diana. 'A coffee? That would be perfect, thank you, what a kind and considerate boss you are.'

'Seriously, though,' said Max, getting up to put the kettle on, 'who's so keen to stop us freeing Rebecca Cley, and why?'

The trouble, of course, with working for a living was that it prevented you from getting on with anything important. As, indeed, was the trouble with working for Eliot Oakcroft MP, who, with the eyes of the Whips upon him, went into overdrive that Monday demanding bullet points for speeches in the Chamber, written Parliamentary Questions he could send into the Department for Law and Order, and endless cups of tea in the office he had suddenly decided to inhabit all day every day.

The pleasure of a Westminster working week, though, was that although it started in earnest about noon on Monday before the Commons went into session at 2.30 p.m., it drifted into tidying the inbox and doing the admin by late Thursday afternoon. The days in between were long and intense, but by Friday morning the chances of finding an MP within twenty-five miles of the Palace of Westminster resembled the chances of finding a Brit within the top twenty-five ranking places at Wimbledon. Eliot Oakcroft, exhausted by three-and-a-bit days assiduously doing his job, drove off to the constituency as usual after lunch on Thursday, leaving

Max and Diana free to work in peace without him. And to go to Tim Cley's office in Kensington first thing on Friday morning.

'We've been on the case a week and a half, and I've got absolutely nothing to tell him,' said Max when they met in a Costa half an hour before their 8 a.m. meeting with Tim. 'Ronni's still working on the Parallel Parking thing and Tony's gone quiet on whether that phone number's traceable.'

'You don't want to tell Tim too much anyway,' said Diana. 'He's bent as a three-pound coin.'

'I can't say I like the man, but we've got no reason to think he's a crook.'

'He claims he has no money but he wears a Savile Row suit and writes with a Montblanc pen,' said Diana. 'Gold cufflinks, tie pin, aftershave you don't get at Lidl.'

'He and Charlie ran a very successful business.'

'He's a PR man,' said Diana. 'Of course he's a crook.'

'I've still got nothing to tell him.'

'Make something up,' said Diana. 'Tell him you've got three positive sightings of Charlie in Northumbria or something.'

'And when nothing comes of them?'

'Nothing comes of them,' said Diana. 'False sightings, bloke looks just like Charlie Cley – after all, he's not that distinctive, terribly bad luck, we keep on looking. It all takes time. I mean, it's not like we're private detectives he's actually paying to do this.'

'That reminds me of something Ronni said,' said Max. 'If Tim was serious about finding his brother, wouldn't he have hired a professional to do this instead of coming to Eliot Oakcroft?'

'You might have a point there,' said Diana, 'or, rather, your much smarter sister might have a point there.'

'Thank you,' said Max.

'But Tim Cley didn't realise he was getting the brains behind Eliot Oakcroft MP on the case, did he?' said Diana.

Max looked at her as she grinned at him across her flat white. He chose not to ask whether she thought the brains behind Eliot Oakcroft MP was Maxwell Murray or Diana Burton.

Tim Cley's office filled the ground floor of what had once been a four-storey Victorian townhouse behind Kensington Church Street, now home to Tim and Charlie's PR company, a psychiatrist and a physiotherapist on the first floor, and the blandly named TL McKenna Ltd on the top two floors. Max and Diana were shown into what once must have been a drawing room. Max's first impression was of a small-scale Oval Office, with two sofas facing each other over a coffee table arranged in front of the partner's desk Tim was sitting behind in the bay window. Tim Cley rose to meet them wearing a white zip-up jumper over a check shirt and above brown chinos and shoes. His clothes could not more clearly have said *I'm leaving for the country for the weekend the second I'm done with this probably pointless meeting.* His face wasn't giving a different message. He dismissed his receptionist with a brief wave. This was clearly going to be a meeting without coffee.

'Well,' said Tim Cley, sitting on one of the sofas, and signalling Diana and Max to take the other opposite him. A fan of magazines was laid out on the coffee table, most of them travel publications as far as Max could see. Lots of blue skies and golden beaches on their covers. A far cry from Kensington on a damp, grey London morning. Diana picked one up and began skimming the pages.

'I thought we should update you on progress,' said Max.

'Which you could have done over the phone,' said Tim. 'Miranda's filled me in on your visit to the prison last week. Including everything Rebecca said about me.'

'She doesn't seem to love you much.'

'She's in jail for murdering her husband and she's looking for someone to blame,' said Tim. 'Have you got any progress to report? I understand you went on to Cromer to interview an ice cream seller, and I'm guessing from the lack of action since that he didn't have Charlie hidden in the back of the van with the flakes and hundreds and thousands sprinkles.'

'He gave me reason to believe your brother might have been the man Miranda photographed,' said Max stiffly.

'Did he?' said Tim Cley. 'And that reason has resulted in what, exactly?'

'I'm still making enquiries,' said Max.

'Do you have anything new to tell me, or have I wasted a Friday morning I could have spent out in the country waiting for you to come and have a nose around my office?'

'You have, really,' said Diana, leaning across the coffee table and tapping Tim playfully on the knee with a rolled-up travel magazine. 'You're dead right. We just wanted to get in here and see how kosher you are.'

'What my associate means . . .' spluttered Max, then sputtered to a halt. Tim Cley's face had darkened and a vein was pulsing in his neck. Then, he leant back on his sofa and let out a burst of laughter.

'How much is this guy paying you?' he said to Diana. 'I'll double it if you want to come work for me.'

'I thought you were broke and couldn't pay anyone right now,' said Diana, unrolling the travel magazine. 'Although if you're looking at villas in Jamaica, you must have a few quid stashed in the biscuit tin, mustn't you?'

'Does she have any kind of an off switch?' said Tim to Max. 'I mean, seriously, does she talk like this to everyone?'

'She kind of does,' said Max.

'Ha,' barked Tim. Max couldn't quite believe it but the man seemed to be genuinely amused by Diana, who was sitting smiling at him as if butter weren't melting in her mouth. 'So what is it you two clowns actually wanted from me?'

'Why does Rebecca think you killed your brother?' said Diana. Tim, even though he'd invited it, sat back as if he'd been slapped.

'Becky's suspicious of everyone right now,' he said carefully. 'Her husband's dead, in case you'd forgotten.'

'Or missing,' said Max.

'Or missing,' said Tim, 'though I doubt anyone still believes that preposterous kidnapping nonsense.'

'Ah,' said Max. 'We did find out how that story got started. I think you can safely rule that one out now.'

'Three years without a ransom,' said Tim Cley. 'I didn't need to hire you to figure that one out.'

'You didn't actually hire us at all,' said Diana. 'You haven't spent any money hiring anyone rather than coming to us.'

'As Miranda has pretty vigorously pointed out to me,' said Tim Cley. 'But why waste money on a wild goose chase? I think we know Charlie wasn't kidnapped, so Charlie's dead, whatever Miranda thinks she saw down on Cromer Pier. Miranda's mother's in prison. She doesn't know who to trust. And that includes you two – she told me she thinks Eliot Oakcroft's useless and we should get a private investigator in to find Charlie.'

'Ah,' said Diana, looking levelly at Tim Cley, 'but you're not dealing with Eliot Oakcroft. Maxwell Murray is on the case, and he's smarter than he looks.'

'He's not the only one,' said Tim Cley, holding Diana's gaze.

'Why don't you get a professional in?' said Max. 'If you're serious about finding Charlie, that would be much better than relying on us.'

'Two reasons,' said Tim Cley. 'First, I don't believe Charlie is alive, even if I don't think it was Rebecca who killed him. He's my brother and I love him like one, but, frankly, Charlie was about smart enough to open his mouth when he needed to eat, and the chances of him hiding out this long without screwing it up are a big fat nil.'

'And second?' said Max.

'And second, as you've just correctly pointed out, you guys aren't costing me anything. Look, I'm going to level with you. I am struggling. I'm close to broke. I can just about keep this place going, and just about pay Arabella out there to make it look like I've still got a staff, but we've got no clients and no money coming in, and no assets I can put my hands on right now to pay back the debts we ran up. Now, do you actually have any information for me, or are we done here?'

'Have you ever heard of an Anthony Green?' said Max. Tim raised an eyebrow at the change of direction, but not more than that.

'Can't say I have,' he said. 'Should I have?'

'How about a company called Parallel Parking?'

'Nope,' said Tim. 'What do they do?'

'Apart from providing donations to political parties and some MPs, they don't seem to do anything,' said Max.

'They'll be even more bust than I am, then,' said Tim. 'What's the connection with me, or with Charlie?'

'I don't know,' said Max. 'Just one of a number of lines we're pursuing.'

'OK,' said Tim, rising. 'So, you've had a look at where I work and I've told you I'm just keeping the façade up until something turns up. I think we're done here.'

'Were you serious about employing me?' said Diana. Max looked at her, surprised.

'I would if I could,' said Tim. 'I like your style.'

'I'll bear it in mind,' said Diana, rising coolly and putting out a hand for Tim to shake, which, surprised, he did. 'I'll be in touch,' she said, ushering Max out of the room as Tim stood watching them go and wondering why he suddenly felt like a guest in his own office.

'You'll bear it in mind,' said Max, as they walked down Kensington Church Street towards the Tube station. 'What do you mean you'll bear it in mind? He's a crook. You can't go working for him.'

'I just wanted to surprise him,' said Diana. 'See what his face does when you tell him something he wasn't expecting.'

'And?' said Max.

'And everything,' said Diana. 'Everything you said before that, he already knew. Including, if you ask me, who Anthony Green might be. Tim Cley is lying through his over-whitened, expensively capped teeth.'

Back at Westminster, Max took the lift to their fourth-floor office while Diana virtuously climbed the stairs. Once, when he'd first met her, Max, admiring the impulse, had courteously joined her, but found himself stopping on the first-floor landing for the lift rather than continuing to try to take the steps three at a time. Today, arriving at the office he found the door open and a Lord-a-lurking, or more accurately a-lounging, in the overstuffed green armchair that Eliot Oakcroft insisted filled the small square of space between the three desks in the room. Tony Wenhamville's lanky form splayed across it like a septuagenarian spider in a tweed suit and waistcoat, peering at a folded *Daily Telegraph*.

'Morning to you, Maxwell,' said Tony Wenhamville. 'Obstinate as the monster of Knossos, four letters and six letters.'

'Bull-headed,' said Max. 'I thought you were a *Times* man, Tony. *Telegraph* crossword not a bit down-market for you?'

'Did *The Times* over the boiled egg and coffee, my boy. Found this rag lying on your lord and master's desk. He appears to have given up yesterday morning after an erroneous attempt at 3 Down. Surprised not to find you at home this morning, Maxwell. I took you for an early starter.'

'Usually am,' said Max. 'We had an early meeting. Tim Cley.'

'Ah, the wicked uncle,' said Tony. 'In fine fettle, was he?'

'I think we're off his Christmas card list.'

If Diana was surprised on walking into the room to find an elderly man with springy hair leaping to his feet to greet her, she managed not to show it.

'You must be Miss Burton,' said Tony, bowing to her courteously. 'Your employer speaks extremely highly of you.'

'Eliot Oakcroft speaks highly of me?' she said, her sangfroid deserting her at that one. Max had never seen her look quite so shocked.

'Forgive me, my dear. I meant, of course, your manager,' said Tony, collapsing back into the armchair, like a puppet who'd had his strings cut. 'Oh, dear me, the very idea of Eliot Oakcroft MP as anyone's employer had escaped my wildest imaginings.'

'Not as much as it escapes his,' said Diana, sitting on the arm of the chair. 'Has my manager managed to get you a coffee yet?'

'No need, dear girl, no need,' said Tony. 'I'm assuming, by the way, given your disrespect for the Honourable Eliot, that the expression "dear girl" is unlikely to have you bar me the room for threatening the safety of its space?'

'You assume right, old chap,' said Diana. 'And I'm assuming I'm OK not calling you My Lord or any of that old-fashioned, hierarchical flummery?'

'We appear to have an understanding, Miss Burton.'

'Diana, please.'

'Tony,' said Tony. 'You're right about this one, Maxwell, smart as a whip and an absolute charmer.'

'Did you really say that about me, Chief?' said Diana, smiling sweetly at Max. 'You'll be offering me a pay rise next.'

Max, aware that he had reddened, felt the need to take some control of the conversation.

'Don't think me impolite, Tony, pleasure to see you and all that, but wasn't our door locked when you arrived this morning?'

'I was a criminal defence barrister for a fair few years,' said Tony. 'Sometimes they paid in kind rather than cash, you know. Handy to know a few tricks of the trade.'

'Fair enough,' said Max. 'Stupid of me to have asked.'

'Talking of which,' said Tony, 'trade trickery also tells me that that phone number you wanted checked out is for a pay-as-you-go phone – a burner, they tell me, is the technical term – of the type often used by drug dealers and ne'er-do-wells who wish to remain unidentified.'

Max could see that Diana was keen to ask questions about that and signalled her to sit down and shut up, which, for once, to his shock and amazement, she did. He knew that Tony had more for them and that the old man, missing his time on the bench when he could theatrically delay telling a guilty accused exactly how long he'd be spending in chokey, would take his own good time to spin it out. The more they interrupted him, the longer it would be before he spilt whether he'd found out where Charlie Cley – or at least the owner of this burner phone – was hiding out.

'Most such users, of course,' said Tony, settling himself comfortably in the chair, if splaying one leg over its arm and the opposite arm over the back of it could reasonably be described as comfortably, 'use these phones but once and then throw them into the nearest river. Your chap, and from this we must presume, I surmise, that he is not dealing crack, tranq or Kalashnikov rifles, is not such a user, and while he, or she, or indeed in these troubled modern times of ours, they, has been an infrequent caller and texter over the past month or so, the user, as I shall now so call this person in order to avoid the troublesome choice of a pronoun, has been out and about.'

'Do you know where?' said Max, unable to restrain himself any longer.

'I do,' said Tony. 'Remarkable thing, modern technology. Crime should be so much easier to solve these days, now that we can prove where anyone is at any given moment just by tracking a telephone from signal mast to signal mast. Your prey seems a restless soul, frequently on the move, but also a homing bird, rarely far from a quite tightly confined triangle.'

'Which happens to include Cromer?' said Max.

'Not within the last month, though not beyond the bounds of previous possibility,' said Tony Wenhamville. 'Did you have a date for your believed sighting of him in the crab capital of the North Norfolk coast?'

'Eight or nine weeks ago,' said Max. 'It doesn't really matter, though, if he's in Norfolk somewhere.'

'Very well,' said Tony. 'Although if you can give me a precise date, I'm sure I can call in another favour.'

'Fine,' said Max. 'I'll get it from Miranda Cley. Now, is there any chance that you might tell us where we can find Charlie?'

'If your quarry is, in fact, the allegedly deceased Charlie Cley,' said Tony Wenhamville.

'Tony, please,' said Max, 'could you just, sometime within, say, the next hour or so, tell us where to look for the owner of this phone?'

'I have an hour of your valuable time at my disposal,' said Tony Wenhamville, smiling broadly at Diana. 'Perhaps I will have that cup of coffee I believe I was being offered a few moments ago.'

'Tony!' yelled Max.

'I jest, dear boy, I jest,' said Tony, beaming again at Diana. 'Do you know, young lady, when Maxwell here was a boy I used occasionally to dine at his father's house, and nothing presented more pleasure than watching his pretty impatience as I spun out a card trick or watched him try to solve his Rubik's Cube.'

'He's very hasty,' said Diana. 'His worst quality, I'd say.'

'The worst of many, no doubt.'

'He has his strong points, too.'

Max glowered silently, biting his tongue, knowing that silence was the only way to get them to get on with it even if there was plenty he could be saying, and not all of it suitable for the ears of young ladies, or elderly gentlemen either.

'And yet he has the patience to work for Eliot Oakcroft MP for fifteen years,' said Tony Wenhamville, studying the ceiling. 'Remarkable when you come to think of it. And, by the way, Maxwell, since I've been making these discreet enquiries on behalf of the Great Legislator, taking his name occasionally in vain, perhaps you might find some means of bringing them to his attention without his particularly noticing it? Best that he's informed; best, too, that he has very little idea what we're doing.'

'Not a problem,' said Max, 'I'll write something in his Monday morning briefing. On page six.'

'Page two should do the trick, I should think,' said Tony. 'If not the third paragraph of page one. In any event, to cut a long story short—'

'Too late,' said Max.

'I could provide further and deeper detail if desired,' said Tony.

'I could listen to you all day,' said Diana, then spoilt it by bursting out laughing at Max's face.

'Please,' said Max.

'Very well,' said Tony. 'After all, I'm a busy man with places to be and things to do and can't hang around here all the livelong day.'

'Tony, for the love of God, please.'

'Your telephone owner appears to be based in Norfolk, as you surmised from the Cromer connection and the information you received from your artist friend, Lulu Marchbanks – ghastly work, by the way, I looked her up online, she'll never sell a canvas—'

'Tony!'

'Your man, and for the purposes of ease at this stage of proceedings, I shall assume it is a man, travels principally within the triangle bounded by Swaffham, King's Lynn and Fakenham. Not terribly far north-west, indeed, from where Charlie Cley's car was found and from where he disappeared. Not terribly far, too, of course, from the family home near Wymondham, although your man has struck west of that area and well clear of the more populous settlements such as Norwich and King's Lynn itself. He tends to switch on his phone between 8 a.m. and 9.30 a.m., and then again in the later afternoon. Triangulating as carefully as we can from the locations at which he's been identified, our belief is that he may have set up camp either in or in the vicinity of Fincham.'

'Fincham?'

'Small village, largely owned and rented out by the local squire. I seem to recall what one might term a somewhat shonky pub.'

'Shonky,' said Diana. 'Is that a legal term from your many years at the Bar and on the bench?'

'Alas, no,' said Tony, 'but it is, I think, sufficiently precise, or at least suitably onomatopoeic, to require little further definition.'

'I think you're right,' said Diana. 'We all know a shonky pub when our feet stick to the carpet.'

'Precisely so,' said Tony.

'Fincham's pretty small,' said Max, who'd been using the time to google the village. 'Barely a hamlet. You think we might find Charlie Cley there?'

'I think it possible,' said Tony. 'Indeed, if he happens to be at home and receiving, I think you might find him here.' He handed over a slip of paper and Max read: *Primrose Cottage, Low Lane, Fincham.*

'You had an address for him all along,' said Max.

'Oh, yes,' said Tony Wenhamville. 'I wouldn't want to drop in here just to waste your precious and valuable time.'

Tony Wenhamville knew the pub in Fincham was shonky because he'd been there – as a guest of the local squire, Roger St George, a former MP who happened to be a fellow member of the House of Lords and maintained some pretty decent shooting on his estate out near Hunstanton. *Something of a chum of your Eliot Oakcroft*, Tony Wenhamville had told

Max. *Thick as thieves; the pair of them, not to mention planks.*

Diana Burton, hearing this while Max figured out a route from London to Fincham and closed down the computers and office for the weekend, argued strongly that His Lordship should join them on the journey to Norfolk to search for Charlie Cley. But, to Max's relief, Tony had demurred, saying his days chasing criminals were long behind him now and wishing them Godspeed and good fortune. The fact that the final weekend at Wimbledon would be starting about twenty minutes after their departure might also have played some part in his refusal. The absence of the elder Peer of the Realm also meant that Max and Diana took the Tube rather than a taxi out to Westbourne Park to pick up his car and its keys, giving them little chance to talk about the chances of finding Charlie Cley. Max found himself amused by Diana's desperately suppressed excitement, hoping that he was himself projecting an air of calm, as if tracking down a supposedly dead person was just a routine part of the day for one as experienced and world-weary as himself.

'Should we tell Miranda Cley we're going up?' Diana said as soon as they were out of Westbourne Park Tube Station.

'Absolutely not,' said Max. 'We need to know what we're dealing with here before we tell anyone.'

Reaching the door of his building, Max fished out his key and told Diana to wait until he collected his car keys from his first-floor flat.

'If you think I'm missing my chance to see inside the ancestral mansion of the Maxwell Murrays, you've got another think coming,' she said, clopping up the stairs behind him. 'Nice building, by the way. You don't need a lodger, do you?'

'You've got a decent flat, haven't you?'

'On what you and Eliot pay me?' said Diana. 'In London? It's got four walls and a roof, and even the cockroaches struggle with the rent.'

'Well, if you're coming in, come on then,' said Max, opening his door. The car keys were in the small bowl on top of the hallway bookcase where he always kept them. Pick 'em up, turn around and get out of here as fast as possible was his plan. In which it differed dramatically from that of Diana, who slipped past him and into the bay-windowed, high-ceilinged living room where he heard her say, 'Oh, hello.'

'Hello,' said an out-of-sight Ronni, and Max walked into the room to find his assistant and his sister grinning at each other across his coffee table. 'Ronni, this is Diana; Diana, my sister,' he mumbled.

'Diana, lovely to meet you,' said Ronni. 'I've heard so much about you.'

'Really,' said Diana, looking for once in her life a little disconcerted. 'He's told me a bit about you,' she said, recovering a little. 'He wanted to be a journalist himself, he said, but he's too lazy.'

Ronni laughed and came forward to give Diana a hug and her brother a look that could only be described as wide-eyed approval. He found himself smirking inanely back and realised that he'd just inadvertently introduced two of his favourite people in the world to each other. Curiously, since Ronni's tiny frame, lost once more inside one of his old rugby jerseys, and dark hair contrasted with Diana's height and vermilion crop, they seemed to him to be nearly alike, as if they were the siblings and he the awkward visitor.

'I thought about journalism myself once,' said Diana, 'but I was worried about the ethics of all that nosing into people's lives.'

'So you went into politics,' said Ronni, 'and you work for Eliot Oakcroft. Not entirely sure you sidestepped the ethical question there.'

'Max said I'd like you,' said Diana, stepping back to inspect Max's bookcase. He saw her running a finger rapidly past the shelf of black-spined Penguin Classics, even more rapidly over the political biographies, and settling happily on the battered second-hand paperback Terry Pratchetts.

'He speaks very highly of you, too,' said Ronni. 'Best researcher he's ever had, apparently.' Max, noting Diana's quick glance of pleasure, also noted Ronni's smirk at him.

'I'm really surprised he doesn't alphabetise his books,' said Diana, 'even if he conforms to expectation by organising them by type.'

'I think you'll find they're chronological rather than alphabetical,' said Ronni. 'I moved *A Tale of Two Cities* once and I heard about it for about a year.'

Diana pulled three of the Pratchett paperbacks off the shelf and scanned the inside pages. 'Oh, my God! He really does have them in date order.'

'I wrote about that in a feature once for a magazine,' said Ronni. 'Anonymised him, you know, but included it in freaky things your flatmates do. Editors cut it, though. Said it was too unbelievable.'

'Shall I just leave the room and leave you two to pull me to pieces?' said Max.

'Much more fun if you're here,' said Diana. 'Never really got why you'd talk about people behind their backs.' She rapidly shuffled the three Pratchetts and put them back on the shelf. 'Now, does it hurt that they're all mixed up?'

'Of course not.' Max restrained himself from going across to put them back in the right order. He'd be able to do it when he got back. Before bed. Before he tried to sleep.

'Getting back to politicians and ethics, by the way,' said Ronni, 'I've had a very interesting morning on the phone with an old friend of yours, Max. Estella Chamberlain. She'd rather have spoken to you, but apparently you've blocked her number.'

'What did she want?' said Max, neutrally and avoiding Diana's interrogative eyebrow.

'She wants to know why your sister's making enquiries about whoever it is who makes donations to her.'

'How does she know you were investigating?'

'I used my own name for my Companies House searches on your Anthony Green and his Parallel Parking,' said Ronni. 'I didn't know the Secretary of State for Law and Order would find out about it and I don't know how she did, but I'm clearly on to something.'

'Did she say why Mr Green's giving her all that money?'

'Old family friend, all above board, all properly declared, no story to find here, nothing to see, please move along now.'

'Family friend,' said Max. 'Someone she's seeing, maybe?'

'Still not a trace of the mysterious Mr Green in all my searches,' said Ronni.

Diana, leaning now against the floor-to-ceiling bookcase, went straight to the point. 'If she knows you're Max's sister, she'll think it's him who's digging into her background.'

'She does,' said Ronni. 'If she does find a way of unblocking her number, I wouldn't take her calls if I were you, Max.'

'She'll get on to Eliot,' said Max. 'He's not going to like this.'

'So what?' said Diana.

'So he could fire us both,' said Max.

'And you could get a proper job at last,' said Diana. 'Hadn't we better get out to Norfolk before he does sack us, though?' She skipped past Max and into the hallway.

'Hear, hear,' said Ronni. 'I can see why you like this girl, Max.'

'I don't,' said Max. 'I mean, I do, obviously, but also, you know, I don't.'

'Yeah, yeah,' said Ronni. 'I think that's the definition of misleading the House.'

As she shut the door behind him, she whispered, 'By the way, I'll put your books back,' and blew him a kiss.

* * *

'You should go into journalism,' said Max, as he manoeuvred the Bentley off the ring road and onto the M11. 'You'd be very, very good at it.'

'What makes you think that?'

'You're nosy, you ask rude questions and somehow persuade people to answer them. I can see you with your foot stuck in someone's door asking them why they're a disgrace to society.'

'Flattery, flattery,' said Diana. 'You don't get rid of me that easily. And Eliot isn't going to fire us. Well, he might fire me, I suppose, but he's tried that already, and he obviously can't fire you. Who else would he get to do his job for him?'

They'd made it as far as the Stansted Airport turn-off before Max's phone rang.

'Eliot,' he said, engaging speakerphone.

'Max. You're not in the office.'

'Running an errand before the weekend. All quiet on the Westminster front. You know what Fridays are like.'

'Yes, yes of course,' said Eliot. 'Fridays, eh?'

Diana's face was a picture. Max was fairly sure that in her four months working for him, Eliot had managed to be elsewhere on every Friday so far. He wasn't entirely convinced that in his own fifteen years working for Eliot, the MP's Friday appearances had made it into double figures.

'However,' Eliot was continuing, 'while the Whips are watching, I really would prefer it if the place looked like we were working. You know, shoulder to the wheel, nose to the grindstone.'

'Finger to the bone,' muttered Diana.

'Eh?' said Eliot.

'Nothing,' said Max. 'I'm driving at the moment. Might be a bit of interference on the call.'

'Right, then. Fair enough. All work and no play makes Max a dull boy and all that. But surely that girl should be there, filing or something or other. Keeping up appearances. Are you sure, by the way, that she's quite the ticket? I wonder if we couldn't do better. Alex Rattray's just recruited a lovely girl.'

'Hello Eliot,' yelled Diana. 'I'm just reading the Independent Complaints and Grievance Code's paragraphs on sexism.'

'Who's that?'

'Diana,' said Max. 'She's here. With me. Running the errand . . .' He tailed off.

'Oh, ah,' said Eliot. 'I see. Right. Well, be that as it may, that's not why I'm calling. Do you know I had the Secretary of State for Law and Order on the line this morning and do you know why?'

'I had heard a whisper,' said Max.

'I bet you had,' said Eliot. 'Your sister – I didn't know you had a sister, by the way, Max, you really shouldn't keep your private life so secret.'

'We've talked about her plenty, Eliot, and you've met her at least five or six times.'

'Estella Chamberlain claims your sister's a journalist. I had no idea of that.'

'She's interviewed you for the *Sunday Times*.'

'Did she,' said Eliot. 'What did I say?'

'They didn't print it,' said Max. 'Pressure of space. Big news week.' This was, of course, a white lie; Eliot had said so little of consequence, Ronni had told Max after he'd pressured her into doing an interview she'd never been keen on, that she hadn't even bothered filing anything.

'Shocking the way these people treat you,' said Eliot. 'You give up your valuable time and they print not a word of what you say. Never a good news story, is it? Scandal, that's all they're interested in. Scandal and tittle-tattle. Which, by the by, brings me back to Estella Chamberlain again. Why is your sister investigating her political donations?'

'Search me,' said Max. Another little white lie. 'I don't really tell Ronni what I'm doing so that she doesn't feel she has to get a story out of it, and she doesn't really tell me in return.'

'Quite right, too,' said Eliot. 'An attitude that does you proud. Never trust a journalist.'

'Unless they're buying you lunch,' said Diana.

'That was a mistake, and I believe I suggested we never talk about it again,' said Eliot, sounding hurt.

'Good lunch, though?'

'There's something very wrong with a political system in which journalists have better expense accounts than Members of Parliament,' said Eliot.

'What else did Estella Chamberlain have to say?' said Max.

'Rather a lot,' said Eliot. 'I didn't catch it all, as I drifted off when I realised she was planning to go on a bit. You know how it is in the Chamber when someone starts droning on and you can sort of half-listen for the bit that might involve you.'

'I have some experience of that sort of listening, yes,' said Max.

'But the gist of it seemed to be that she wanted me to make you stop your sister poking her nose in where it didn't belong. So I told her I would.'

'I can't do that, Eliot,' said Max. 'Ronni's a professional reporter. I have no control over her.'

'I told her I would tell you,' said Eliot, with the air of a man who'd made a killer point. 'I didn't say you would tell her. In fact, suits me fine if your sister carries on digging.'

'Really?' said Max. 'I thought you supported Estella and the Government's law and order policy.'

'Of course I do,' said Eliot. 'Law and order is the first duty of government. On the other hand, if Estella's been up to something that might get her sacked, then the department's going to need new blood, isn't it?'

'Ah, right, I see.'

'After all, if she's got anything dodgy in the finances, the public have a right to know, don't they?' said Eliot. 'When did you last update mine, by the way? All in order, are they?'

'Apple-pie order, Eliot,' said Max. 'So, I can tell Ronni to keep on the trail, then?'

'I thought you and your sister didn't discuss work,' said Eliot, and Diana laughed as she saw Max remember that Eliot had his occasional flashes of lucidity.

'I meant it metaphorically,' said Max, confident the lucidity would stretch only so far.

'Ah, well, that's all right then,' said Eliot. 'Now, our esteemed Secretary of State also wanted to know what progress we're making on this business of the missing businessman. I have to say it had rather slipped my mind, but what's the story, morning glory? I could give that rather dishy girl a quick call this afternoon to update her on progress. And to remind her I'm taking her to lunch whenever it's convenient.'

'How's your wife, Eliot?' said Diana brightly. 'She's about the same age as you, isn't she?'

'My good lady wife is very well, thank you very much,' said Eliot, 'and spending the weekend in the constituency, which I happen not, on this occasion, to be. What was that girl's name again?'

'Miranda,' said Max. 'But we've nothing much to tell her. We're off to Norfolk now to investigate a couple of leads.'

'Ah, yes,' said Eliot. 'Old Roger St George mentioned you'd had Tony Wenhamville asking him about something out in his neck of the woods.'

'I didn't know you knew St George that well,' said Max.

'Shooting chums,' said Eliot. 'He's invited me out for a weekend. Very swish, lots of good party connections.'

'You've never fired a gun in your life,' said Max.

'There is more in heaven and earth than is dreamt of in your philosophy, Maximilian,' said Eliot. He had three Shakespearean quotations that he recycled through his speeches, and was unbearably proud of each of them. He had once, and once only, appeared in a parliamentary sketch in *The Times*. Jasper Montgomery, the paper's three-piecesuited sketch-writer, had enjoyed him calling the Leader of the Opposition and his front bench team 'Double, double, toil and trouble'. *To gain laughter from an essentially meaningless insult half-remembered from schoolboy* Hamlet *is a skill much to be prized*, Montgomery had written. *This is one to watch.* (Though however much watching Jasper had since done of Eliot, he hadn't again felt moved to mention it, and nor had he replied to Max's email letting him know that it was *Macbeth.*)

'I've been practising on the firing range,' said Eliot. 'I'm getting quite handy.'

'Firing range,' said Diana. 'What firing range?'

'The Houses of Parliament one,' said Eliot, 'and very useful it is, too. Right, then, must be off, things to do.'

'Lunch to eat,' said Diana. 'Nap to have.'

'Good luck with the errand, then,' said Eliot. 'St George told me where you're looking – Bingham, is it, Langham, Congham?'

'Fincham,' said Max.

'Fincham,' said Eliot. 'And if your sister does get any dirt on Estella Chamberlain, be sure I'm the first to know, won't you?'

'So that you can warn her?'

'So that I can comment first when she's sacked,' said Eliot. 'Get my name out there when they're looking for replacement ministers. Pip pip, and carry on.'

* * *

'There's a firing range in the House of Commons,' said Diana as they came off the M11 and onto the A11 towards Wicklewood. 'We're a quarter of the way through the twenty-first century, and the House of Commons spends public money to maintain a firing range?'

'House of Lords, actually,' said Max. 'In the basement. House authorities keep trying to close it down to replace it with a nursery, or something. Lords keep resisting.'

'Well, you would resist a nursery, wouldn't you, if you were all 108,' said Diana. 'What use would a nursery be to a member of the House of Lords? If any of them has a child under fifty, I'll be mildly shocked.'

'Ageism is a protected characteristic, Diana,' said Max, mildly.

'Maybe if they offered them a nursing home,' said Diana. 'Meanwhile, I'm only being outraged about this so that I can blot the image of Eliot wielding a rifle out of my head.'

Max had also been speculating on the nightmare scenario of Eliot Oakcroft at a shooting party. New Barbour, new tweeds, new boots and no chance of much risk to the pheasants of North Norfolk. Into which region the Bentley had now carried them as Max navigated down a narrow, hedge-lined country road into the village of Fincham. A low flat building sat on the left side of the road ahead of them – the shonky pub. And outside it stood a builders' van.

'That's Patrick Alderton's van,' said Diana as Max slowed to pass it. 'Pull up. We should find out what he's doing here.'

'Could just be coincidence,' said Max. 'Guy's a builder. He's got to work somewhere.'

'Absolutely,' said Diana, 'and Eliot could be Prime Minister after the next leadership contest.'

'I'll pull up,' said Max.

The single-storey pub looked unwelcoming from outside, little more than a grey-brick municipal toilet block. Inside, though, they found a cheerfully lit wooden bar and an interior decorator's nightmare – a dartboard at one end of the room, a stag's head at the other. And a surprisingly busy pub with a pretty clear class divide – men in T-shirts and jeans sitting alone with a pint and a lunchtime pie in one half, and in the other three men in pink shirts, tweed jackets and the further throes of an anecdote fuelled by at least two empty bottles of Cabernet Sauvignon. One of whom wolf-whistled at Diana as she and Max walked over to the bar.

'Weekend bankers,' said Max.

'Absolute bankers,' said Diana.

The only woman in the bar was standing behind it. Tight blonde curls, mid-forties and smiling a toothy smile at her new customers as she held out two menus.

'I thought you'd be back,' she said to Diana. 'Got your scarf behind the bar.'

'Sorry?' said Diana.

'Lovely bit of silk, that,' said the barmaid, holding up a purple silk scarf. 'Wouldn't want to lose it, would you?'

'I would not,' said Diana. 'Not mine, I'm afraid, though.'

'Oh, right, sorry, my mistake,' said the barwoman, sliding the scarf back below her bar. 'Now, then, table for two, is it, for you and your dad?'

'Sorry, we're not here for lunch,' said Max, trying to ignore Diana's snort.

'You'll go hungry then,' said the barwoman. 'Nothing beyond here 'til you get to Thornhamwood and we've a lovely steak pie special on today, if I can tempt you?'

'We're very tempted,' said Diana, 'but actually we're looking for someone.'

'Lot of that about today,' said the barwoman, still smiling, if a little less toothily, as she put the menus back in their holder. 'What you drinking?'

'Pint of Adnams for me, lime and soda for him,' said Diana. 'He's driving.'

'So's one of that lot,' said the barwoman, nodding at the three posh men. 'We don't worry too much about that sort of thing around here.'

'Even so,' said Diana, 'but maybe a little Southern Comfort to wash down my Adnams as well?'

'You're a girl after my own heart,' said the barwoman, pouring the Adnams. 'Who was it you was after?'

'Patrick Alderton.'

'Never heard of him.'

'His van's parked outside. We thought he might be in here.'

'Oh, him,' said the barwoman. 'Funny thing. He came in looking for someone, too. Wouldn't give me a name, mind you. Just wanted to know if there was anyone new in the village, posh bloke, bit loud, one for the girls if you know what I mean.'

'And is there?'

'Oh, yes, in the cottage up the back of Low Lane. Tony he calls himself. Champagne Charlie I call him. Very flash, very swish. In here every night for his first week 'til he realised he wasn't going to find much in the way of ladies around here.'

'I'm sure he flirted with you,' said Diana.

'I won't say he didn't buy me the occasional Baileys and ice,' simpered the barmaid, 'but he keeps himself to himself most of the time. So I told the man with the van and he went up there to find him. Probably be back any minute, I should think. Excuse me,' she said, fishing out a bottle of Cabernet Sauvignon and heading for the posh blokes' table.

'Alderton knows Charlie's here but doesn't know where he's hiding out,' said Max. 'We should get up there.'

'Half a mo,' said Diana, and sank her pint in two gulps, the second punctuated by the Southern Comfort. 'Right you are, then. To Primrose Cottage.'

Max drove cautiously down Low Lane as Diana navigated. Primrose Cottage was in a cul-de-sac just off the lane, the only building there, a two-storey white house with an angled roof and a patch of lawn in front of it, well maintained but with no frills. The cottage was attractively proportioned, with two ground-floor windows and one window above and between them below the roof gable, and surrounded by woodland. The front door was to the right, and was open. And in it as they got out of the car appeared Patrick Alderton. He was carrying a wine bottle and looked half drunk. He began to walk down the path but saw Max and Diana coming towards him. He stopped as if he were going to say something, but then turned and leapt over the small picket fence to the side of the property and disappeared into the woodland.

Max instinctively made to follow him, but found himself jerked back by Diana pulling at him.

'We should follow him,' said Max.

'He's got a club, Max.'

'It wasn't a club, it was a bottle.'

'Really, Max,' said Diana. 'Not being rude or anything, but the guy's younger than you, taller than you, fitter than you and has biceps like melons on him. Do you really want him smashing a bottle over your head in deserted woodland?'

'Maybe not,' said Max. The open door of the house beckoned, and they walked up the path and into a small hallway, a living room to their left, a kitchen and probably a bathroom just visible ahead, and a staircase to the upper rooms right in front of them. Diana picked up two brown envelopes on the hallway table and handed one to Max.

Anthony Green, c/o Primrose Cottage, Low Lane, Fincham. Too much of a coincidence to be a coincidence. Max little doubted now that Charlie Cley and the mysterious Anthony Green were one and the same person. And the alias Charlie had been using while he hid out here in the back of nowhere.

'Why would he use a false name to give Estella donations?' hissed Max, putting the envelope back on the table. Diana stuffed hers into her pocket.

'Put that back,' hissed Max. 'We can't go stealing his mail.'

'The guy's a crook who's been pretending to be dead and using a fake name,' said Diana. 'He's not going to sue me for nicking his electric bill. Besides, your sister's going to need some evidence we've found Anthony Green, isn't she.'

Max supposed she was right, but wished he'd thought to take a photo with his phone before Diana began pinching the post. It occurred to him that although he'd been whispering, she'd spoken in her usual voice at a volume calculated to carry across a crowded pub. If there was anyone here, they must have heard her, but the house was silent, still.

'I don't think he's here,' said Max.

'Me neither. You take a shufti round here and I'll go through his stuff upstairs.'

'We really shouldn't. We must be committing burglary or something.'

'Oh, do shut up, Max. We've driven 150 miles and probably found Charlie Cley's hideout. Do you really think we're going to turn around and drive back again because he's popped out for a bit?'

'We could wait for him to come back.'

Diana barely gave him a look before she was going up the white-carpeted staircase two steps at a time. With a sigh,

Max walked into the living room and was struck by what a pleasing cottage Charlie had managed to find for himself. The front window let the sunlight in and though dust motes danced in the beams, the room was well furnished with a comfortable-looking sofa facing a large television set and in front of a substantial oak bookcase filled with hardback novels and history books. On the coffee table sat two wine glasses with a centimetre of red in one, while the other was more or less full. A couple of magazines – *Spectator*, *Economist* – were scattered on the table, too. And some travel brochures, sun and sand in the Caribbean. A quiet, discreet, tastefully decorated room but with no sign of any personal touch anywhere.

Then he heard Diana calling him from upstairs.

'Max,' she shouted. 'Max, could you get up here, please?'

He was up the stairs three at a time to find her on the small white-carpeted landing, between three doors leading to two bedrooms and a shower room. She signalled the larger of the bedrooms, the one facing out into the garden at the front of the house, and Max walked towards it.

'Miranda Cley was right about her father being alive and well on the pier at Cromer that day,' said Diana, behind him as he passed through the door.

Stretched on the bed in an open-necked blue shirt, white jeans and open waistcoat lay a handsome man in his early forties with swept-back black hair and a vacant expression, casually holding a gun in his right hand.

The gun would have worried Maxwell Murray a whole lot more if Charlie Cley had not been flat on his back, training the pistol on the window, and very, very dead.

Chapter Ten

Eliot Oakcroft MP had dreamt all his career of being front-page news. All that weekend, his dream came true, but it was an unfortunate fact of most MPs' lives that they only became famous when something went catastrophically wrong. Where the successful policy initiative might have merited a footnote in a history book, it was the scandalous and salacious that got an MP's face and name on the front pages and into the public mind. Twenty years of quiet and dedicated public service – *nada*, *niente*, not a single column inch. Take a few hundred quid for asking some parliamentary questions or go dancing in a nightclub when you've dined not wisely but too well, or leave your clothes on a beach to escape to Australia when you've gone bankrupt, and fame and ignominy await.

MP's aide arrested for murder, said the *Daily Mail* over a huge picture of a beaming Eliot and a smaller inset one of Max and Diana being hustled into King's Lynn Police Station. Eliot sipped his coffee and surveyed the front pages of *The Times* and the *Sunday Times*, *The Telegraph* and the *Sunday Telegraph*, *The Mail* and the *Mail on Sunday*, *The Express* and the *Sunday Express*, and *The Sun* and the *Sunday Sun*. *The Guardian* he'd set aside, as his interest in rising greenhouse gases in Guatemala, never high, was eclipsed by his mixed feelings about seeing himself on all other front pages. *The Observer* had just about managed a brief mention alongside its lead story about the wind farm industry's decline in Campbeltown. On the one hand, having one's name attached to the word 'murder' wasn't unmixedly good publicity, but on the other, one's name and face were out there, and all publicity was good publicity, as Shakespeare, or someone, had once said.

'We weren't actually under arrest,' said Diana when the MP proudly laid out all 'his' front pages on Monday morning. 'Just helping police with their enquiries.'

'I'm not sure that sounds a whole lot better,' said Max.

'Never mind,' said Eliot Oakcroft. 'Never mind, never mind, all sorted now, eh?'

Max nodded and thought back to the shock of finding a dead man and the frankly bigger shock of finding himself suspect number one for five or six hours. Diana had called the police while he'd run back down to the village to try to stop Patrick Alderton leaving – unsuccessfully, as the man's van was already gone from the front of the pub. He'd come back up to the cottage to find Diana calmly making a cup of tea in Charlie Cley's kitchen and rooting through the cupboard for biscuits.

'You'll be getting fingerprints all over the place,' said Max.

'They're going to be expecting our fingerprints, Max,' she said. 'Body was still warm, by the way. He hasn't been dead long.'

'Well not if Alderton killed him,' said Max. 'And how do you know he's still warm?'

'Thought I best check for signs of life,' said Diana. 'Custard cream with your tea? By the way, I found this in his trousers pocket.'

She was holding a wallet and Max leapt back as if it were an electric cattle prong.

'The police are going to want that.'

'They're never going to know it wasn't just lying on the kitchen table,' she said, wiping it with a dish towel and tossing it onto the surface. 'Three credit cards, all in the name Anthony Green. And I thought you might find this interesting.'

She handed him a business card. A House of Commons business card. A House of Commons business card with the name *Maxwell Murray, Researcher for Eliot Oakcroft MP* written on it.

'Must have been printed before Eliot promoted you to Chief of Staff,' said Diana.

'I don't have Chief of Staff business cards,' said Max.

'I'll sort some Monday,' said Diana. 'Sit down, drink that tea, and I'll put some more sugar in it.'

'I don't take sugar.'

'Max,' said Diana, helping him into a chair where he realised his hands were trembling, 'for this cup of tea you take four or five sugars, OK?'

He sat sipping the sweet milky tea. He took a bite of a custard cream. He remembered how he would always eat custard creams like a normal human being while his sister, Ronni, would prise off the top of the biscuit to eat it, then lick out the cream filling, then eat the bottom half of the biscuit. It was one of her most annoying habits. I mean, why, why would you do that, when it meant eating the biscuit separately from the creamy part instead of putting it all together the way the biscuit-baker—

'Max,' said Diana. 'Before you vanish inside your head completely and before the police get here, why do you think Charlie Cley has a copy of your business card in his wallet?'

'I have no idea.'

'Turn it over,' she said. He read the handwriting on the back of the card: *Oakcroft's an idiot but watch out for this one*, it said.

'Someone who knows you,' said Diana, 'and knows Eliot, of course.'

The sound of a siren in the lane outside heralded the arrival of Norfolk Police. Max slipped the business card into his own wallet and finished his tea. Three uniformed officers were in the hall and Diana was ushering them upstairs.

A man in a brown suit introduced himself as Detective Inspector Bernie Adrian and sat down with his notebook.

The rest of the evening passed in a blur, most of it at King's Lynn Police Station, where Max discovered what it was like to have your fingerprints taken and that Diana's were already on file – 'loads of times', she said when they asked if she'd had them taken before. Max made a mental note never to ask her why. If she hadn't included it on her CV when she applied for the job, it was probably best he didn't know.

'This guy, Patrick Alderton, was carrying a wine bottle, you said,' Inspector Adrian asked sometime late in the evening. Max by this time had come to rather like Inspector Adrian, a man of about thirty with a rumpled suit and creases round his eyes that spoke of limited sleep and a fair amount of good humour and laughter.

'Looked like a wine bottle,' said Max.

'There were glasses on the coffee table in the living room,' said Adrian. 'Red wine in one of them. We didn't find a bottle. You're free to go. Don't leave the country without letting us know.'

On the long drive back to London, Diana told Max her investigating officer had let slip that they thought Charlie Cley had been poisoned and were working on the theory the poison had been in the wine. Someone Charlie knew, they reckoned, since there was no sign of a break-in, no sign of a fight. And since Alderton used to be his next-door neighbour and had been identified from his pictures by the barmaid and others in the pub as well as by Max and Diana, and since Alderton had left carrying the wine bottle, the police were pretty confident they had their man, or at least knew who it was they were looking for.

'Why, though?' said Max. 'What reason could Patrick Alderton possibly have for killing Charlie Cley?'

'More to the point, how did he find Charlie ten minutes before we got there?' asked Diana.

'Why isn't my mother out of jail yet?' asked Miranda Cley later that following Monday morning. 'She can't have murdered my dad if he was still alive.'

'She certainly has an unbreakable alibi,' murmured Tony Wenhamville.

'Exactly,' said Miranda. 'Why is she still in prison?'

Gathered for what Eliot Oakcroft had grandly, if with questionable accuracy, titled a Council of War were Miranda Cley, Tim Cley, Eliot himself, Tony Wenhamville, and Max and Diana. Eliot's office was too small to hold such a gathering and the open area of Portcullis House too public for a meeting with a young woman whose father had turned up alive only to be found dead while her mother was in prison for murdering him three years earlier. Max had booked a corner meeting room in the Portcullis House building, where the six of them sat around a circular table with windows looking out over the Palace of Westminster, the River Thames and the former Greater London Council building on its other side. Eliot Oakcroft had almost refused to use the room because of the circular table – he found it impossible to know where to sit to chair the meeting and wondered how anyone would know he was – but Diana had found him a bigger chair than everyone else's and bought him a coffee from the café on the floor below to keep him happy.

'What exactly happens now?' said Tim Cley. He was sitting next to his niece and holding her hand. Max had been nervous about inviting Miranda in for a meeting quite so quickly after her father's death had been discovered – indeed, before Charlie Cley had even been buried. But Miranda, though pale, seemed composed and calm, focused less on the death of a father who'd already been assumed dead by almost everyone than on the fact that her mother had clearly been wrongly convicted of killing him but, for the moment at least, appeared still to be stuck in jail.

'There will have to be a hearing at the Court of Appeal with a view to quashing Mrs Cley's conviction,' said Tony. 'Due process, all that.'

'Can that happen today?' said Miranda.

'Afraid not,' said Tony. 'It's one of the central principles of English justice that justice be seen to be done. Unfortunately, it's also one of the principles of English lawyers that it can be best seen to be done if it is done extremely slowly.'

'How long will that take?'

'Hard to say,' said Tony. 'Papers to prepare, finding a date for the Court of Appeal to fit it in – two or three months perhaps, if we're lucky.'

‘She can’t stay in prison all that time,’ said Miranda. ‘She hasn’t done anything. What are you going to do about it?’ she added, turning her attention to Eliot Oakcroft.

‘Eh,’ said Eliot.

‘What are you doing to get my mother out of prison?’

‘Oh, steps are being taken, channels pursued, buttons pushed,’ said Eliot. ‘I mean, obviously, I know all the avenues we’re exploring, but perhaps, Max, you’d like to outline them for our guests.’

‘Eliot’s written to the Secretary of State for Law and Order,’ said Max.

‘I have?’ said Eliot. ‘I have. I have!’

‘And he’s applied for an Urgent Question,’ said Max.

‘When you say urgent,’ said Tim Cley, ‘is that like urgent in the normal world, or six weeks next Thursday in parliamentary terms?’

‘It really is urgent,’ said Max. ‘A debate in the Chamber today with a law and order minister having to say what they’re doing about it.’

‘Estella Chamberlain, is it?’ said Tim Cley. ‘She’ll have to give answers herself?’

‘Probably not,’ said Max, wondering why that answer seemed to give Tim Cley some relief. ‘She’d usually send one of her junior ministers for an Urgent Question.’

‘And what does that mean,’ said Miranda Cley, ‘a vote and some action to get my mum out of jail?’

‘Not quite,’ said Max. ‘Forty-five minutes to an hour’s debate, no vote, but the issue gets publicity.’

‘Right,’ said Miranda. ‘And that’s it, is it? They don’t even vote on it? That’s what Parliament does with something urgent?’

Eliot Oakcroft felt the need to pour oil on a troubled fire, reaching across the table to pat Miranda’s hand. ‘Keeps up the pressure on the Government, you see, my dear, focus intensified, thumbscrews applied.’

‘What else have you got?’ said Miranda Cley, turning to Max after a second’s appalled silence.

‘We can petition the Secretary of State for Law and Order to release Rebecca on licence until the courts have had time to quash her conviction in full,’ said Max.

‘Which any reasonable person would instantly do,’ said Tony Wenhamville. ‘Such a pity we have to ask the Secretary of State in this case.’

‘I’ll put in a call to her straight after this meeting,’ said Eliot. ‘Won’t I, Max?’

‘I’ll get on to it,’ said Max. He nodded to Diana to slip out of the room to make the call setting up a conversation or a meeting between Eliot and Estella Chamberlain.

‘I might be able to contact her myself,’ said Tim Cley, shifting nervously again in his chair. Max was struck once more by how uncomfortable Tim had seemed throughout their meeting. ‘I’ve done some work for the party in the past, met her at the odd event at HQ.’

‘Excellent, excellent,’ said Eliot, turning his attention back to Miranda Cley. ‘I’m sure you can see, my dear, that we’re doing all we can to ensure your poor mother is back with you as soon as she possibly can be.'

'We need her out of prison,' said Miranda, leaning forward to look Eliot in the eye. The intensity of her gaze was, thought Max, open to interpretation; while Eliot Oakcroft's goggle-eyed response suggested the MP thought it was a heartfelt plea to a powerful and mighty man, it was likely that everyone else in the room realised Miranda had discovered that she'd bet her house on a donkey. 'Please do whatever you can to make that happen.'

'Absolutely,' said Eliot. 'Nose to the wheel, shoulder to the grindstone, no stone left unturned. I don't suppose I can offer you a spot of lunch?'

'It's quarter past eleven in the morning,' said Miranda, leaning back and picking up her shoulder bag.

'Coffee,' said Eliot, hopefully.

'We'll leave you to get on with the work,' said Tim Cley, guiding his niece out of the room. 'Keep us in touch.'

As Miranda Cley and Tim Cley left, Diana Burton returned holding her phone and shaking her head.

'The Secretary of State might be able to squeeze you in on Tuesday next week for ten minutes, Eliot,' she said.

'Ah, excellent,' Eliot said. 'Splendid.'

'Don't we want something a little speedier?' murmured Tony Wenhamville. Max had the mildly mean thought that this was rich coming from a former Appeal Court judge, but remembered to be glad that Tony's expertise was so useful to them. He also had a feeling the older man would be using his contact book to see whether Rebecca Cley's hearing could be speeded up as much as possible. Before he could reply that he'd be on to the Department for Law and Order to get quicker action on a call or meeting for Eliot, his own phone buzzed, and he was surprised to see Estella Chamberlain's name on his screen. Excusing himself, he stepped into the corridor outside the meeting room to take her call.

'Estella?'

'I didn't know until now that the Secretary of State for Law and Order had the power to have a phone block lifted, Maxwell,' said Estella Chamberlain. 'Thank you for that particular learning experience.'

'I assume you have to have a reason to use that power?' said Max.

'I do, but I don't have to tell anyone what it is.'

'Parliament in all its wisdom gave you that authority?'

'It did,' said Estella. 'Having fully scrutinised and thoroughly understood section 36 of the Interception of Communications Act 2001.'

'You didn't abuse section 36 so that we could have a chat about the limits and failings of parliamentary scrutiny of legislation, though, did you?'

'I did not,' said Estella. 'I need a favour. Get Eliot Oakcroft to withdraw his Urgent Question and I guarantee you we'll have Rebecca Cley out of prison tomorrow morning.'

'This afternoon,' said Max. 'And I want that in writing, or I want you to agree to having this phone call recorded.'

'Don't play silly buggers, Max,' said Estella. 'I've got the nation's press on my back to let this woman out of jail, and party donors bugging me. I'm getting her out as fast as I can, and, though I doubt you'll believe this, I'd like her out within the next hour, but there are tedious administrative reasons why it has to be first thing tomorrow morning – bloody civil servants, can't get a thing done around here, and that's the best I can do.'

'Eliot's UQ would keep up the pressure,' said Max. 'Why should he withdraw it?'

'Because if I have to spend the next two hours preparing to answer a Commons debate and then another two hours having one, that's four hours I can't be spending on the phone to judges and prison governors making sure Rebecca Cley's free tomorrow morning.'

Max paused to think for a second. He had no reason to trust Estella Chamberlain. He had no reason to do her the favour of sparing her a public hearing. But she might, just might, be making some decent points.

'OK,' he said. 'But I still want an email from someone at the Department for Law and Order within the next twenty minutes saying that Rebecca will be out of prison tomorrow morning.'

'Can't we dispense with formalities on this one, Max?'

'Let's keep it formal this time,' he said. 'Deadline for pulling the UQ is noon. You've got about twenty minutes. As soon as I get an email – doesn't have to be from you, but I want at the very least a senior civil servant's name on it – I'll tell the Speaker's Office we've withdrawn it. Deal?'

There was a brief silence before Estella muttered, 'Deal.'

'Excellent, thank you, a pleasure as always,' said Max. 'Before you go, though, would you mind telling me who Anthony Green is and why he was giving you £10,000?'

There was a longer silence, so long that Max wondered if Estella had hung up on him.

'I don't know,' she said, just as he was about to disconnect the call himself. 'The donations came in, we didn't ask.'

'Do you know now?'

'If you're asking if I know that Charlie Cley was using the name Anthony Green, I do,' said Estella, cautiously. 'By the way, this is all off the record, and I'm assuming you stick to your rule of not telling your sister anything you hear in confidence.'

'Ronni's perfectly capable of finding out her own stuff without asking me,' said Max. 'We have a deal. Anything you tell me stays with me, and if she finds out about it, she doesn't get it from me.'

'You were always revoltingly ethical,' said Estella. 'Weirdly, you're one of the few people I would actually trust.'

'Thank you, I think,' said Max. 'Forgive me if I don't return that compliment. So, you had no idea Charlie Cley was providing you with funding?'

'I still have no idea Charlie Cley was providing me with anything,' said Estella. 'Anthony Green's a common enough name. Could be a coincidence.'

'Could be,' said Max. 'Isn't though, is it?'

'I think we're done for now, Max. That email should be with you by now. Could you acknowledge with confirmation that the UQ's being withdrawn?'

'Soon as I see the email,' said Max. Estella had already cut the call.

Chapter Eleven

It was a phrase Max wouldn't use often, but the Secretary of State for Law and Order proved as good as her word. There was a huge media scrum outside His Majesty's Prison Norton St Meald at 8 a.m. the next day, flashbulbs flashing, arc lights lighting, TV reporters preening, and their grubbier colleagues from what was left of the print media scattering cardboard coffee cups and crumbs from sausage rolls, pastries and doughnuts from their cars to the gates of the prison.

On the dot of 10 a.m., Rebecca Cley, pale but smartly dressed in a grey trouser suit and perfectly coiffed, walked into the sunlight flanked by her daughter, Miranda Cley, equally coiffed and in a black trouser suit, and Eliot Oakcroft MP, butter-coloured hair gleaming in the sunlight, blue and white striped shirt and lime-green tie merrily clashing beneath his charcoal-grey suit. Cometh the hour, cometh the Eliot. As the flashbulbs started popping, Eliot raised Rebecca's arm as if she'd just won a prize fight. Which meant that most of the pictures that appeared online immediately afterwards showed a startled, wide-eyed woman looking towards a beaming red-faced man who might have just won the National Lottery.

The big set-piece speech was one of a politician's great moments. The best of them looked and sounded effortless simply because so much work had gone into them, and Max and Diana had worked late into the night crafting a searing indictment of a justice system that had let Rebecca Cley down so badly at every step, building an argument, reaching a crescendo, polishing every phrase until it glittered and shone and rang down the ages.

'Thanks,' said Eliot Oakcroft, sticking his printed copy into his jacket pocket, 'but I think I can just busk this one, don't you?'

Eliot Oakcroft stepped forward to address the waiting reporters while Rebecca and Miranda Cley stood demurely behind him. Max and Diana stood behind the bank of reporters and photographers watching Eliot beaming widely and raising his arms for silence.

'The British justice system is a jewel in the nation's crown,' he announced, 'the finest in the world, the envy of the globe.'

'And that's why it banged up Rebecca Cley for two years for no reason at all,' muttered Diana. Max hushed her. They were far away from Eliot so no risk of him overhearing, but it wasn't impossible a journalist might pick up the cynicism, and the media already had their own surplus of that.

'And,' went on Eliot, 'there is a golden thread that runs through that system, that we are all innocent until proven guilty by a jury of our peers.'

'Rebecca Cley was proven guilty by a jury of her peers,' yelled a man who might have been from the *Daily Express*. Eliot Oakcroft had been long enough in the House of Commons, though, to know when to ignore an inconvenient heckle.

'Justice delayed is justice denied,' he went on, 'and Rebecca Cley has been denied justice by the delay in releasing her from detention for a crime she did not and could not have committed. It has required tireless effort, not mine alone—'

'Not yours at all,' murmured Diana to another hard stare from Max.

'To bring about her thoroughly deserved freedom today. No stone has been left unturned, no avenue unexplored, no question unasked.'

'No cliché unspoken,' murmured Diana. 'Darkness before the dawn, light at the end of the tunnel.'

'And yet, even in the darkness before the dawn of Rebecca's release, we held fast to the light at the end of the tunnel,' said Eliot Oakcroft, 'and this is a great day for truth, for justice, and for the Great British sense of fair play.'

With which, Eliot ushered Rebecca and Miranda forward and put his arms around them as the cameras clicked and zoomed in. Smart move, thought Max, to get himself in the middle like that – years of experience of being stood on the end by photographers who knew they could crop him out had given Eliot a sixth sense on where precisely to place himself.

'You wrote such a beautiful speech, Max,' said Diana, as journalists started yelling questions at Rebecca and Miranda, apparently in the belief that the Great British sense of fair play required the nation to know whether two women who'd lost their husband and father would be celebrating with champagne in a hot tub.

'Someone actually wrote that crap?' said a voice behind Max and Diana, and they turned to find Inspector Adrian looking as if he'd slept in his suit. And not for very many hours at that. Even grey-skinned, though, the crinkles round his eyes looked more like laugh lines.

'Up to a point,' said Max. 'How's the search for Patrick Alderton going?'

'We'll find him,' said Adrian. 'He can't stay out of sight for ever. He'll use his bank card soon and we'll have him.'

'You've been to his house?'

'No, sir,' said Adrian, with a grin. 'We hadn't thought of doing that. If only we had some interfering amateurs from London to come out here and tell us how to do our jobs.'

'OK,' said Max. 'Point taken.'

'We might be able to help, though,' said Diana, linking her arm through Adrian's. Max noticed that the inspector had no objection. 'If there's anything we can tell you, it's all yours.'

'He hasn't been back home since you two saw him in Fincham,' said Adrian, not moving to get his arm back. 'He's had the sense to turn his phone off. We're assuming he had some cash on him, but who carries much these days? He's going to need cash or petrol or food sometime soon, so we'll pick him up.'

'Like she said,' said Max, 'if there is anything we can do to help, we'd be glad to.'

Adrian finally removed his arm from Diana's. 'Give me your phone numbers and I'll be in touch if I can think of anything.'

'Smooth work, Inspector Adrian,' said Diana, getting her phone out. 'Do you really want his too?'

Adrian grinned as he tapped Diana's number into his own phone. 'I suppose I can reach him through you if I need him. Meantime, there is something you can do for me. Any chance you two could get Rebecca Cley discreetly out of that scrum and into my car?'

'Why?'

'I'm driving her back home so that I can find out exactly what her relationship with Alderton is.'

'You should take Miranda, too,' said Diana, 'or instead, maybe.'

'I'm taking Rebecca,' said Adrian. 'She'll speak more freely without her daughter in the car.'

'What about Eliot?' said Max. 'He's going to want to stay with Rebecca.'

'I'm sure you can find a way to keep him out of my hair,'

said Adrian. 'Now, do you want to get Rebecca Cley out of there quietly, or do you want it to look like I'm arresting her all over again?'

'Could we get him a ride in a police car?' said Diana. 'If we promise him sirens all the way to Norfolk, he'll be fine.'

Adrian sighed, and waved to a waiting constable.

Extricating Rebecca proved easier than it looked, not least because she herself wanted to be anywhere but Norton St Meald Prison. Max saw how tired she looked beneath the make-up and the haircut her daughter had arranged for her. It was hard to imagine what mix of feelings were surging in her, her freedom the result of the discovery that the husband she'd loved and knew she hadn't murdered was nonetheless now dead. Miranda Cley had wanted to get into the unmarked police car Inspector Adrian took Rebecca to, and Max hadn't heard whatever sharp words had left the younger woman glaring at the departing car and close to tears. He watched as Diana walked over to Miranda and put an arm around her shoulders as she directed the girl towards Max's own Bentley. Finally, he glanced back at Eliot Oakcroft, still talking to a rapidly declining pack of journalists while a mystified-looking constable waited to usher him to a marked police car.

As the police car set off, sirens indeed blazing, Max began to walk towards his own car, only to find a young man with a shock of hair and a notebook in his hand diffidently stepping in front of him.

'*Norton St Meald Express*,' said the young man. 'Can you tell me something?'

'Sorry,' said Max. 'I can only talk to you on background, off the record, but you should have pretty much all you need by now I'd think.'

'Yeah, yeah,' said the young man. 'I just wondered if anyone could tell me who that guy who made the speech was?'

Miranda Cley had headphones on before Max started the Bentley, and Diana Burton also seemed lost in her thoughts as they drove back across Norfolk to Wymondham and the Cley family home.

Which, when they arrived, had four cars and a police car already crammed into its driveway, over which a seriously disgruntled constable was standing guard. He guided Max into what little space remained, then goggled at Diana Burton and Miranda Cley as they stepped out of the bottle-green Bentley, clearly feeling that life was fairer to some men than others.

'Is that guy, the MP, your boss?' he asked Max as the two women walked into the house.

'Was it you who drove him here?'

'He wanted me to do seventy all the way. I told him, there's a speed limit, it's the law. He said he was the law.'

'Give me your name, and I'm sure he'll write to your chief constable saying what a brilliant job you did.'

'Does my chief constable know who he is?'

'I think they've met, yes.'

'If it's all the same to you, then,' said the PC, 'I'd be grateful if he didn't.'

Max grinned and walked into the house. A low hubbub of conversation told him to head for the dining room, where he found what looked like a business meeting arranged around the long table. Eliot sat at the centre flanked by Rebecca Cley and Miranda, with Tim Cley opposite him and Diana Burton and Inspector Adrian on either side.

'So, that's agreed, then,' Eliot was saying. 'We establish a new charity to campaign for the release of wrongly imprisoned women, which Rebecca is kindly funding.'

Max could see straight away that Rebecca Cley was staring into some faraway space, wanting nothing more than to be somewhere alone. Only Eliot could think that a woman returning to her home for the first time since she'd been arrested and on the day after her husband was confirmed dead would want to be sitting around a dining table talking about anything to do with him. He wondered why Tim hadn't put a stop to this, but the man seemed to have aged fifteen years since they'd seen him in his Kensington office four days ago.

'Now, we'll need a name, of course,' Eliot was blissfully continuing, 'and if you wished to use mine, say the Eliot Oakcroft Foundation, then of course I'd be more than honoured to lend it, although I ought to make it clear right from the outset that the demands of parliamentary life mean I might find it difficult to find the time to commit to taking part in any events.'

'I think we'll call it the Rebecca Cley Foundation,' said Tim Cley, leaning back in his chair and staring at the ceiling. 'Since it's Becks' idea and her money and she'll be doing all the work.'

'But I get to be its patron,' said Eliot. Tim looked at Rebecca, who nodded. Max thought that she would at that moment nod to anything that might end this discussion and let her be alone. 'Excellent,' said Eliot. 'Right, then, perhaps I might take you to dinner, Rebecca, to discuss the outlines. And whatnots.'

'Yes, OK, whatever,' said Rebecca, pushing her chair back to rise.

'This evening, shall we say? Anywhere near here worth eating in?'

'I'm a little tired today,' said Rebecca, walking towards the door. 'And, if you'll forgive me, in spite of all your help and how grateful I am for it, I could do with just settling back in tonight, if we're finished here?'

'Of course, of course,' said Eliot. 'Insensitive of me. How about tomorrow evening?'

'We should probably have a talk about your schedule, Eliot,' said Max, stepping into his way to block him from following Rebecca. 'How about you leave it to us to fix something up?'

'Fair enough,' said Eliot, sitting back in his chair and beaming around the table. 'Right then. Time we let this poor woman rest instead of bothering her with all sorts of rubbish. Her husband has just died, you know, after all.'

Rebecca managed to get out of the room before Eliot could say anything else. Miranda followed her mother with a scowl at him and a silent appeal to Max to follow her.

In the hallway outside, as they watched Rebecca drift slowly upstairs, almost seeming not to recognise the surroundings of her own home, Miranda turned to Max. There was a tear in her eye. Max realised it was the first tear he'd seen from any of the Cley family – Rebecca, Tim and, until now, Miranda, none of them crying, at least in public, about the death of Charlie Cley. 'Please,' said Miranda, 'please, get that man out of my life and my mother's life and make him forget all about us now.'

'He means well,' said Max.

'I wish I'd never seen Dad alive on Cromer Pier,' whispered Miranda. 'I wish I'd never come to you.'

Max watched her run up the stairs and returned to the dining room. Tim Cley was on his feet, leaning across the table towards an unperturbed, seated Inspector Adrian.

'So what do you propose to do now?'

'We're pursuing a number of lines of enquiry.'

'Why aren't you pursuing Patrick Alderton? My brother's murderer.'

Adrian frowned. 'We are pursuing Patrick Alderton, sir. We'll get him into custody soon enough. To help with our enquiries.'

'What do you mean help with your enquiries?' Tim Cley exploded. Max noticed Inspector Adrian clock the spittle that had flown from Tim's mouth and sprinkled the oak tabletop. He also noticed that Tim's hands were clenching and unclenching around his Montblanc pen. He wouldn't bet against Tim spearing someone with that. He wouldn't bet either against Tim Cley collapsing. If Rebecca was frozen by the death of her husband and her resulting freedom, Tim was the one showing the most open grief that his brother was dead. 'What do you mean, helping with your enquiries? That man murdered my brother.'

'That's one line of enquiry,' said Adrian, evenly.

'Two people saw him running away from the house carrying the murder weapon while Charlie's body was still warm,' shrieked Tim Cley. 'What more do you need?'

'Motive,' said Adrian, still calm. 'We have no idea why Patrick Alderton would want your brother dead. After all, it wasn't him Charlie owed all the money to. And we could do with an explanation of how Alderton found out where your brother was hiding out after his little disappearing act, and who it was who was helping him out there.'

Max exchanged a glance with Diana at that one, as Tim Cley threw his pen on the table in frustration and his arms behind his head to stare at the ceiling. Eliot Oakcroft leant forward as if he was about to say something, then relapsed back into silence. Whatever was going through his mind, thought Max, he'd had enough sense to realise it wasn't relevant to whatever was happening around the table.

'We know,' went on Adrian, 'that Alderton had to ask directions to your brother's hideaway. Mr Murray here and Miss Burton established that the landlady of the pub had to tell him where to go, and their story's checked out.'

'He can't have got there long before us,' said Diana, and Adrian nodded, but hushed her.

'Chances are Patrick Alderton's our man, Mr Cley, but it's not as cut and dried as it might look.'

'Why's he on the run then, eh?' said Eliot Oakcroft, emerging unexpectedly from his haze. 'That's not the act of an innocent man.'

'It might, sir, be the act of a man who was seen by two witnesses running away from the scene of a crime carrying the wine bottle he'd just figured out might be poisoned,' said Adrian.

'Christ,' said Tim Cley. 'It's no wonder every criminal in the country's on the loose if you're the best the police can offer.'

'We'll have our hands on Patrick Alderton soon, sir, and, as I said, chances are he's our man once the Ts have been crossed and the Is have been dotted. We're watching his house – we know he has some survivalist skills from courses he's done, but they were tuppenny-ha'penny stuff, toy soldiers out in Wicklewood Forest for an evening's piss-up. He's not going to survive out in the open for long. He'll use his cash card soon enough, or his phone, and then we'll have him.'

'Be sure you do, Inspector,' said Tim Cley, getting up. 'Be sure you do.'

There was a silence after Tim had swept from the dining room. Diana Burton picked up the Montblanc pen he'd forgotten to recover from the centre of the table. Little flecks of his spittle were still disfiguring it and she picked up a cloth from the sideboard behind her and dabbed them away. Max watched Inspector Adrian quietly shutting his notebook and putting away his own Bic ballpoint pen, and noticed the smile curling the corner of the inspector's lips. Not everyone would take being yelled at like that so phlegmatically. The inspector seemed quiet and unassuming, but Max sensed a bit of steel beneath the tired exterior, a man not entirely discontent at having ruffled some feathers.

'I suppose we ought to show ourselves out,' said Max. Little point further bothering their hosts, and little excuse for an MP, his two staff and a police inspector to keep on sitting in the Cley family dining room.

Outside on the gravel, Adrian wearily agreed that his now very disgruntled constable should drive Eliot Oakcroft into Norwich to get a train back to London.

'Why can't he go in the car with those two?' said the constable, pointing at Max and Diana.

'He has a very important engagement back in London and we're not sure we'd be able to get him there as fast as the train,' said Max. *And*, he added silently, *Diana told me she'd murder me slowly and painfully if she had to spend the best part of three hours in a car with him.*

Once Eliot was safely on his way, and the siren had Dopplered off into eventual silence, Max turned once more to Adrian.

'You're right about Alderton not having any obvious interest in killing Charlie Cley,' he said. 'And there's still a heck of a lot of money missing from the company account.'

'Thus explaining Tim Cley's little performance in there,' said Adrian evenly. 'Rebecca Cley can put her hands on the assets belonging to her and her former husband, but wherever it was Charlie Cley was hiding whatever he embezzled from his brother, neither we nor, by the sign of it, Tim Cley have any idea.'

'Charlie made two donations to the Secretary of State for Law and Order using a false name,' said Max.

'Anthony Green,' said Adrian. 'We've checked it out. No sign of Green having any bank account except the one that money went out of. Twenty grand was the opening deposit, account for Parallel Parking, based in Wandsworth, London. No other transactions since he opened it, except the transfers to Estella Chamberlain's constituency party. Bank asked me if we were going to pay the overdraft for charges due for it as a business account.'

'The payments were made to the constituency,' said Diana. 'Not directly to Estella Chamberlain.'

'All above board,' said Adrian, 'assuming there's no need for any due diligence on who exactly it is paying you what most of us would think were decent sums of money – but then that's more your bag than mine, isn't it, that sort of thing?'

'Are you asking Estella if she knows why Charlie Cley was funding her office?'

'I've got an appointment,' said Adrian. Max recognised a slight change in the policeman's easy-going tone, or the appearance of one. Adrian had turned defensive.

'With Estella Chamberlain?'

'With my chief constable, who wants to know why I've put in a request to him to seek a meeting with the Secretary of State for Law and Order.'

'At a time,' said Diana Burton, 'when the annual police grants are three weeks from being announced.'

'The chief's office did mention that that might be a factor in precisely when he might consider my request,' said Adrian. 'I'm seeing him in the morning.'

'Will you let us know what he says,' said Diana.

'This is a police investigation, Mr Murray,' said Adrian, turning away from her. 'I've already shared more information than I normally would with civilians. I'd be grateful if you two would consider your part in this investigation now formally at an end, but I'd be a fool if I thought you were giving up, right?'

'Well,' said Max.

'You're right,' said Diana.

'We'll get Patrick Alderton into custody soon,' said the inspector. 'I could do with any co-operation going from any of you if he gets in touch.'

'With us,' said Max. 'Why would he get in touch with us?'

'Who else is going to help that shiftless, friendless bastard out,' said Inspector Adrian, and recognising a good line, got into his car. 'You hear from him, I hear from you, OK?'

'He's not going to contact us,' said Max.

Adrian smiled and drove away with a little wave.

'Well, that was just idiotic,' said Max, opening the

passenger door of his own car to let Diana step in. 'There's no way Patrick Alderton's going to contact us.'

'I don't know, though,' said Diana. 'That inspector's a pretty smart cookie.'

'Oh, it was his intellect you were interested in, was it,' said Max, then wished he'd kept that to himself. He looked off into the trees behind the house, knowing that Diana was looking at him coolly.

'He seems like a nice guy,' she said evenly. 'And I like his style. He's not daft, is he? He knows what he's doing. Look how he's winding you up.'

'He is not winding me up,' said Max, realising that he sounded like a six-year-old denying he'd stolen a biscuit.

'Look how he's winding up Tim Cley, then,' said Diana, 'to try to make him let something slip.'

'Such as?'

'Our only evidence that there are missing millions from the company account and that Charlie stole it and hid it away comes from Tim Cley. But nothing we've heard about Charlie Cley suggests he was a criminal genius, does it? Criminal dunderhead about sums him up.'

'So?'

'So if Charlie was too dim to steal the money and Rebecca hasn't got it, then there's only one person who knows where that money is.'

'You can't accuse Tim Cley of embezzling his own firm,' said Max, 'not least when you've stolen his Montblanc pen.'

'I haven't stolen it.'

‘I saw you pick it up and put it in your pocket, Diana,’ said Max. ‘Come on, do you know how much those pens cost? Five hundred, six hundred quid, those things.’

‘I know,’ said Diana. ‘I can’t believe anyone would pay that for a pen when you can get one from the stationery cupboard for free, and who needs a pen these days anyway, frankly? But I didn’t steal it. I just picked it up and inadvertently forgot to give him it back so that I’ve got an excuse to go and meet him again to return it. After I’ve got his fingerprints off it, of course.’

‘Charlie Cley may not have been a criminal genius,’ said Max. ‘I’m not sure Eliot Oakcroft realises he’s employing one, though.’

‘I mean, seriously,’ said Diana, fishing in her bag for a piece of paper, ‘how can a pen be worth paying anything more than a pound for?’ She put the paper on top of Max’s Bentley and unscrewed the cap of the pen. She signed her name on the paper. ‘Ooh, it does feel nice, though,’ she said. ‘You barely have to touch the page and it just flows out like this.’

Max glanced at her signature. He looked at her. She looked back, right eyebrow raised.

‘What stirs in that great brain, oh Chief of Staff?’ she said.

‘Shut up,’ said Max, finding his wallet in his pocket. ‘Shut up and scribble me something. Write “Oakcroft’s an idiot”.’

‘Would you like me to write that out a hundred times, sir?’

‘Once is fine, thanks.’

As Diana wrote on the paper on top of the car, he fished his own business card from his wallet and placed it face down next to Diana's piece of paper. *Oakcroft's an idiot*, said Diana's paper. *Oakcroft's an idiot*, said the first line on the business card. Each of them in thick, liquid royal-blue strokes.

'The business card we found on Charlie Cley,' said Max, seeing Diana's quizzical right eyebrow raised again.

'Well, we've proved that isn't my handwriting,' said Diana. 'Only sixty-five million three hundred and ninety-eight thousand to go.'

'We might just have proved that that is Tim Cley's ink,' said Max, softly.

Diana's right eyebrow shot up towards her little cap of hair and she picked up the paper and the business card and held them to the light. 'Oh, clever Max. Clever, clever Maxwell Murray.'

'If Charlie got my card from Tim Cley,' said Max, 'then Uncle Tim knew all along that his brother was alive and well and living in Fincham. We need to tell Adrian this.'

Max was opening the driver's door on his Bentley when his phone rang. Unknown number.

'Hello,' he said cautiously, expecting a sales call.

'This is Patrick Alderton,' said the voice. 'We need to talk.'

'Idiotic, you said,' said Diana Burton, happily. 'There's no way on God's good earth Patrick Alderton's going to contact us, you said.'

'All right, all right. No need to rub it in,' said Max, turning the Bentley off the London North Circular towards Diana's flat. 'Not for the eighteenth time, thank you. The first seventeen were plenty. Inspector Perfect was right and I was wrong.'

'So do we tell Inspector Adrian, or don't we?'

'I don't know,' said Max.

'The longer you wait, the harder it's going to be to explain why you've waited two hours and rising.'

Max eased the car down a wide road made narrow by the cars parked on both sides of it. Too many London streets had become one-way tracks. One day, someone was going to do something about the fact that almost every street was obstructed by traffic that not only wasn't moving but didn't move from week to week, just sat outside houses and flats in residential bays or any spare space. He pulled up outside Diana's flat and switched the engine off.

'We should make our minds up,' he said.

'Your call, Max,' said Diana. 'I know I've been taking the piss ever since we left Norfolk, but this is serious stuff. I know what I would do.'

'Which is what?'

'No clues. This one's your call.'

'You'd keep it to ourselves,' said Max.

'No clues,' said Diana. 'But I think when we started I thought this was fun, and now I'm beginning to think we've got in over our heads.'

'We could get Eliot in a lot of trouble if we keep this to ourselves.'

'We could get ourselves in a lot of trouble, Max. There's a lunatic out there threatening to kill us.'

She opened the door and got out of the car, and gave him a worried little wave over her shoulder as she walked up the path to her apartment building. Max leant back in his leather-upholstered seat, his hands on the steering wheel, perfectly at ten and two o'clock, and thought about what Patrick Alderton had said and why he, Max, hadn't yet kept his promise to let Inspector Adrian know about any approach. Back in his university rugby-playing days, he'd had drilled into his head the acronym T-CUP, thinking correctly under pressure. He'd never been good at it on a rugby field; he'd proved useless at it driving away as fast as he could from an isolated village where a madman had been firing gunshots at him. Or in his vague general direction, anyway. The concentration needed to drive a car back to the safety of London might have driven what Alderton had said out of his mind, at least as far as Diana would let it. He smiled as he realised how much her mickey-taking had done to keep him calm enough to get them home. Then he laid his head against the headrest to run through again what precisely had happened to scare the wits out of him.

'This is Patrick Alderton,' Alderton had opened. 'We need to talk.'

'Yeah, sure it is,' said Max, still insouciant. 'Is that you, Adrian? Just checking up on me?'

'I'm Patrick Alderton,' said the voice. 'And you are Max

Murray and you're standing in front of Miranda Cley's house and if you don't start talking to me and start talking to me right now, I could just shoot you, or your little girlfriend there, and see if you think I'm just checking up on you.'

'Oh, come off it,' said Max. 'No one knows I'm here except you, Adrian. Look, if he gets in touch, I'll call you, OK?'

Max jumped as a shot rang out somewhere in the woodland away to the right of where he was standing, out beyond the edge of the Cley house and the end of the village. Diana ducked behind the car as Max dropped behind his side of it.

'Get in,' he shouted at her, and she did, double-quick.

'What the hell?' she said through Max's driver seat window.

'Patrick Alderton,' he replied. 'He can see us, wherever he is.'

'That was just a warning shot, nowhere near you,' said Patrick Alderton. 'If anyone comes out the house, tell them it was far away in the woods and they'll just think it's a poacher.'

Max glanced back at the house. Rebecca Cley, Miranda Cley and Tim Cley were all still in there, doing who knew what. Rebecca could be sleeping, Miranda taking a bath, Tim venting his rage at the financial and other predicaments he found himself in. Whatever it was they were doing, it wasn't coming to the door to find out who was firing a shot in their vicinity in the late afternoon. Maybe it wasn't that unusual out here in the Norfolk wilds. A bit of hunting, a bit of poaching. Maybe it was as normal as the scream of an urban fox or an ambulance siren in West London.

'What do you want?' said Max into his phone. Diana's head popped out of the window, and he turned up the volume to let her listen as much as she could to what Alderton might say. He glanced back at the house again, worrying that if anyone in there heard the conversation, they'd be out to join it. Still silence from there. Not a curtain twitching, far less a door opening.

'Got your attention, now, have I,' said Alderton. 'Now listen, and listen good.'

'I'm listening,' said Max.

'Shut up. I need money. I need a burner phone. And I need a guarantee of immunity from prosecution if I tell the cops who killed Charlie Cley.'

'You killed Charlie Cley,' said Diana.

'Oh, no I didn't,' said Alderton, 'and if you say that again, I'll blow your pretty little head off for you.'

'Who was it, then?' said Diana.

'Oh, no, oh, no, you don't get me that easy,' said Alderton. 'I'm going to want a whole lot of money and a promise I'm all right before I tell anyone that. But I'll tell you this. I got a message to get out to Fincham to find Charlie Cley, and when I got there, I did find Charlie Cley, dead on his bed, just like you did, and then I walked down to his living room and figured out someone was there before me. Took one sniff at the wine bottle, realised I was going to have to get rid of that with my fingerprints all over it, all over the joint. I figured I was being stitched up like a kipper so that when you or the police or whoever it was turned up, Charlie'd be lying there dead and there'd be muggins looking down the wrong end of twenty years in jail. And I'm telling you now that not one hour of jail time am I doing.'

'But if you know who sent you and think you were set up,' said Max, 'you could just tell Inspector Adrian and let him get on with it.'

'Norfolk plod,' said Alderton, with a laugh like a bark. Max glanced surreptitiously out towards the woodland, wondering if he might see the glint of binoculars, or a rifle sight. The idea that there was a man with a laugh at the end of his tether out there plus a gun of some sort didn't inspire a whole lot of joy. 'Norfolk plod,' repeated Alderton, 'would put me in the nearest cell and chuck away the key and tick the box on their case-solved file and tell the *Eastern Daily Press* they'd met their targets.'

'Was this someone paying you to go find Charlie?' said Diana. 'What were you supposed to do with him when you found him?'

'That was the promise,' said Alderton. 'Only I haven't been paid, have I? Haven't had much chance to be in touch. I was meant to tell him his cover was blown, get him out of there. Up to then, I thought he was dead, like everyone else. Could have knocked me down with a feather when I heard he was still alive.'

'Bet the money was good,' said Diana. 'Someone rich paying for all this, are they?'

'Oh, very clever, missy,' said Alderton, 'very smart you think yourself, don't you. Be a shame if I blew your clever little brains out your pretty little head.'

'Don't like women much, do you, Patrick,' said Diana. Max glared through the window at her. He'd begun to get used to her overstepping the mark, but taunting a possible murderer who was pointing a gun at them was really pushing it.

'I want money – if you've got cash on you, leave your wallets on the drive when you go. I want a burner phone. Get hold of one, I'll be in touch to pick it up. And I want you two hours away from here before you tell Adrian I spoke to you.'

'OK,' said Max. 'We can do all that.'

'And don't think you can call Adrian five minutes after I let you drive away, because I'll still be here and if I get a whisper of a sniff of any copper anywhere near that house, I'll be in and out in ten minutes, and Rebecca Cley won't be enjoying being out of prison much, and I'll enjoy cutting the smile off that Miranda's face.'

Diana twirled her finger at her temple to signify that Alderton was mad. Max didn't need the prompt.

'OK,' he said. 'I'll guarantee you we'll be back in London before I tell anyone about this call. I've got forty quid in my wallet and I'll leave it here. Diana?'

'Who carries cash these days, Max?' said Diana.

'OK, so she's got nothing, and forty quid's the best we can do,' said Max.

'Right,' said Alderton. 'So you tell Adrian I was set up and I'm happy to talk when I get immunity promised, in writing, OK?'

'OK,' said Max. He laid four £10 notes beneath a stone beside the car, opened the driver's door, turned on the ignition and drove the car slowly out of the gates of the Cley house and down the lane towards civilisation. The idea that somewhere out there was a madman with a gun trained on his Bentley didn't help with manoeuvring it through the gateway and down the narrow road away from the Cley house.

Diana was silent for twenty minutes, until the first time she said, 'Idiotic, you said. There's no way Patrick Alderton's going to call us.'

Max waited until he was back in his flat before he made the call. Ronni, not quite knowing what he had to do when she saw how grim his face was, had gone to her bedroom and probably wouldn't be listening, even if she'd somehow know exactly when to come back to the sitting room when the deed was done.

Inspector Adrian, predictably, was furious that Patrick Alderton had two hours' start on him by the time Max called to tell him what had happened. On the one hand, Max could see his point: Adrian himself had clearly been standing within view of his number-one suspect outside the

Cley house and explaining why he still hadn't laid a hand on the man. On the other hand, he hadn't pulled his punches.

'He told me not to call for at least two hours or he'd do some damage to Rebecca or Miranda,' said Max once some of the initial fury had abated.

'And how exactly was he going to do that when he was getting as far away from there as fast as he could once you'd hung up on him?'

'I couldn't know he wouldn't stay close.' Max held his phone away from his ear as Adrian let loose a stream of curses you wouldn't utter in front of your mother.

'Of course he wouldn't stay close,' yelled Adrian. 'What would be the point hanging about where the police might be turning up? And if the police were turning up, what kind of idiot would be breaking into the house to do some damage?'

'I couldn't take the risk,' said Max.

'And you're an advisor to an MP,' said Inspector Adrian. 'Explains a lot about the state this country's in.'

'At least you know he was still in Norfolk,' said Max, realising that he hadn't really thought logically about how great the risk was. The experience of hiding behind his car in fear that someone with a gun might actually shoot at him wasn't really what being an advisor to an MP usually encompassed. Death from boredom was the routine weekly risk; being physically threatened by email and phone wasn't pleasant, to be sure; but actually being shot at – well, shot near – in the service of Eliot Oakcroft MP was beginning to make him question his dedication to his lifework.

'Well, he probably isn't in Norfolk now,' said Adrian, 'unless he's even dimmer than I think he is. Or dimmer than you.'

'There's no need to be offensive.'

'Really? Are you sure about that?' And Adrian hung up.

Max replaced the landline receiver in its cradle and lay on the sofa. And saw that his sister had padded into the room, her arms swamped in one of his jumpers, her feet quietened by thick socks as they crossed the floorboards. He shuffled up to halfway and watched her sit quietly opposite him, saying nothing.

'If that was the police, you might want to call them back,' she said. 'I've got Estella Chamberlain and Tim Cley bang to rights.'

'Shit,' said Max. 'I forgot to tell him about Tim Cley.'

'Tell him what?'

'I think Tim knew Charlie was living in that cottage in Fincham. I think they were in this together to get money out of the firm before it went bust.'

'So Tim killed him?'

'No,' said Max, remembering Tim Cley's ashy face at the prison release that morning. 'No, I don't know why he would want Charlie dead after all this time. It must mess up whatever scheme the two of them had in place, and whatever Rebecca and Miranda were feeling about Charlie being found dead, it was Tim who looked shattered this morning.'

Ronni nodded at him. 'I think you're right about Tim

embezzling the firm,' she said. 'Tim is Anthony Green, and I think I know why Estella Chamberlain tried to get you to leave the case alone.'

'Do you mind,' said Diana Burton, glancing into the tree-lined square, 'telling me exactly how you know Estella Chamberlain's private home address?'

'I have my sources,' said Max. It was the third time Diana had asked him the same question, the first when he'd called her to tell her to meet him and Ronni here, the second when the three of them had met around the corner at Oval Tube Station, and the third now they were walking into this quiet square. Max was fairly certain she already knew the answer, but confirming it for the MPs' staffers' gossip network wasn't on his agenda. He was glad that Ronni was keeping her counsel, too. He had a vague memory that she'd come down here once with him for a party Estella was throwing when they were still together.

'Are they sources who see you in the shaving mirror every morning?' asked Diana.

'You might think that; I couldn't possibly comment.'

It was a thing in London, you found really posh neighbourhoods nestling just next to the kind of place you wouldn't want to walk through alone even before dark. One such posh neighbourhood was a small Victorian square just behind Oval Tube Station, found through a tiny alley off Kennington Road. One minute, you were walking along a major traffic artery breathing in fumes and tripping over

Big Issue sellers; the next, via an alley lined with green, black and blue wheelie bins, you were in a tree-lined square of discreet four-storey Victorian houses with a gated park at its centre. Or, if you were Max Murray, you were remonstrating with the plain-clothes police officer who'd just emerged from behind one of the trees and asked you why you and two young ladies were walking up and down the road casing the houses. An officer who was running the considerable risk of having two young ladies kicking him in the shins.

'I'm here to see the Secretary of State for Law and Order,' said Max.

'Oh, yes, sir,' said the copper, and Max could almost hear the man trying to sniff his breath, 'and what makes you think you'll find him here, then?'

The fact that I slept with her for three or four months behind one of these doors and can't remember the number of her house, thought Max. As he stared at the solid face of the police protection officer, he realised that this was an argument likely to have him arrested. Not to mention that it might make Diana Burton throw up.

'First,' he said, 'I know the Secretary of State's a she, not a he. And secondly, the fact that her police protection leaps out the second someone comes into the street.'

'Ah,' said the copper. 'I'm not police protection, just out on my beat.'

'Your beat's this quiet square no one knows exists, and you're in plain clothes?' said Diana.

'Modern policing's a complex business, miss.'

'Should I stop worrying my pretty little head about it?' asked Ronni, sweetly. Max noted that the six-foot-three, sixteen-stone police officer wouldn't stand a chance against his five-foot featherweight of a sister, and that the man had no idea how close he was to finding that out.

'Look, officer,' he said, 'I'll be sure to tell the Secretary of State how assiduous and discreet you've been. She's clearly safe in your hands.'

'If,' said the copper, 'and I'm admitting nothing here, you three did have an appointment with the Secretary of State, if he, or she, happened to live anywhere near here, why are you walking up and down the street instead of arriving in a civil service car and knocking on the door? Not that there is, necessarily, a door to knock on, that is, I mean to say.'

'Why don't you ask her for yourself,' said Max, resorting to desperate measures on his mobile phone and hoping Estella hadn't changed her number. 'Estella,' he said, when it turned out she hadn't.

'What the hell do you want?'

'Your police protection officer's doing a superb job out here. Fully passed the test. Would you like to tell him I can come in now?'

'Are you outside my house?' said Estella. There were about six Ss in 'outside' and 'house' – she susurrated like the women from ABBA – and Max recognised the effect of a white wine bottle or two on his one-time girlfriend. Recognised and remembered, with a twinge of affection and a stab of pain.

'Mystery shopper test over and done,' said Max. 'Would you have a word with him?'

He handed his phone to the surprised policeman and watched the guy put it to his ear.

'Good evening, ma'am,' he said. 'Forgive me, but what's the codeword?'

Max watched as the copper got the codeword right in his ear with both barrels. He wanted to stay straight-faced and not look smug but suspected he'd missed both by a mile. The policeman handed him back his phone without a word and curtly nodded Max into the square. Max was just steeling himself to ask for the number when a Victorian-gas-lamp-styled electric light clicked on above one door and light flooded a neat pathway bisecting two squares of billiard-table lawn as it opened.

'I'll let you know when we leave,' said Max to the back of the police officer as he merged once more into the square's central garden.

'Don't you worry, sir,' came a voice from the gloom. 'I'll know.'

Max, Ronni and Diana walked up the pathway to Estella's front door and pushed it open. No effusive welcome on the doorstep, then. They entered a narrow wood-floored hallway, to the right a white staircase leading up, to the left a darkened drawing room, and straight ahead a well-lit kitchen and dining room with what appeared to be a well-lit Estella Chamberlain suddenly appearing in front of him. For public consumption, the Secretary of State for Law and Order favoured deceptively simple trouser suits of fairly severe cut, but the one who let her hair down at home was in old grey sweatpants and a Snoopy T-shirt and carrying a large wine glass. Any tabloid photographer who could catch a snap of this would make a fortune.

'You're not alone,' she said.

'My sister Ronni you know,' said Max. 'And my assistant, Diana.'

'Part of Eliot's stable,' said Estella. 'Can't you find a proper job?'

'She's younger than you were when you did it,' said Ronni, smiling sweetly at Estella.

'And at least I'll still have a job after tonight,' said Diana, following suit.

'Drink?' Estella said, and she led them into the kitchen. Max noticed that the hand not waving the wine glass was holding a bottle of Chardonnay and a corkscrew. Something was playing quietly in the background, piano music, Chopin maybe, and he remembered that while Estella had told *Desert Island Discs* her favourite song was some Taylor Swift thing, she'd always had a taste for classical music of the kind they didn't excerpt on Classic FM. 'Glasses are up there,' she said. 'Help yourselves.'

Max found three wine glasses in the open oak cabinet on the left-hand wall of the long, light kitchen and took a seat at the dining table. At the far end, by the French window leading to a small garden behind the house, Estella had left an open laptop and an open red box of Government papers, a three-inch pile of which was neatly stacked beside it. She'd also left another empty bottle of the same Chardonnay next to the sink, along with a box of crackers and what was left of a piece of cheese.

'Working?' he said. 'Just the average evening in, is it?'

'Always working,' she said, plonking a very full glass of wine next to his hand. Some of it sloshed over the rim as it landed. 'I'd say you should see some of the crap a minister has to work their way through, but since you work for Eliot Oakcroft, I doubt you ever will.'

'Good to see you living the dream.'

'Don't give me a hard time, Maxwell,' she said, sitting at the opposite end of the table and draining about a third of her glass. Max sipped his own wine, noting how perfectly chilled it was, cold but warm enough to release the flavours. This Chardonnay wasn't the kind the supermarkets bought in bulk from Australia. It deserved some care and attention as it went down, and it shouldn't come in a glass that contained two-thirds of the bottle. 'Your sister gave me a courtesy call earlier this evening. I wasn't entirely expecting you to come dancing on the remains.'

'I'm not here for that,' said Max.

'And you don't have to worry about his sister,' said Ronni. 'She's not filing a story on you.'

Estella looked steadily at Ronni. Well, almost steadily. 'What're you waiting for?' she said. 'What more do you want from me?'

'Nothing,' said Ronni. 'Except your resignation.'

'For a story you're not going to print?'

'I'll be telling the police what we know about you interfering in an investigation into a murder. But I'm not writing about you having an affair. I'm a serious reporter, Estella, not interested in celebrity flim-flam. Who cares about who's been sleeping with you?'

'Anthony Green isn't sleeping with me.'

'Anthony Green doesn't exist, but I note the use of the present tense,' said Ronni. 'Don't underestimate me, Estella. Remember I knew you when I did care who you were sleeping with.'

Estella gave a little 'humph' of a laugh and drank deeply of her Chardonnay. 'Poor Max,' she said. 'Always had little sis to look after him.' Max began to worry about how drunk she really was. How she'd begun to cope with the realisation that her political career was probably about to crash. He had to remember, yet again, exactly how Estella had dumped him in that Premier Inn. To remind himself that he didn't, couldn't, mustn't still have the slightest affection for her. And really, really couldn't still fancy her a bit.

'So, what is it you want?' said Estella, dragging her glare away from Ronni to Max and on to Diana. 'And what's Mary's little lamb doing here trailing along behind you?'

She'd more or less drained her glass and half-reached for the bottle again before restraining herself.

'Tim Cley,' he said. 'We want to know exactly what Tim Cley did to stall the investigation into Charlie's disappearance and why.'

'You know why,' said Estella.

'We think we do,' said Max. 'We want to hear it from you before we go talk to him about it.'

'You're going to talk to Tim? You better hurry.'

'Why?' said Max.

'And why on earth would I talk to you about any of it?' said Estella. She got up and took her glass to the kitchen sink and rinsed it out. She filled it with water from the tap and drank it down. Max wondered if the empty bottle of Chardonnay by the sink was the only one she'd had before he arrived, and recognised that she was becoming aware of how drunk she'd been getting when she hadn't expected any visitors.

'What were you working on there?' he said, pointing at the red box. Her name was printed on it in gold lettering, and her title, above the golden crown that signified it was a Government case. He'd give her time to get her thoughts together before he got back on to Tim Cley's donations to her constituency party, to Tim Cley's alter-ego existence as the no-longer-mysterious Anthony Green.

'Usual crap,' she said, returning to her chair with another full glass of water. 'Never be a minister, Max. They fill your day with meeting after meeting and then they send you home with one or two of these boxes.' She riffled through the pile of paper. 'Reports, surveys, letters to sign, letters to read, submissions, minutes, policy papers, all of it long and complicated and dull beyond belief. It's no way for a woman to spend her nights, Max.'

'You wanted it.'

'I know,' she said. 'So did you.'

'You could give it up tomorrow,' said Diana. 'And let's face it, you're probably going to have to.'

'Tomorrow,' said Estella, with a sad little smile. 'Two more boxes arriving by special delivery first thing tomorrow. Unless the news programmes have got me sacked by then.'

'Would it be such a bad thing?' said Diana. 'If this is your life?'

Estella smiled at her, a slow, sad smile. For all that he'd trust her as far as the French window behind her, Max felt another stabbing reminder of why he'd found her attractive in the first place. 'Of course it would,' she said. 'I'd do anything to keep on doing this. Ask Max. He knows more than most how much we all want it. I expect it keeps you up nights yourself, dreaming of a life like mine.'

Max looked at the table and swirled his wine for a moment. In an alternative life, this could have been him, ministerial office and decisions that could mean life or death. Diana, across the table, simply smiled and shook her head.

Estella looked slightly disconcerted as she turned away from him and poured herself a fresh large glass of wine. Max recognised the way she'd tilted her chin upwards, her automatic fight back against a slight. One of the sharper newspaper cartoonists had spotted her using the mannerism at the despatch box in the Commons when her back was against the wall and always drew her with an elongated, pointy chin up in the air.

'I didn't know who he was at first,' said Estella. 'I met Tim Cley at some party things, fundraisers, you know how it goes. Two hundred pounds a plate dinner, revolting food, filthy wine, and you get stuck next to someone who might cough up a bit more for the party and the pleasure of meeting me. This guy was funny, he was charming, but I had no idea he was donating to me personally.'

'Because he was doing it as Anthony Green.'

'I'd never heard of Anthony Green either. You know how it is, Max. So much stuff comes into the office. I never see it, never know what replies are going out in my name. My office thought the donations were kosher, declared them in full and on time, met all the requirements. You know how it is.'

'I know how it is,' said Max, although he also knew that some MPs' staff were more rigorous than others in checking out donors before they accepted the money. The way they were supposed to be but hardly ever had the time or training for.

'We can't survive without donations, can we?' said Estella. 'Offices cost, campaigns cost, posters cost, and we get nothing towards all that except what we can raise for ourselves.'

'I know,' said Max. He chose not to mention that no government, including Estella's, was brave enough to regularise political party funding, no one willing to ask a public for money who already thought that politicians were a thorough waste of it. 'So when did you find out that Tim Cley was Anthony Green, and when did he start calling in some favours?'

'He asked me out to dinner a few weeks after we met. I turned him down, but he wrote me back – no strings, no ulterior motives, just enjoyed meeting me and wanted to see if we'd enjoy getting to know each other.'

'Have you sold the rights to the screenplay yet?' said Diana.

'He was charming and funny and good-looking.'

'Not to mention rich,' said Ronni.

'I've never pretended that didn't help.'

'No one's accusing you of hypocrisy,' said Diana. 'Cheating, lying, dishonesty, being a moral and emotional self-centred and over-ambitious vacuum, maybe, but at least you're no hypocrite.'

'Thank you,' said Estella, ironically.

'What we see is what we get.'

Estella stared at Ronni unblinking for a moment or two, then turned her unfocused gaze back on Max.

'So we had dinner a few times and Tim told me about his brother being murdered and his sister-in-law being in jail for it, and then, one night, he said his niece was stirring things up a bit and could I do him a favour and call Eliot Oakcroft off, because it was just going to make the poor girl sadder and madder if we pretended her father might still be alive when he was so clearly dead.'

'So you called Eliot in to find out what was going on.'

'I didn't want to see him,' said Estella. A grin broke out across her face. 'I wanted to see you.'

'I'm touched.'

'To find out what you were up to,' she said. 'I mean, when he told me an MP was looking into it, I was going to take him seriously. But then he told me it was Eliot Oakcroft and I put two and two together and came up with Maxwell Murray.'

'Uncle Tim pretended he was supporting Miranda Cley when he came to see us,' said Max. 'Telling you he was sparing her pain was a pretty low trick.'

'He's a bit of a shit,' said Estella. 'I'm not used to people not taking my calls.'

'He's a crook,' said Max. 'I'm sorry it's going to hit you, but we have to tell the police what we know.'

'You said we need to hurry if we want to find Tim Cley,' said Diana. 'Why? Where is he?'

'Darling Tim is fleeing the country tonight,' said Estella. 'I suppose he had the decency to let me know.'

'We have to stop him,' said Diana. 'Where is he now?'

'He's out of Heathrow at ten,' said Estella.

'You can stop him.'

'Right,' said Estella. 'And then the police can arrest him and he can drop me right in the crap.'

'Hate to tell you,' said Ronni, 'but you're already neck-deep in that, Estella. If you let him leave the country, I will change my mind and write everything I know to any paper that'll print it.'

'Blackmail,' said Estella, toying with her mobile phone. 'That's a crime, you know. I'm the Secretary of State for Law and Order. I could have that guy outside the door come in here and arrest you all right now.'

‘You’re not going to,’ said Ronni. ‘You’re going to pick up that phone to Border Force right now. Get them to hold Tim Cley at the airport. And we want half an hour with him before they hand him over to the police.’

‘And what’s in that for me?’ said Estella.

‘We’ll keep you out of it for as long as we can. Give you time to resign quietly.’

Estella put down her wine glass and poured another glass of water. ‘So I lose my job,’ she said. ‘Not really selling this to me.’

Max got up from the table and walked across to her. He looked her in the eye. He saw something unfamiliar, the dullness of the knowledge of defeat, not yet admitted but deeply understood. ‘If you resign quietly you can come back,’ he said. ‘Personal reasons, health, time with your family, whatever it is – you can spend a couple of years with your head down and make a return. But if you go because you helped a suspected murderer to fly to Jamaica because he’s been funding your office, well, there’s no way back from there, is there?’

‘I guess I don’t have much choice, do I?’

Max shook his head.

‘It’ll still get out,’ said Estella. ‘The police are leakier than Downing Street.’

‘Best we can do,’ said Max. ‘If someone gets you, it won’t be us. It won’t be me.’

‘Why?’

‘Does that matter?’

'Yes, it does,' said Estella. 'If anyone's got a reason to bring me down, it's you. Why would you let that go?'

'Why do you think?'

'I'd love to think it was because you still held a flame for me and hoped we might get back together. I mean, here I am, still single, no time for any kind of liaison with anyone other than a dodgy businessman who's been using me as much as I've been milking him. I'd love to think it was something like that, Maxwell, but somehow I suspect it's not.'

'You're right,' said Max, knowing how much what he was about to say would hurt her. 'We've just got bigger fish to fry than you.'

Estella finished her glass of wine and rested her hand on the pile of papers next to her governmental red box. She picked up her mobile phone and walked out of the kitchen, dialling a call.

'You OK, Max?' said Diana.

'I'm sorry for her.'

'Don't be,' said Ronni. 'We're giving her more than she deserves. She'll be fine.'

Estella came back into the kitchen, and fished a piece of Home Office stationery out of her red box. 'It's done,' she said, as she scribbled a line on the paper and added her signature. 'They'll hold him until you can get there. You can travel back with him in the back of the police van.'

'Thank you,' said Max. Ronni said nothing as she led Diana towards the door out of the kitchen.

'You think it might be a few more days before the press find out I'm connected to him?'

'Maybe weeks,' said Max. 'Maybe never.'

'I guess I owe you some thanks,' said Estella. She'd picked up a paper from the top of her pile of documents. 'Now, I'm afraid I have work to do.'

Max left two-thirds of his wine in his glass as he let himself, Ronni and Diana out into the night, giving a wave as he went to the invisible policeman out in the private garden at the centre of the square.

'It's not even as if we're actually going anywhere,' Max told the operative driving the little truck that eventually transported him, Ronni and Diana, at 5mph, through Terminals 2, 4 and 5 to reach the Border Control secure facility where Tim Cley was being held.

'Neither are they, chum,' said the operative with the sort of lugubrious joy that only a British transport worker in sight of three hundred passengers sleeping on their own suitcases can muster. He'd clearly been on the same training programme as the operative who'd met Max, Ronni and Diana at the Border Control information desk, read four times their letter of authorisation from the Secretary of State for Law and Order and called his supervisor, who paged her supervisor, who texted their Director of Service Delivery, before asking Max and Diana to wait for forty-five minutes in the Caffè Nero for clearance to be confirmed. The only consolation was that even if Inspector Adrian was haring down the M11 and around the M25 with blue lights flashing and sirens blazing, he'd have to be at least an hour behind them before he hit the immovable brick wall of British bureaucracy.

Finally, though, they were on their way to the secure facility, a small set of Nissen huts on the airport perimeter where Tim Cley had been kicking his heels since his attempt to check in for his flight to Jamaica had raised the red flag. Even if they were moving at a pace the average Parkrunner would find a bit too comfortable.

There was an officer outside waiting for them: stocky, blue jumper, peaked cap, clipboard in hand. He handed it to them to sign as they climbed off the airport transit vehicle, and Diana handed him back the Bic ballpoint that came with it to sign with a flourish with Tim Cley's Montblanc pen.

'Last chance,' she said to Max. 'Guess I have to give it back to him now.'

'I'll have that,' said the officer, 'if it's the property of the detainee, that is.'

'It is,' said Max. 'He left it with us by mistake.'

'Can't be letting prisoners have pens, sir,' said the officer, disappearing it into his black trousers pocket. 'No knowing what mischief might arise from a pen. I'll see it's logged and returned to him at the appropriate juncture.'

'You'll get about £200 for it on eBay,' said Diana.

'Naturally, no such thought had crossed my mind,' said the officer.

'Could we have a receipt for it, please?' said Max. 'It's not entirely impossible the police will want to see it.'

The officer's eyes narrowed as he reappeared the pen from his pocket, unscrewed the cap and scribbled a note on his clipboard, ripping it off and handing it to Max. *Fancy pen provided by the MP's nark*, read the receipt in thick blue strokes. *Near enough, I suppose*, thought Max as he followed the officer's broad blue-jerseyed back into the Nissen hut.

Tim Cley was sat at a small square table by a small square window in the small square prefabricated room they were shown into. He was also handcuffed and looked up at them with tired, defeated eyes as they sat in the two chairs opposite him.

'I knew you two clowns were trouble,' he said. 'Who's your friend?'

'My sister, Ronni,' said Max.

'I should tell you I'm a journalist,' said Ronni. 'I like to keep things honest.'

'That puts the tin fricking lid on it, doesn't it,' said Tim, laying his head on his hands. 'So, what happens now?'

'You tell us what happened.'

'What's in it for me?'

'Depends on whether you killed Charlie,' said Max.

Tim sat up straight and stared at the three of them. 'Charlie?' he said. 'Of course I didn't kill Charlie. You're not fitting me up for that. I loved him like a, like a—'

'Like a brother,' said Ronni, reaching across to take Tim's

hand. The Border Force guard coughed, and she pulled it back again. But Tim was looking at her with a tear forming at the corner of his eye. 'Why don't you just tell us what happened, Tim?'

'I knew these two were trouble,' he said, still looking only at Ronni. 'Ever since Toby Cuthbertson told me to send Miranda to Eliot Oakcroft, I knew these two were trouble.'

'Cuthbertson's Miranda's MP,' said Max to Ronni. 'He's the one who passed Miranda on to Eliot.'

'"Oakcroft's useless", he told me,' said Tim. '"Doesn't know his Arras from his Elba. You can fool the girl into thinking he's on the case, but nothing'll happen." He clearly knew zilch about you two.'

'Why didn't he want to take it on himself?'

'You're here to ask me about dodgy donations. One thing I should have learnt from Cuthbertson is giving MPs money's a one-way street. I give a donation, I expect a favour when I need one.'

'They can't do that,' said Max. 'Against the rules.'

'His idea of a favour was passing me on to a patsy dumber than he is.'

'It's not something I'll say often,' said Diana, 'but, frankly, you're being unfair to Eliot Oakcroft there.'

'I really was serious about offering you a job, darling. You could make serious money if you got out of this game and put yourself to work,' said Tim, almost smiling ruefully at her. 'At least Oakcroft knows how to employ smart ones.'

'Is that why you gave Charlie this?' said Max, sliding his business card across the table. Tim picked it up and turned it over and barked.

'Ah, Charlie,' he said, 'God love him. I was wondering how you got on to me and here all along it was my idiot brother not doing his admin properly, hanging on to bits of paper that should have been in the shredder.'

'There was a lot of paper that went through the shredder, wasn't there, Tim,' said Ronni kindly. 'How about you just tell us all about it?'

'I want a solicitor,' said Tim Cley, folding his arms and sitting back in his chair.

'We're not the police, Tim,' said Ronni, 'and unlike the police, who'll be here in a bit and a lot less nice than us, we don't think you killed your brother.'

Tim unfolded his arms and leant right across the table, almost as if he'd been slapped.

'Who thinks I killed my brother?'

'Inspector Adrian,' said Max. 'Norfolk's finest. You're the only person who knew where Charlie was hiding out. Charlie was stealing money from your company. Whoever it was who killed him was someone he trusted enough to be drinking a glass of wine with him – a glass, what's more, of his favourite wine that his guest had brought for him. You are, as I believe the saying goes, bang to rights.'

'Patrick Alderton killed him,' said Tim.

'Probably not,' said Diana, 'but assuming he did, someone must have hired Alderton, and that someone didn't know where Charlie lived, so Patrick had to ask in the local pub. And that means that if you hired him, you were either very incompetent about telling him the address, or it wasn't you.'

'Of course it wasn't me,' said Tim, leaning back and looking at Diana carefully. 'And you know it wasn't me.'

'We think it wasn't you,' said Diana. 'We think you were the brains behind you and Charlie shifting as much money out of your PR company before it went bust.'

'And why would I do that?' said Tim, unconvincingly.

'So that Charlie could disappear and everyone would assume he'd stolen it all and then, when it had all blown over, you and he could fly away into the sun with as much as you could take with you and start all over again abroad somewhere. Jamaica, wasn't it, you were trying to go to tonight? Was that always the plan?'

'Charlie wanted the Dominican Republic,' said Tim. 'I chose Jamaica. Dominican Republic, I ask you. What does anyone know about the Dominican Republic? Charlie chose it because I wouldn't let him go to America and he loved baseball. Baseball! I ask you! My brother was an idiot.'

'But you loved him,' said Ronni.

'He needed looking after,' said Tim, simply. 'Mum and Dad told me when I was a kid he'd need looking after, and I looked after him. We started the firm together because he needed a job. He'd had six and they'd all fired him – loved him for a week and then realised he was a lazy so-and-so who'd nick the pennies off a corpse's eyes if he thought no one was looking. But he made me laugh, how he got away with everything, how he got a cracking bird like Rebecca to marry him.'

'I don't doubt he had a heart of gold,' said Max, 'but you and him got Rebecca life in prison for killing him when he wasn't even dead.'

'She was on to us,' said Tim. 'Worst mistake we made was making Rebecca the company secretary. She knew exactly what was happening with the money vanishing out of the firm, only she thought we was siphoning it off to cope with Charlie's gambling debts.'

'He had gambling debts?' said Max. 'We hadn't heard anything about gambling debts.'

'One brilliant thing he did,' said Tim. 'Let Rebecca think he was a gambler once she'd noticed the odd ten thousand was missing here and there. But it wasn't – we was channelling it into a Cayman Islands account, where Rebecca couldn't find it and the taxman had no way of getting his grubby little mitts on it.'

'Why?' said Max.

'Classic mistake,' said Tim. 'We started that PR firm over a shop in Hackney, you know, one room, a photocopier and a phone. And we grew and grew. Charlie was brilliant at talking people into being our clients, I did the work and hired good people to write stuff for us, and Becks did the accounts and whatnot. And then we grew, two offices, then four, then fourteen. And a headquarters in Kensington instead of Hackney and Shoreditch, and a posh bird on the reception desk, all that.'

'You overextended,' said Max.

'We funded it all on borrowing,' said Tim. 'Thought if we could keep servicing the debt, we could just keep expanding. Best PR firm in London said *PR Monthly* four years ago, biggest client list, innovative, the hip firm to be with and Charlie the charismatic frontman. Only me, the boring back-office bloke, had realised interest rates were rising and we couldn't keep up. Charlie got the clients in, 'cos they loved him and he made them laugh, but then he did something crass, like shag their daughters, and the ten-year future relationship turned into two years, and future projections got a bit iffy, and we started paying our creditors out of more borrowing, and I thought, time to get out of this game and get out to the sun and the sand somewhere before it all goes splat.'

'And that was Jamaica,' said Diana.

'That's about the size of it,' said Tim. 'Plan was Charlie would disappear. Leave the car in the woods, vanish into thin air, as if he'd nicked all the company cash so that I could declare bankruptcy and our creditors could go sing for their money. No real victims, all of them could afford it.'

'Bet they didn't see it that way,' said Max.

'They could cope,' said Tim. 'Almost everyone we were owing money to was rich-kid stuff – family trust, inheritance, not one of them worked for it. We worked for it. I worked my fingers to the bone for what I had.'

'Which was nothing,' said Max. 'Nothing you didn't owe to anyone else.'

'Whatever,' said Tim. 'Charlie would vanish. We'd wait for the fuss to die down, then him and me would go off to Jamaica, new identities, couple of million quid, quiet life of luxury. Only it went wrong, didn't it? My idiot brother had to gild the lily a bit. Blood all over his bloody car. Murder inquiry. Rebecca banged up for it. More publicity than you could shake a stick at.'

'So sorry your imprisoning that poor woman for two years was just bad luck,' said Diana.

'You think butter wouldn't melt in her mouth,' said Tim. 'Let me tell you this. When Rebecca realised we were shifting money out of the company, she got her share as quick as she could. She probably ended up with more than we did. Why do you think she didn't tell the police we were nicking company funds?'

'She was protecting Charlie,' said Max.

'Like hell,' said Tim. 'She was shagging the handyman, what's his name, the one that killed Charlie.'

'Patrick Alderton.'

'Alderton,' said Tim. 'There's a piece of work.'

'She spent two years in prison,' said Diana.

'Rebecca's a smart girl,' said Tim. 'You think she didn't know Charlie was alive? You think she didn't know she'd get out of there sooner or later and live on what she took out of the company?'

'She says she didn't have an affair with Patrick Alderton,' said Max.

'Charlie up in London working Monday to Thursday,

Mr Muscles living three doors down from Rebecca. You do the maths. If you're really asking who hired Alderton to kill my brother, then the answer is staring you straight in the face.'

'You think Rebecca had Charlie killed,' said Diana.

'As you said, she got two years inside,' said Tim. 'She was always going to get herself out somehow.'

'How could she know where Charlie was living?' said Max.

'That I don't know,' said Tim, 'but Charlie wasn't exactly discreet, was he? Ice creams on Cromer Pier, for God's sake. When Miranda first came to me with that photograph, I nearly went up and killed him myself. Lie low, I told him, six months just living quietly out of sight and the rest of our lives lying on a beach in the sun with a couple of million quid. But he couldn't, could he? Couldn't just sit in of an evening when he could be out making an arse of himself with some bird half his age. I mean, have you seen that Lulu Marchbanks he was with on Cromer Pier that day?'

'I have, actually,' said Max, not looking at Ronni, noting Diana's curious eyebrow.

'Well, there you are, then,' said Tim. 'My brother. Caught out because some flighty piece who'd sleep with anyone caught his eye. Stupid bastard got himself killed because he couldn't keep his pecker in his pants for a few weeks.'

And with that Tim Cley laid his head on his arms on the table and began to bawl his eyes out. Diana signalled to Max that they should withdraw and leave him alone with his grief, and the three of them got up quietly and made their way to the door.

Before they got there, though, it flew open, and a short, angry man in a leather jacket burst into the room. Inspector Adrian, red of face and short of breath, shot Max, Ronni and Diana a surprised, furious glance, and then turned his attention to the man crying into his arms.

'Timothy Frederick Wilson Cley,' he announced, 'I am charging you with the murder of Charles Anthony MacAllister Cley. You do not have to say anything, but it may harm your defence if you do not mention when questioned something which you later rely on in court. Anything you do say may be given in evidence.'

Tim Cley didn't move, still weeping into his outstretched arms. Inspector Adrian looked at him for a moment, waiting for his prey to acknowledge his presence. When Tim continued not to, he turned in his wrath to Max, Ronni and Diana.

'What, and this better be good, in the hell are you two doing here with my suspect? And who the hell is she?'

'Let me tell you a little story, about financial fraud and peculation,' said Ronni, putting her arm through Inspector Adrian's and leading him towards the door. 'Once you've got your constables to put Tim Cley in a police van and we get rid of Max and Diana, we can find a quiet bar and a bite to eat.'

Adrian looked around him with a wild surmise. Then he looked at Ronni again, her tiny frame, her dark hair, her open smile.

'We'll, er, just, you know, get the Tube back to Central London,' said Max, ushering Diana past the pair of them.

'OK,' said Inspector Adrian, signalling to two constables hovering outside the door.

Chapter Twelve

Max waited the next morning on the street outside the Palace of Westminster with Ronni, to meet and escort Inspector Adrian into the building. And was surprised to see Adrian grinning and waving at him as he approached from the Westminster Tube side. Until, lumbering not untypically a few yards behind the uptake, it occurred to him that perhaps the wave was for Ronni, who was waving equally enthusiastically back.

Like every senior police officer since Sergeant Cuff, as a rule Inspector Adrian had about as much time for interfering amateurs as he had for the Royal National Opera or women's football. But if he had to trust one, then Ronni Murray was the ideal. Serious, thoughtful and apparently giving him the whole story without actually planning to claim all the credit.

Not to mention matching him glass for champagne glass in the Heathrow Terminal 4 Seafood House and Caviar Bar and insisting on paying for her half. Romance had been born in less likely locations, and the heart of Inspector Bernie Adrian, never lightly given, had been fully trothed as he sat, mildly drunk after a night on the town, on the District Line back to the Earl's Court Premier Inn the Norfolk Police accountants would be querying come the end of the month's expenses claim.

'What on earth did you do with him?' said Max, who'd been waiting up for Ronni.

'Showed him a few of the sights,' said Ronni. 'He's never been to London before.'

'Never?'

'It's not the centre of everyone's universe, Max. There's a whole country outside the North Circular. I've promised to show him Scotland Yard when we're done meeting tomorrow morning, by the way.'

'He'll be wanting 221b Baker Street next.'

'We did that.'

'Do I want to know what else you did?'

'We walked, we talked, I showed him Soho, then sent him off to his hotel a happy man.'

'Really?'

'Patrick Alderton might still be at large,' said Ronni, 'but it's only a matter of time. And being gift-wrapped all the evidence he needs to finger the collar of Tim Cley for embezzling funds from his company and helping Charlie hide out in the country is going to be a major feather in his cap.'

'We still don't know who killed Charlie.'

'OK, but after the bollocking he got from his chief constable for not laying his hands on Patrick Alderton yet, he'll take whatever credit's going. And spending Norfolk Police's expenses on three courses and a couple of bottles at Mon Plaisir's cheered him up no end.'

And, though the citizens of Norfolk might never know it, that was clearly money well spent. Gone was the tired and grumpy inspector who'd licked his pencil and scribbled in his notebook in Norfolk. If this were a silent movie, Adrian would have been whistling and clicking his heels as he gavotted his way along the front of the Palace of Westminster to the visitor entrance. If he'd had a hat, he'd have been wearing it on the side of his head.

'London air seems to be good for you,' said Max as Adrian berthed alongside him.

'Might give the capital a go one of these days,' said the inspector, leaning over to give Ronni a quick peck on the cheek. 'Scotland Yard, all that, might be just the thing to pick me up.'

'It's just around the corner,' said Max. 'Over there, behind that glass building.'

'Perhaps I'll pop in when we're done,' said Adrian. 'See what the market might be for a highly talented, undervalued, overworked policeman. Now, then, how do we get into the House of Comedians, then?'

'You sure it was only the two bottles?' whispered Max as the inspector foxtrotted down the ramp towards visitor security. 'I think he's still pissed.'

'Minibar at his hotel?' said Ronni, looking mildly worried. 'Could you let him know that I'm usually on assignment abroad and hardly ever in London when you get the chance?'

'Do your own dirty work,' said Max, grinning.

Security cleared, Max escorted the two of them into Westminster with visitor badges around their necks and into a tiny, shabby conference room off Westminster Hall. He saw, as he had so many times with other guests, how Adrian took in the grandeur of the Hall itself, its high oak ceiling and vast stone space, before looking slightly shell-shocked by the state of the place as soon as they were behind the scenes in the little corridor where the meeting rooms were housed. Five minutes inside one of the tiny conference rooms with their off-off-off-grey and peeling wallpaper, damp ceilings and rickety conference tables was usually enough to convince most visitors that the horror stories about needing to spend £60 billion or so on refurbishing the place before it fell into the River Thames were pretty much on the mark. The cracked windows the wind was whistling through and the crooked paintings that looked like they might pull the plaster off the grubby whitewashed walls if you tried to straighten them up were pretty effective signs, too. Just to help things along, an anti-Brexit protestor who hadn't caught up with history yet was on the pavement just outside the palace, blasting Beethoven's Ode to Joy and 'Yellow Submarine' on a continuous loop.

'Thank you so much for coming in, Inspector,' Max said when Adrian and Ronni had walked in to find five more people looking at them from the oblong conference table they'd presumably had to build inside this tiny room, since it couldn't have fitted through door or window. 'We've got a lot to tell you, and we thought you might benefit from meeting one of the finest legal minds at our disposal.'

'Always glad to be of assistance,' said Eliot Oakcroft MP.

'I suspect dear Max may have meant me, old boy,' murmured Tony Wenhamville, managing both self-deprecation and exasperated accuracy. Adrian sat down next to Ronni with the others around the table – Eliot, Tony, Diana Burton, Miranda Cley and a shattered-looking Rebecca Cley, whose perfect hair and expensive clothes couldn't hide the prison pallor. For the next fifteen minutes, Ronni Murray's revelations about Rebecca's husband's plans to flee the country did nothing to bring the roses back to her cheeks.

'Let me get this straight,' said the policeman, slightly hazy on what Ronni had told him the night before about why he should trust a journalist, 'you've done all this digging, you've uncovered a major crime with the embezzlement, cleared up the question of who was helping Charlie Cley to hide out, and revealed a secret affair between this dodgy criminal and the Secretary of State for Law and Order.'

'That's right,' said Ronni.

'And you're not writing about it.'

'*Sub judice* if you charge Tim,' said Ronni, 'so I wouldn't want to influence his trial.'

'And the Estella Chamberlain stuff?'

'Someone'll write about it eventually,' said Ronni. 'Once it becomes public. But I'm not interested in political tittle-tattle.'

'Hang on a second,' said Eliot Oakcroft. 'Hang on a second. Let me work this one through. If you don't write about it, Estella won't have to resign. There'll be no reshuffle, no new ministerial jobs.'

'Not necessarily,' said Ronni.

'Oh,' said Eliot, looking like a four-year-old holding a cone whose ice cream has just hit the pavement.

'Sometimes I wonder how she makes a living,' said Max, giving voice to the idea in Inspector Adrian's head and everyone else's except for Eliot Oakcroft, who'd retreated into musing on the best strategy for asking Rebecca Cley to come out to lunch with him.

'To business,' said Tony Wenhamville. 'Perhaps you'd care to explain, Miss Murray, precisely what it is you've found out about Tim and Charlie Cley.'

'Yes, please,' said Rebecca Cley, though whispered might have been more the *mot juste*. Miranda Cley held her mother's hand and looked at her, concerned. 'Yes, please do tell me exactly why my husband and his brother had me locked up for two years.'

Ronni's story was surprisingly simple. Extensive searches via Companies House and through contacts she didn't want to be too clear about when there was a policeman in the room had established that Tim Cley had always had full control over all the money in his and Charlie's company, until about six months before Charlie's disappearing act. At that point, for no obvious reason, the power of sole signature on various accounts had been switched to Charlie, and money had been quietly shifted out of the accounts to other accounts that Ronni's contacts hadn't yet been able to trace.

'When you say contacts,' said Inspector Adrian, 'that sounds like the serious crime boys.'

'On one or other side of the fence,' murmured Tony Wenhamville.

'I'm happy to share my findings, Inspector,' said Ronni, smiling at each in turn, 'but I'm not giving any clues who my contacts are.'

'Fair enough,' said the inspector.

The company's main accounts had been more or less cleaned out three nights before Charlie's disappearance, leaving just enough for Tim to keep the firm running day to day, so long as no one came asking for their bills to be paid. And then, with Charlie disappeared and the money apparently vanished with him, the accounts were frozen, leaving creditors waiting for their payments until they wrote them off or went bust themselves.

'What complicated things for them was the ransom story and all the blood in the car,' said Ronni. 'Tim was hoping it would be assumed that Charlie had just staged his disappearance. He never figured there would be so much press interest, and they never imagined that the finger would start pointing at Rebecca.'

'They didn't mean to frame me?' said Rebecca.

'I don't think it occurred to them,' said Ronni. 'And it wouldn't have if Charlie hadn't tried to make it all more exciting.'

'Sounds like my Charlie,' said Rebecca, staring at the scratched tabletop.

'I'm not sure that's not worse than actively trying to frame you,' said Tony Wenhamville. 'Thoughtless, careless, greedy man.'

'I'm not sure it makes any difference,' said Miranda Cley, offering a handkerchief to her mother, who was clearly holding herself tightly under control. 'They got her sent to prison whether they meant to or not.'

'I can't believe Charlie let that happen,' said Rebecca. 'Once they sent me to prison, why didn't he reveal himself and get me out?'

'Because he never loved you, Mum.'

There was an embarrassed silence for a moment, each of them keeping their thoughts to themselves. Tension you could cut with a knife. A solemn stillness broken only by the sound of 'Yellow Submarine' replacing the Ode to Joy again on the anti-Brexit boombox outside on the pavement. Max tried desperately to think of something to say to break the strain. Anyone. Anything.

'Right, then,' said Eliot Oakcroft, suddenly becoming

aware that everyone had stopped talking, 'if we're all done, perhaps I might take you for lunch, Mrs Cley?'

'We're not quite finished here, I think, Eliot,' murmured Tony Wenhamville.

'He did love me,' said Rebecca, quietly. 'Charlie can't have known I was in jail.'

'Of course he knew,' hissed Miranda, rummaging in her handbag. 'Can't you see, Mum? He slept with every woman he met who would let him. He was nothing but a charming bastard.'

'He's your father,' said Rebecca, glaring at her daughter. 'Have some respect.'

Miranda took a photograph from her bag and slid it across the table. Cromer Pier. The ice cream van. Charlie Cley with his arm around a laughing Lulu Marchbanks.

'Look at him,' she said, as Rebecca looked over her shoulder into the distance. 'You were rotting in prison, and that's my dad.'

'The girl's very pretty,' said Ronni, looking at Max, who wondered how obvious his blushes were. Diana's eyebrow also told him he'd better be prepared for junior staffer's question time when this meeting was over.

'I think, my dear,' said Tony, taking Rebecca's hand, 'you have to accept your husband was something of a rogue.'

Rebecca's eyes came back from far away as she looked into the kindly face of the white-haired old man holding her hand. 'Of course he was,' she said. 'Why on earth do you think I married him? He was the most fun human being on the earth, and he made me feel like nothing in the world could possibly go wrong when I was with him.'

'A knave and a scoundrel, my dear, and far too wicked to have won a prize such as you.'

Rebecca smiled at Tony Wenhamville at that. Max was aware of seeing the reactions of seven people all at once. Miranda furious with her father and her mother and the world. Diana slightly repelled but fascinated by the old-world charm that was bringing Rebecca back into the room. Ronni quietly watchful. Inspector Adrian examining Ronni. And Eliot, well, Eliot away in wherever Eliot's happy space was until the meeting was over and he could go to lunch.

'I know you're right,' said Rebecca Cley, focusing her attention only on Tony Wenhamville, 'of course you are. But I have to tell myself that I loved him and he loved me and I had the best times of my life with him, and I don't know what I'm going to do with my freedom and my money now that he isn't here to share it with me.'

'For God's sake, Mum,' said Miranda. 'You were shagging Patrick Alderton while he was still alive.'

'What?' said Inspector Adrian, his hand automatically reaching inside his jacket for his police notebook.

'I flirted with Patrick,' said Rebecca. 'I flirted with him to make Charlie jealous. But Charlie just laughed. He knew I wouldn't be with anyone except him.'

'You had a relationship with Patrick Alderton?' asked Adrian.

'I think she just said she didn't,' said Ronni Murray.

'It wasn't me Patrick was interested in,' said Rebecca, glancing across at her daughter. Miranda Cley got to her feet.

'This is ridiculous,' she said. 'I'm wasting my time even being here.'

Miranda squeezed her way around the conference table towards the door. Making a dramatic exit wasn't easy when a room was too small to hold eight people and furniture. Max signalled Diana to follow her, and Diana's eyebrow said no.

'She'll need an escort out of the building,' he said as Miranda made it through the door, and Diana grimaced at him as she followed.

'Are we done?' said Eliot. 'I wonder if you have any plans for lunch, Mrs Cley.'

'Do be quiet, Eliot,' said Tony Wenhamville. 'Mrs Cley, I think you have to accept that your husband was prepared to see you remain in prison so long as he made off with the money.'

'I know,' said Rebecca.

'What exactly was your relationship with Patrick Alderton?' said Inspector Adrian.

'He did some work for me. I flirted with him once, one weekend, when Charlie was home, just to annoy Charlie, when Miranda had told me, yet again, that Charlie had been coming on to one of her friends when he picked her up from a concert.'

'And that's it?'

'That's it, Inspector. I threw Patrick Alderton out of the

house when I found him attempting to kiss my daughter in the kitchen one Saturday afternoon.'

'He was kissing Miranda?'

'I prefer to think so. That was the last time I saw him until my trial, when he was allowed to stand in the witness box telling all those lies about having an affair with me. And if I ever see that man again, I will kill him.'

The sheer intensity of Rebecca's final words left an awkward silence hanging in the room. Adrian opened his mouth to ask another question, but Ronni put a hand on his arm and shook her head at him. Max poured some water from a carafe on the table and slid it across to Rebecca, who was staring into space somewhere outside the window again. If she noticed the mild film of dust in the glass as she drank it, she gave no sign. Tony Wenhamville was still holding her hand, and patted it. Eliot Oakcroft was reading a message on his phone and beaming gently.

It was Tony, dropping Rebecca's hand at last, who broke the silence.

'It is, I think you'll agree, Inspector Adrian, pretty clearly established that Tim Cley, fully aware that Charlie was alive, and taking back full control himself of the company finances as soon as he could, was keeping Charlie under cover at his cottage in Norfolk.'

'He's admitted as much,' said Adrian. 'When we first picked him up yesterday evening he denied it all, but a night in the cells seems to have made him figure he isn't getting out of anything at this stage. He admits he and Charlie cooked up the plan to filch all the money. The company was going bust, there was no real work coming in – lots of bills to pay, lots of people who'd given them loans demanding their interest and wanting their capital back.'

'So he was keeping Charlie fed and watered and informed about what was going on.'

'Needed Charlie to lay low until the dust settled, and the plan was they took off together for Jamaica or wherever later this year. He couldn't curse Charlie enough for being dumb enough to get his photo taken on Cromer Pier.'

'My husband,' said Rebecca Cley, coming out of her trance. 'Tim can't have known him well if he thought Charlie wouldn't be off on a spree the second his back was turned.'

'He did,' said Inspector Adrian. 'But he couldn't keep watch on Charlie all the time, could he? With the cat away, Charlie was out looking for a good time, not knowing he was signing his death warrant.'

'But who executed it?' said Ronni Murray. 'Tim Cley didn't kill Charlie, did he? And we have no idea how Patrick Alderton fits into this, how he found out where Charlie was, and why he would kill Charlie, if he did kill Charlie.'

'No,' said Max. 'No, we don't know that yet.'

'Isn't it obvious?' said Inspector Adrian. 'Uncle Tim couldn't be there to keep an eye on Charlie or deliver things to him. He had to have some sort of go-between, and Patrick Alderton would do anything for money.'

'But we've established that Alderton didn't know exactly

where Charlie Cley was living,' said Max. 'He had to ask at the pub where he'd find him.'

'It is, in my judgement, unlikely that Alderton is the killer,' said Tony Wenhamville. The old man left a silence after his remark, almost as if he were still an Appeal Court judge knowing that no one would speak while he was addressing them from the bench. 'I can see no reason why Alderton would kill Charlie Cley. Steal from him, certainly. Cuckold him, without a doubt. Beat him up, unquestionably. But there is no obvious reason in this case why Patrick Alderton would wish Charlie Cley dead when he was so obviously in a position to provide Alderton with money and quite a substantial portion of the stuff. And if a man like Alderton were going to murder a Charlie Cley, he wouldn't do it via something as subtle as a drop of poison in a glass of Burgundy.'

'He still hasn't turned himself in or made arrangements to meet Mr Murray once more,' said Inspector Adrian. 'For now, he remains suspect number one.'

'As is reasonable, my dear inspector,' said Tony Wenhamville, 'given the absence of any other clear suspect. But two key questions remain to be resolved. The first and perhaps most obvious is why Patrick Alderton would murder Charlie Cley. But who put him up to it by telling him that Charlie Cley was there is a much more interesting line of enquiry, wouldn't you say?'

Rebecca Cley had left immediately after the meeting, once more ignoring Eliot Oakcroft's offer of a very decent lunch at the Chopsteak Club, entirely at his own expense.

'Another time, perhaps,' said Eliot, hopefully. They were in the vaulted Westminster Hall by now, and Miranda Cley, looking like thunder, was tapping her foot, impatient to be away, while Diana Burton stood next to her.

'Another time, yes,' said Rebecca Cley, backing away from Eliot. 'I'll be in touch when I get my diary sorted out. And when Miranda's free to join us.'

'Me?' said Miranda. 'I'm not coming to dinner with him.'

'Charming as your lovely daughter's company is,' said Eliot, 'perhaps it would be better tête-à-tête. To discuss the aims of the new charity, that is. I'm visiting my old friend Roger St George up at Fincham Hall over the weekend. Perhaps we might squeeze in dinner nearby.'

'Are you seriously suggesting my mum and I meet you for dinner at Fincham,' said Miranda, appalled. 'Do you remember my dad died there?'

'Well, perhaps not absolutely in Fincham itself,' said Eliot. 'I doubt there's a decent eatery there anyway, from what St George says about the locals.'

'Just the one pub,' said Diana.

'It's just about horrible enough for him,' said Miranda, glaring back over her shoulder at Eliot as she led her mother away from him and Diana. 'Seriously grim pub.'

'I think I've got a date, there,' said Eliot once they'd gone.

'It *is* a seriously grim pub,' said Diana. 'Interesting, interesting.'

Eliot himself had sloped off shortly afterwards, very

possibly in the direction of the Chopsteak in the hope of finding someone to share a steak and claret with him, and even better pick up the bill.

'He's coming on a bit strong with the grieving widow, isn't he?' said Inspector Adrian to Max as Max escorted him back out of the Palace of Westminster. 'I looked him up before I came down today, and Wikipedia reckons that there's a Mrs Eliot Oakcroft waiting for him at home.'

'There is,' said Max. 'Married eighteen years, two kids, both safely packed off to school.'

'Just goes to show,' said the inspector, looking moonily at Ronni Murray again. 'Someone for us all if the likes of him can find someone to marry them. God have mercy on her soul.'

'I wouldn't worry about her too much,' said Ronni, who'd met Max's boss's wife twice. 'There's only one thing worse than being married to Eliot. And that's being married to Mrs Oakcroft.'

'Would you be busy for lunch?' said Adrian to Ronni.

'Circle Line from Westminster goes straight to Liverpool Street,' said Ronni. 'You can be back in Norwich cop shop by about three if you leave now.'

'Right, of course, fine, absolutely,' said Adrian, handing Max his visitor badge and walking sadly towards the exit.

'Bit harsh,' said Diana. 'Seems a nice guy.'

'I'll give him a call later,' said Ronni. 'Easier to avoid the cow eyes if he's a hundred miles away. Now, how do I get out of here without running into him at the Tube station?'

When the inspector and Ronni were safely off the premises,

Max walked back up to the office to find Diana boiling the kettle. 'Any idea where Eliot's gone?' she said.

'Nope, but he's got votes at seven so I expect he'll be back before then,' said Max. You could say what you liked about Eliot, and there was plenty that could be said, but he was punctilious about being in the Commons for every vote – the Whips weren't going to have to text him or ring him up to find out why he'd missed one. And there were worse MPs to work for. Well, at least, there were MPs no better focused but who kept their staff on a much tighter leash. It wasn't every MP who'd have let their staff effectively take a couple of weeks off from the accumulating routine work of their office. Max skimmed quickly down the 342 unopened emails in his inbox. Such a flood of information, it was hardly surprising so little got done in MPs' offices. He arranged the emails by sender rather than date received, and began the satisfying task of deleting everything from Party Central Office, the House of Commons authorities and the various GOV.UK and news feeds he subscribed to. Never anything in them that required any action, even if they distracted him too often with snippets of handy gossip. He sometimes thought of simply cancelling or blocking them all, but hearsay was such a Westminster currency that he couldn't quite bring himself to choke off the supply. Five minutes' rapid scanning and deleting brought the tally down to a more manageable 147, and he set himself to a couple of hours of concentrated work.

'It's not really satisfying, though, is it?' said Diana after about five minutes' worth.

'Hmm?' said Max. He was reading, for the third time, an email from one of Eliot's regular constituent correspondents, trying to figure out, for the sake of a reply, whether the man was for or against the tax cuts he FELT SO STRONGLY ABOUT. Even in his comparative youth, Max could still remember when the House of Commons had received letters written on paper, often in green ink and sometimes in crayon. He felt almost nostalgic for the deranged correspondents of his early years in the job; so much more effort made than simply putting the caps lock on and hitting 'send'.

'We still don't know who killed Charlie Cley,' said Diana, 'and I don't know about you, but I'm not honestly concentrating very hard on the Government's new plans for urban regeneration in the coalfield communities when I could be trying to find out who that was.'

'Very important, the coalfield communities,' said Max.

'Yes, but they have been for about forty years and this is new plan number twenty-three, so there'll be another one along next year and we could be spending our time doing something useful instead.'

'Nothing we can do,' said Max. 'The police will find Patrick Alderton eventually.'

'He didn't do it,' said Diana. 'Tony doesn't think he did, and nor do I.'

'No, me neither,' said Max. 'You're right – why kill the golden goose? He'd want money from Charlie and Tim if he knew what they were doing.'

'And where is he?' said Diana.

'We all want to know that.'

'No, I mean why hasn't he called you back?'

Max steepled his fingers beneath his chin. She was right. Why hadn't Patrick Alderton been back in touch? It was twenty-four hours since the man had demanded money, a phone and a guarantee of immunity, and he'd sounded desperate then. The radio silence since that call made no sense at all.

'He really can't have got far on that forty quid I left him,' he said. 'And he still hasn't used his cash card.'

'I think Adrian's wrong about him needing that,' said Diana. 'Alderton's a fly-by-night handyman. He's a cash-in-hand kind of a guy. He won't be putting everything he earns through the books, and he won't be putting it all in a bank account, either. I bet he had a stash hidden somewhere at home. I bet that's why he was out in the woods that night. Waiting to get home to dig it up.'

'So why ask us for money?'

'He needs someone to talk to. He's been framed for murder and he doesn't have any friends.'

'Someone's got to be sheltering him.'

'Not necessarily.'

'Where is he then?'

'Where would you be, Max,' said Diana, 'if everyone had been hunting you for days and thought you were as far away from home as you could be?'

'You do know this is crazy,' said Max as his Bentley pulled off the road at Wymondham once more and turned down the long narrow lane towards Patrick Alderton's place and the Cley mansion. The light had faded now, and a smattering of rain had created a damp smir that meant looking at the lane through the windscreen was like looking through gauze.

'You only live once,' said Diana cheerfully.

You only live once. And potentially not for long if you were driving in the dark in the middle of the back of beyond to the home of a desperate man on the run from the law who possessed to your certain knowledge at least one fully functioning rifle. As he dipped the lights to begin the approach to Patrick Alderton's house, Max glanced across at his junior researcher, happily humming to herself whatever was playing on her headphones as she sprayed bits of crisp across his white leather upholstery. For a careful, considered, even cautious man who had, after all, spent fifteen years working for the same fairly unsuccessful MP, this madcap escapade should have been scaring the willies out of him. The rewards of the MP's researcher were small – a freed prisoner here, a constituent helped out of debt or other trouble there, a minor amendment to a piece of legislation, a few column inches for a well-written speech or a well-coined phrase. But

Max valued those rewards and would be glad to be back to obtaining them as soon as all this was over. For now, though, as he slowed to a stop in the lane outside Alderton's house, spiders dancing lightly up his spine, adrenalin coursing through his veins, he realised he felt more alive than he had in a decade.

The house, hidden behind hedges, was dark, no sign of occupation. Alderton's van, as it had been since the police had driven it back after he disappeared, was in the yard in front of the single-storey building – a yard that was probably once a small lawn or garden before the imperative of parking any vehicle as few steps from the front door as possible was established. Further up the lane, the Cley house, so much larger, was also in darkness. If Rebecca Cley and Miranda were home, there was no sign of it, but they could be at the back of the building, or in the furthest wing. Diana and Max walked to the end of the hedge outside Alderton's house and paused to make sure no one knew they were there.

The house was an oddity – a single-storey white-plastered building of little distinction, picture window to the left of a small porch hiding the front door.

'I think he's here,' said Diana, as they walked cautiously up the path to that front door, 'or he's been here.'

She pointed to a small woodstore off to the side of the house. Its door was swinging open, and two logs lay between it and the porch. Diana picked one up – dry in spite of the rain that had stopped an hour or so earlier.

'Or someone's here,' said Max. The picture window looked

tightly closed, so no chance of getting into the house that way without breaking it and alerting anyone on the premises. He was about to scout windows round the back for an easier one to jemmy open when he saw Diana tiptoeing onto the porch and trying the front door. And the spiders on his spine began an eightsome reel as it swung open and she turned back to him with her eyebrows as high on her forehead as they could go.

He walked quickly across to make sure he was going in first. Max was not, he thought, a brave man, but if anyone was going to be hit or threatened it was definitely him, not Diana. He should never have allowed her to talk him into this. He should never have allowed her to come with him. He slipped from his pocket the £500 he'd withdrawn from a cash machine so that he could wave it at Patrick Alderton if the man appeared in front of him wielding his rifle, a signal that he'd come to keep his part of the bargain they'd struck. But there was still no light in the house, not a sound, beyond the slight creak of the door hinge, to suggest that there was anyone here.

'It's fine,' he hissed to Diana, then screamed as something ran across his foot and realised that twenty-five £20 notes were confetti-ing their way through the damp air.

'Rat,' said Diana as she scooped them up, and Max shuddered from top to toe again. He hadn't loved the idea of confronting a gun-toting lunatic, but the idea of confronting a gun-toting lunatic while rats were running at him he really hadn't bargained for.

He stepped carefully into the hallway, hearing the creak of a floorboard as loud as if it were Eliot Oakcroft addressing the House of Commons. The place smelt of dust and damp, and a clutter of paint tins, toolboxes and discarded overalls littered the narrow passageway in front of him. Diana was behind him, her hand on his arm. Through the gloom, he saw a dim glow in what looked like the kitchen towards the back of the house, a lamp rather than an overhead light. Or, as it turned out when the two of them crept into the kitchen, a torch laid on the long, cluttered table. A man as fastidious as Maxwell Murray would normally have been troubled by the uncleaned plates and metal takeaway cartons on the table, the pile of unwashed pots, pans and dishes by the sink. He might in other circumstances have been revolted by the flies buzzing round the torchlight or the stink of a kitchen bin that hadn't been emptied for days.

But house pride didn't mean much when the body of Patrick Alderton lay sprawled in the chair at the far end of the table.

'Making something of a habit of this, aren't we?' said Inspector Adrian. 'Some police officers might take a dim view of a couple who keep finding dead bodies in quiet houses in the country.'

'We're not a couple, Inspector,' said Diana, smiling sweetly at the police officer.

'That wasn't entirely my point, Miss Burton,' said Adrian, smiling cheerfully back at her, 'but good to know.'

‘How did he die?’ asked Max.

‘Doc’s still having a look, but I’d put my money on the same poison that killed Charlie Cley,’ said Adrian. They were seated in the living room of Patrick Alderton’s house, just as filthy and untidy as what Max and Diana had seen of the rest of the place. Adrian had asked if they wanted tea after the shock of finding the body. Max had thought of the grime of the kitchen and politely declined.

‘Has anyone told Rebecca Cley he’s dead?’ asked Diana. Max had been avoiding asking the same question himself. With Tim Cley in police custody, he had assumed it wouldn’t be long before Inspector Adrian was walking up the lane to ask Rebecca and Miranda Cley what they’d been doing that evening.

‘Not yet,’ said Adrian. ‘And if you’re assuming we’re looking at them as suspects, you’d be right.’

‘They can’t have done it,’ said Max.

‘They’ve got motive,’ said Adrian. ‘Alderton’s lies got Rebecca Cley imprisoned for two years; Miranda Cley thinks he killed her father. They live a quarter of a mile up the road; they’ve got enough money to trick him into thinking they’d pay him for something. Poisoning him just like he poisoned Charlie Cley? Poetic justice. Some would say they’re bang to rights.’

‘But you don’t think he did poison Charlie Cley,’ said Diana.

‘Doesn’t matter what I think if they believe it,’ said Adrian.

‘Alderton must have had dozens of enemies,’ said Max.

'Hundreds. Christ, if you look at the state of his kitchen, it's surprising he hadn't accidentally poisoned himself years ago.'

'Curiously enough, our pathologist wondered whether he might have just eaten something botulitic,' said Adrian, smiling grimly. 'But I think we know he didn't die accidentally, don't we? Right now, my only question is whether they did it together, or one of them did it without the other one knowing.'

'Can we come with you when you go to see them?' said Diana.

'Course you bloody can't,' said Adrian, giving a nice-try smile and getting one in return. The smile was wiped off his face by a police officer walking into the living room, the constable who'd had to drive Eliot back from Norton St Meald a few days before.

'Well,' said Adrian.

'No one there, sir,' said the constable. 'Scarpered, if they were there at all tonight.'

It turned out they were not there at all that night. Rebecca and Miranda Cley had gone to York for a few days' luxury rest and recreation and, if the statements taken from hotel staff were to be trusted, had both been on massage tables or in a sauna at the time when, if the police surgeon was correct, Patrick Alderton had breathed his last.

Chapter Thirteen

'Case of whisky,' said Inspector Adrian, in a phone call Max let Diana listen in to on speakerphone four days later. 'Pretty much drank himself to death. Scotch. Bell's. Not the fanciest whisky in the world, but twelve bottles of it. We're working on the hypothesis that someone paid him for some services rendered with it, and he sat there getting himself hammered until he passed out and choked on his own vomit.'

'So he wasn't murdered?' said Diana.

'People do sometimes die without being murdered,' said Adrian, world-wearily. 'Let it go, Miss Burton. No signs of force. No signs of a second glass. No fingerprints or other forensics to show anyone else was in that house when he died. No suspects.'

'So what next?'

'My current caseload is three murders, sixteen burglaries, an armed robbery, forty-five domestic incidents and more shoplifting than we can count,' said Adrian. 'I had an hour's leave last Sunday and I haven't got the time or energy to spend any of the overtime. I put in a request to my chief for some additional constables. He rang me this morning, and what do you suppose he said?'

'I know you've made this one tricky for us,' said Diana, 'but I'm prepared to bet a year's salary on no extra constables.'

'No extra constables and, by the way, since I haven't completed my mandatory annual community policing and diversity training for the last three years, he's booked me in for three days for a residential course at Hendon so that I can be au fait – he's got a degree, my chief constable, he likes words like au fait – with the cultural standards required of the modern police officer. And when I get back, he wonders if I'd be so kind as to brief the squad – we're not a force or a service or a team now he's in charge, we're a squad – on his new effective policing framework and his plans for an information-sharing hub, and then organise his cross-cutting, cross-community clambake against criminality.'

'And this is modern policing,' said Max.

'This is modern policing. So, since Tim Cley is a criminal and I have the chance to bang him up, I'm going to bang him up, and then I'm shutting the file, putting it in a cabinet and throwing away the key.'

* * *

'I rather think that puts the tin lid on it, Maxwell,' said Tony Wenhamville when he, Eliot Oakcroft, Diana and Max met for a coffee in the House of Lords canteen the following Monday morning. 'You've done what you were asked to do, and far more. Rebecca Cley didn't kill her husband, and she's out of prison. Miranda Cley knows what happened to her father, even if, rather unfortunately, he's somewhat beyond her loving caress these days. Alderton probably killed Charlie Cley, then someone donated a case of whisky to Alderton and he shuffled off this mortal coil.'

'My own thoughts, in a nutshell,' said Eliot Oakcroft. 'Good job, well done, and all wrapped up. Obviously, we'll continue to work with Rebecca Cley on her new foundation now that I'm its patron.'

'She's coming in later to talk about that,' said Diana. 'But there are so many unanswered questions.'

'Ah, well,' said Eliot Oakcroft. '*C'est la vie*. Did you check whether she has time for dinner after our meeting?'

'She said she's got something else on.'

'Ah, shame, see if you can pin her down to a date, will you?'

'We're on it,' said Max. 'But Diana's right about the case and the things we don't know. Someone bribed Patrick Alderton to tell the police Rebecca Cley had had an affair with him when Charlie first disappeared.'

'I think we have to assume that that was Tim Cley,' said Wenhamville. 'I can't see who else had an interest in pinning the blame on Rebecca.'

'So if Alderton was being paid off by Tim for that, could it have been Tim who sent him to Charlie's house once we'd found out where Charlie was hiding out?'

Tony Wenhamville stretched his long legs out beneath the table, his hands steepled in front of him. 'That, I confess, puzzles me. I can't fathom why Tim Cley would want his brother dead when they were more or less ready to leave the country. If Tim and Charlie benefited from having Rebecca in prison, then a dead Charlie was the last thing Tim Cley needed.'

'Someone sent Alderton out there,' said Diana. 'Apart from Tim, though, the only people who knew where Charlie was were you and Max and me.'

'And me, of course,' said Eliot Oakcroft MP. 'You told me you were off to Fincham, didn't you, Max?'

'I did,' said Max, slowly, remembering the conversation. 'You knew the guy who owned the place.'

'Good old Roger,' said Eliot Oakcroft.

'Yes,' said Tony Wenhamville.

'Good old St George.' Eliot beamed into a pregnant pause.

'You didn't,' said Max, 'I mean, you didn't, by any chance . . . You didn't tell Roger St George, did you?'

'Of course I didn't,' said Eliot Oakcroft, drawing himself up to his full height, so far as being seated would allow. 'What do you take me for? You swore me to secrecy. Wild horses wouldn't have dragged it from me – silent as the tomb.'

'Of course,' said Max, apologetically. 'I'm sorry to have suggested it.'

'And I was out to lunch for the rest of that afternoon, as soon as I'd called Miranda Cley to let her know.'

Eliot beamed around the table, wondering why his two staff and a Peer of the Realm were staring at him quite so intently.

About half an hour had passed by the time Eliot Oakcroft remained absolutely unconvinced of the possibility that Miranda Cley could be a suspect in the murder of her father. Or, for that matter, be a suspect in the murder of anyone at all. Miranda was female. She was attractive. She was rich. Miranda showed every sign of having been properly brought up in a good middle-class home (Eliot's idea of middle class rather began with people who earnt six figures a year or more). She'd been to the right kind of schools and had been so properly finished by them that she almost certainly knew the correct method of drinking soup while wearing a ballgown at a Royal Gala. In short, there was nothing in Miranda Cley's person, upbringing and education that fitted in the slightest degree with Eliot Oakcroft's idea of who a murderer might be. And since the one thing harder than getting an idea firmly fixed in Eliot's skull was drilling an idea out of it, progress had been, and continued to be, somewhat slow.

'Inconceivable,' said Eliot Oakcroft, slapping his hand on the table. 'Poppycock, balderdash, an inverted pyramid of piffle.'

On another occasion, Max might have been gratified that

Eliot had not only remembered the string of insults Max had written into yesterday's speech against the opposition's economic policy, but remembered them in the right and rhythmic order. He forced himself to remember that the man had some skills.

'I mean why,' went on Eliot, 'why, I ask you, would that girl – that lovely girl, mark you—'

'Woman,' muttered Diana, for the forty-eighth time in the past half-hour, more or less without caring by now. She had moved her chair back from the table and was sitting slumped in it with her head back and her arms crossed, musing, Max imagined, on why no one had thought to murder Eliot Oakcroft yet. At least she was still awake, mind you. Tony Wenhamville's eyes had closed at least a quarter of an hour ago, and Max wasn't sure he hadn't caught a snore from the direction of the aged peer.

'That lovely girl, mark you,' said Eliot. 'Why would Miranda Cley want to murder the very father she called us in to find for her?'

'Your remarkable mind, Eliot,' murmured Tony Wenhamville, suddenly emerging from his gentle doze, 'has, as it so often does, arrived at the very answer to your own most perspicuous question.'

'Eh?' said Eliot.

'While lesser intellects would struggle to reconcile the conundrum of Miranda Cley's seeking your aid and assistance in discovering the whereabouts of her absconding and recalcitrant father, you have, in your own unique way, cut directly to the quick.'

'I have?' said Eliot. Max glanced at Tony Wenhamville, beginning to realise what the old man was up to. They'd all made the elementary mistake of expecting Eliot to respond to argument, reason, fact and evidence. Flattering Eliot into thinking he'd thought for himself that Miranda might not be all she seemed was an audacious plan, but it might just work.

'After all, Charlie Cley framed her beloved mother for his murder and had her imprisoned, in addition to which he would have left his daughter destitute by abstracting the family fortune. It is impossible to see how the poor girl could let the scoundrel get away with such ungentlemanly conduct. Charlie Cley, let us face the fact, was a mountebank, a cad, a bounder and an outsider.'

'Yes,' said Eliot, uncertainly. 'Yes, but—'

'And if, as a result of your expert exegesis of the puzzle bewitching, bothering and bewildering youthful Maxwell and young Diana here, that idea has now percolated through to an intellect as waning as my own simply because you have adumbrated it so articulately, then all credit to you, Eliot.'

'Eh,' said Eliot once more.

'I think he's saying you've cracked the case, Eliot,' said Max, trying not to look at Tony Wenhamville or Diana Burton for fear of cracking up. 'You've spotted that Charlie was a wrong 'un and that poor, dear innocent girl—'

'Woman,' said Diana.

'—had very little choice but to revenge her mother and claim her inheritance,' finished Max.

'And you,' said Tony, 'you, Eliot Oakcroft, have found your way through the miasma of misinformation, the fog of obfuscation that has surrounded this case with the very particular velocity of your intellect.'

'Well,' said Eliot. 'Well, yes. Well, yes, I suppose I have done that.'

'You are the instant coffee to the slow drip of my own brew,' said Tony, folding his hands in praise of Eliot Oakcroft.

For a second, Max thought the old man had overplayed his hand. But Tony's straight-faced smile of what might have been admiration of Eliot Oakcroft was sealing the deal. Eliot was preening, a cat whose fur had been thoroughly rubbed the right way. Diana, paying attention again for the first time in a while, was staring straight ahead of her, knowing that one glance at Max would make her burst out laughing. Tony, innocent as a choirboy, simply kept on smiling at Eliot.

'Yes,' said Eliot Oakcroft, finally, 'yes. The point is, what do we do about obtaining a confession from Miss Miranda Cley?'

Chapter Fourteen

'I don't like it,' said Max. 'I do not like this at all.'

'It'll be fine,' said Ronni. 'He's rung me three times asking for a date. He'll be fine.'

They were sitting in Max's Bentley in a parking bay in Norwich City Centre at 5.55 p.m., waiting for it to be six so that they didn't have to pay £7.50 to park for 300 seconds. Across a park and two streets further was the Unthank Arms, and in that pub in thirty-five minutes' time Ronni was due for her first date with Inspector Bernie Adrian of the Norfolk Police. A fact Max had found out two hours and a drive from London ago.

'I don't like it,' repeated Max.

'Which is why I didn't tell you I was seeing him. Maybe

try to remember I'm a grown woman and you're my brother, not my dad?'

'On any of the three calls did he say, "Would you like to come out with me and bring your brother with you?"'

'You'll not be staying long,' said Ronni, opening the car door. 'And he likes you. He'll be glad to see you. Think we can risk the traffic wardens yet?'

'I'm giving it until 6.01,' said Max. 'I've parked in Norwich before. And exactly how long do you think he'll be staying when he realises why I'm here?'

'He'll be fine as long as I don't talk about the case.'

'Which leads me to wonder once more what the hell I'm doing here, apart from being your taxi service.'

'It was the one rule we set when I agreed to go out with him,' said Ronni, getting out of the car. 'I don't talk about the case, and he doesn't talk about police work in general and the Charlie Cley case in particular.'

'So what,' said Max, locking the car and checking his watch, his phone and the clock on the 1930s art deco brick tower of Norwich City Hall to be sure 6 p.m. had passed, 'is precisely the point of my being here if we can't talk about the case?'

'I didn't say *we* couldn't talk about it, did I?' Ronni smiled. 'You've got him for fifteen minutes max, Max, and then he's all mine, OK?'

'You're actually going to date this guy?'

'No harm killing two birds with one stone.'

'Anyone ever told the birds that?'

'I like him. Diana likes him. Given my recent dating record, he's got to be worth a try.'

Maxwell Murray looked at the profile of his sister against the darkening sky. Ronni's peripatetic lifestyle since she'd gone into newspapering after university had, he'd always thought, made it hard for her to form much of a long-term relationship with anyone. And their respective dating was one of the few things they didn't talk about, she skirting delicately around the fact that he basically hadn't for years now, he forbearing to ask how she spent the few nights she wasn't at their flat in the weeks when she wasn't abroad covering some famine, war, pestilence or plague.

'I hope I don't spoil it too much,' he said.

'I guess we get to pull the nice-cop, nasty-cop routine on him for once in his life,' grinned Ronni. 'Shall we?'

Max locked the car, watching the skipping form of his sister heading towards the park and giving a cheery wave to the deeply disappointed traffic warden who'd just come round the corner from Bethel Street.

The Unthank Arms was near enough the perfect local pub. Hidden away in residential streets just outside the city centre, bigger inside than it looked from a quite large exterior, it offered decent pub food, a garden, a range of ales and, on its less good nights, local live music. This was not, happily, one of its less good nights, and Bernie Adrian was already sitting at a window table when Ronni and Max arrived, trying not to look as if he'd been there for forty-five minutes already for a date he knew was officially beginning in five more minutes' time, halfway through a pint and pouring peanuts into his mouth.

'He's seen us,' said Ronni as she opened the pub door.

'He looked overjoyed,' said Max, 'but he's here already, it must be love.'

'Don't upset him too much,' said Ronni. 'Vodka tonic for me, Adnams Broadside for him, and I'll be in the loo if he asks.'

'For fifteen minutes?'

'Girls take longer, Max,' she said, and skipped down a little passage as Max entered the bar.

'Mr Murray,' said Inspector Adrian, who'd left his pint and peanuts on the table to glower at him from the other side of the door.

'She's gone to the loo,' said Max, offering a hand, then taking it back. 'Broadside for you, I think she said?'

Adrian looked like he'd been hit by a truck, but managed a nod and turned back to his table in the window. There was a candle on it in a wine bottle. Two menus. Max gritted his teeth and headed for the bar.

'Two pints of Broadside, a vodka tonic and two packets of peanuts,' he said.

'Ordinary or dry roast?'

'One of each,' said Max. He couldn't see what colour of packet Adrian was already eating, so hedging his bets on the peace offering was the best he could do.

'One ordinary, and we've only got the honey-roasted ones, is that OK?'

'Does anyone actually eat those?' said Max.

'You want them or not?'

'Sure,' said Max, hoping against hope that Adrian had no taste buds. As he approached the table, though, he saw that Adrian's previous packet was blue, and steeled himself to eating some of the honey dry roasts in the cause of justice.

'What does she want me to tell you?' said Adrian as Max sat down.

'We think we've got some new evidence,' said Max, pushing across a Broadside and the nuts.

'Case is closed. Tim Cley's been charged. The CPS are taking it from here.'

'We don't think he did it.'

'He's admitted he was keeping Charlie Cley in the cottage in Fincham. Plan was to disappear abroad with the money the pair of them abstracted from the company accounts. Only some of it's still missing and Tim doesn't know where it is. He underestimated Charlie, who filched it, and when he found out, he lost the rag and killed him.'

'With a poisoned bottle of wine,' said Max. 'Chassagne-Montrachet 1978, no less. Charlie's favourite. Not exactly a crime of passion, is it? Not exactly losing the rag and shoving a knife into him.'

'Case is closed, OK. We've all moved on. Plenty more for us to be doing.'

'You don't believe Tim Cley did this any more than I do.'

'I do,' said Adrian, reaching at last for the peanuts and tearing the packet, 'but let's imagine for a second that I don't and there's a better suspect in the frame.'

'Miranda Cley,' said Max.

'And I think we're done here,' said Adrian. 'Have you got a signal you're giving your sister when you and I are done and I can get on with giving her a bit of dinner?'

'Hear me out,' said Max. 'If Tim Cley was providing Charlie with food and drink while he hid out in Fincham, then he wasn't using Patrick Alderton to do it, agreed?'

'He might have been,' sighed Adrian, sipping from his Broadside for the first time. 'He probably wasn't doing the grocery deliveries himself.'

'Granted,' said Max, 'but he has no connection with Alderton, and Alderton didn't know Charlie was there until he turned up on the day Charlie was killed, so what motive does Tim have for killing Alderton?'

'Alderton drank himself to death.'

'With a case of whisky someone thoughtfully provided for him while Tim Cley was already in your custody.'

'He could have bought it himself.'

'With what?' said Max. 'Day before he died, he was begging me to give him some money. Have you tested that whisky to see if it was poisoned?'

'I can't reveal details of an ongoing investigation,' said Adrian, folding his finished peanut packet into a paper aeroplane. Max waited until the policeman looked up and caught his eye.

'You did, didn't you? Same poison as the one that killed Charlie Cley?'

'Tim Cley has been charged with the murder of Charlie Cley and the case is in the hands of the Crown Prosecution Service,' said Adrian. 'You want another pint?'

Max watched as the inspector took three empties to the bar and ordered two more pints. The ice in Ronni's vodka tonic was almost entirely melted and Max wondered if she'd drink the diluted liquid when she finally emerged from the ladies' or whichever part of the bar she'd hidden in. He saw Adrian scanning the part of the bar he could see before the man walked back over with two more pints of Adnams and two more packets of peanuts.

'Honey-roasted for you, eh?' he said, dropping another pack in front of Max. 'I didn't think anyone ate those. Now, am I doing you for drink-driving after that or are you not driving back to London tonight, I take it?'

'Premier Inn,' said Max. 'I hate honey-roasted, by the way. Just didn't know which you preferred first time round.'

'Good man,' said Adrian, raising his Adnams for a glass chink. 'So, Ronni, is she actually going to join us, or is she just cover tonight for you quizzing me about Miranda Cley?'

'She's giving us fifteen minutes,' said Max, conscious that thirteen of them had passed. 'She wants me out of here because she really likes you.'

'She said that?'

'She didn't need to,' said Max. 'It's just kind of obvious.'

Adrian looked at him through narrow eyes and drank a quarter of his pint.

'OK,' said Max. 'She said she quite likes you and you're worth a try, but you ought to know that her job takes her out of the country quite a lot and it's difficult for her to maintain any kind of serious relationship with anyone.'

'Right,' said Adrian. 'To be honest, she kept telling me she'd be abroad a lot that night we went out in London.'

'But you shouldn't take that as meaning that she's not interested at all and just using you to get information for me.'

'Right,' said Adrian, sinking another quarter of his pint. 'That's what she said, is it?'

'Sorry,' said Max.

'No, fair enough,' said Adrian. 'I was trying to figure out what she saw in me, and at least that's honest.'

'She does like you a bit,' said Max. 'She's never been quick to commit.'

'I can work with that,' the inspector said. 'So, one more minute, eh? Until she's back and I get a shot at a date?'

'So, what do you think of Miranda Cley as an alternative suspect for killing Charlie and Patrick Alderton, then?' said Max. 'We think she thought her father was really dead, and then when she found out he wasn't, she hated him for framing her mother and putting her in prison. We think she paid Alderton to go out to Charlie's cottage but got there first and gave her dad a bottle of his favourite wine, nicely poisoned. We think she gave Alderton the whisky when she paid him off.'

'Nice theory,' said Adrian, sinking about a third of his third pint. 'Only Miranda Cley was in London when her dad was murdered, at the National Theatre watching Henrik Ibsen's *An Enemy of the People*. We've got the ticket stub and the programme to prove it.'

'Ah,' said Max. 'Right. But—'

'Evening,' said Ronni, behind him. 'Since I can't cope with my two favourite men in the world being in the same place at the same time, I think it's time you were on your way, Max.'

Max had since childhood been an early riser and hearty breakfaster, and the crack of 7.05 a.m. found him entering the dining room of his Premier Inn after a quick walk round the block to find a copy of *The Times*. He also, or so he told himself, preferred to breakfast alone, although he also admitted to himself that that might be more a preference for eating his sausage, bacon, black pudding, hash browns, baked beans and scrambled eggs without a commentary from his sister on the way his belly bulged over his belt.

He wouldn't be dining alone this morning, though. Ronni, bright-eyed and bushy-tailed, was already sitting in the window seat and waving at him to join her. Vaguely brandishing his paper at her as his eyes took in the black coffee, orange juice, granola, yoghurt and fruit on the table, he wearily collected the same for himself (quietly slipping a couple of pains au chocolat into his jacket pocket for later) and took a seat at the table.

'You've never been up at this time in the morning in your life,' he said.

'What makes you think I've been to bed?' she replied. 'If you're not reading that paper, can I have it?'

Max crunched his way silently through his granola as Ronni scanned the news sections, trying to work out if she was serious. Eventually, he cracked.

'So where did Norfolk's finest take you if you were up all night?'

'The Broads,' she said. 'He knows a little hideout there and we sat watching birds until the sunrise.'

'Wow,' said Max. 'Romantic.'

'He's an absolute gentleman,' said Ronni. 'And he knows a lot about birds. You'd hardly credit how much there is to know about birds.'

'Adrian?' said Max. 'This is still Inspector Adrian we're talking about?'

'He has hidden depths,' said Ronni, 'and he's really sweet.'

'Ah,' said Max. Sweet. The death-knell word. In earlier years, he'd fixed up dates with Ronni for four of his old school or university friends. The clouded, befuddled eyes of three of them when they'd been pronounced 'sweet' had stuck with him. At least he was still vaguely in touch with them; the other one had been a real mistake. He only hoped Ronni would let poor Adrian down gently when the end came. 'If you've finished with that paper, can I have it?'

'No,' said Ronni. 'Finish your muesli and get yourself down to the train station to pick Diana up.'

'Diana?'

'Diana Burton,' said Ronni. 'Remember her? The brains of your office.'

'Ha, ha. Why would she be at the station? How would she be in Norwich even? They don't run trains in this early, do they?'

'Overnight bus,' said Ronni, showing Max her phone. 'She's got something to tell you.'

Maxwell Murray stood at the counter of a café on the banks of the River Wensum, just out the back of Norwich Railway Station, waiting to order a cappuccino for himself, a black Americano for Ronni and an oat milk latte for Diana Burton, and a bran muffin, yoghurt pot, mango pot and banana. He was, he thought, as he stood behind a man in a suit who was trying to remind the boy behind the till that there was a station nearby and trains might be leaving before the crack of noon or the delivery of a flat white, not in London now. He glanced across to where Ronni and Diana were deep in conversation, planning to shrug an apology at how long this was taking. There was no need. Ronni was talking animatedly at Diana and Diana was talking animatedly back.

It struck Max, and struck him quite hard, that he was the only one of the three of them who had had a good night's sleep, and the only one of the three of them who resembled death warmed up. Ronni, for all her night out ornithologising with a lovelorn detective, was alive and kicking. Diana, even worse, had spent several hours travelling through the night on a bus and was fresher than a field of daisies. Max, who'd slept, was exhausted just watching them. How did they have so much to say? How did they manage to take in what the other was saying? When was the boy behind the counter going to make the card machine work? Was the man in the suit going to die of apoplexy – or conceivably old age – before that happened?

Eventually, he walked across to their table with a tray.

'Have you two had breakfast, then?' said Diana, claiming her muffin, yoghurt, mango and banana.

'Premier Inn buffet,' said Ronni.

'Did you let him have the full English?'

'Didn't need to stop him. Collected his granola, yoghurt and fruit like the health-conscious man he is.'

'Have you checked his pockets, though?' said Diana. 'I make him have all that in our canteen, but he usually sticks a pain au chocolat or two in his pocket he can eat later when he thinks I can't see him.'

'Don't let the fact that I'm sitting right here prevent you from talking about me,' said Max, guiltily wondering if he could drop the pastry in his pocket beneath the table before they made him turn his pockets out.

'We won't,' said Ronni, turning to Diana. 'Have I told you about the time he dated Estella Chamberlain?'

'He hasn't dated since, I've heard.'

'To be fair, Estella could put you off for life.'

'Let's save that story for the long winter evenings, shall we?' said Max. 'I'm sure we've got more important things to discuss.'

'Don't let us stop you eating whatever that bulge in your pocket is,' said Diana, taking a bite of her muffin. 'Now, Ronni, getting back to him and Estella?'

'So, what was it brought you haring up the road to Norwich in such a hurry?' said Max urgently. Both women looked at each other and laughed.

'Poor Max,' said Ronni. 'I wish you could see your own face sometimes.'

'Why are you here, Diana?' said Max. 'What's so important you needed to come up on a night bus?'

'A photograph,' said Diana, mysteriously. 'We started this case with a photograph, and I think I've finished it with one.'

'What photograph? What are you talking about?'

'Get your pastries out your pocket and eat them, then get on the phone to Miranda Cley to tell her we're coming out to see her.'

'What's the point?' said Max, pointing at Ronni, and guiltily removing a pain au chocolat from his coat pocket. 'Her boyfriend says Miranda has a cast-iron alibi.'

'My boyfriend's got a cast-iron skull then,' said Ronni. 'Oh, and he's not my boyfriend.'

'Ooh, isn't he?' said Diana. 'How was the date? No good?'

'Lovely, really,' said Ronni, head on one side. 'Sweet.'

'Ah,' said Diana, knowingly. 'Sweet. Never mind.'

'It was always a long shot.'

'Aren't they all?'

'Look,' said Max, 'if I can drag us back from the appalling sweetness, niceness and general loveliness demonstrated by the poor souls who are mad enough to want to date you two, may I just point out that if Miranda Cley was sitting in the National Theatre in London, she can't have been out at Fincham killing Charlie Cley.'

'Anyone can get hold of a theatre ticket and a programme,' said Diana. 'Doesn't prove she was at the show.'

'And how do we prove she wasn't?'

'Let's go ask her, shall we?'

Thirty minutes later, having put Ronni on a train back to London, Diana Burton and Max Murray were on the road out to Wymondham to visit Miranda Cley's house. Diana had been uncharacteristically quiet for about twenty-five of them. They were only about ten minutes away from Miranda's turn-off when she suddenly spoke.

'How much of a detour would it be to swing by Fincham to have another look at Charlie Cley's cottage and that pub?' she said.

'About thirty miles each way,' said Max. 'More than an hour wasted.'

'I've got an idea,' said Diana, lapsing back into silence and staring out of the window. Max was about to ask why they should divert when it dawned on him that the quickest thing to do was whatever Diana wanted, rather than arguing about it for twenty minutes then doing what Diana wanted.

By the time the Bentley pulled up outside the pub, Max had had another half an hour alone with his thoughts.

Inspector Adrian and the Norfolk Police were satisfied that Patrick Alderton had killed Charlie Cley on the orders of Tim Cley. Max Murray believed that they couldn't be more wrong, not least since Alderton had had to ask directions in this pub in Fincham before he could find where Charlie lived, so had clearly not been there before to deliver food to the missing man. And Tim Cley had only lost out from his brother's being murdered, so it was hard to see why he would have wanted Alderton to kill him anyway. No – Adrian, under pressure to close the case, was taking the easy option and he was wrong.

Which left the question of who had killed Charlie Cley and who had sent Patrick Alderton out to Fincham to take the rap for it. And who had then supplied Alderton with the whisky that killed him? And the obvious suspect, the person with the two biggest motives to want Charlie Cley out of the way, was the woman who'd spent two years in prison for 'killing' him the first time round and whose money he'd stolen – Rebecca Cley. Only Rebecca Cley definitely couldn't have been in Fincham killing her husband, because she'd been safely under lock and key in Norton St Meald Prison the day Charlie drank his last glass of Chassagne-Montrachet.

Which left Miranda Cley as the only person with means (her dad's favourite wine), motive (her dad put her mother in prison for a crime she didn't commit) and opportunity (Eliot had told her where Charlie was hiding out). But Miranda had persuaded the police she'd been in London when her father was killed, watching a play.

'Adrian said Miranda was at the matinee of the play, didn't he?' said Max, as he put on the handbrake.

'She wasn't there,' said Diana. 'We have to crack that alibi.'

'Eliot phoned her to tell her where her dad was,' said Max slowly. 'He phoned her soon after we left to drive to Norfolk that day. At about two o'clock in the afternoon. Who takes a phone call in the middle of a matinee?'

Diana stopped staring into the distance and smiled broadly at Max. 'I knew my boss was a genius,' she said.

'Eliot's a genius?' said Max.

'Not that boss, boss,' said Diana, getting out of the car. 'And we've got Eliot's phone to prove he called her then. We've got her. Come on. I think we've got even more than that.'

The shonky pub in its single-storey breeze-block building was no more attractive in the dull afternoon light than it had been when they'd last visited. Inside, this time, it was quiet, though. Well, mostly quiet. There were a couple of people at a table at the back window and the barwoman boredly twirling a tea towel inside a gleaming glass. And three loud posh men at the back table drinking red wine and braying at each other.

'Do you think they've been home since we were last here?' asked Diana.

Max and Diana walked up to the bar and the barmaid looked up at them with her big, welcoming, toothy smile.

'Hi,' said Diana. 'I don't know if you remember, I was in here a couple of weeks ago.'

'Course I do, darling,' said the barmaid, lying through her pearly whites. 'What can I get you?'

'Pint of Guinness for me, lime and soda for him,' said Diana. 'Now, I know it's a long shot, but I think I left my scarf last time I was in. Don't suppose you still have it?'

'I do,' said the barmaid, looking more closely at Diana, then rummaging under the bar before handing over a Hermès silk scarf. 'You're lucky, mind you – there was another girl in just after you and I nearly gave it to her. Surprised she didn't just take it for herself, given how lovely it is.'

'She must be an incredibly nice person, the kind her boss should be offering a pretty huge pay rise,' said Diana. 'And thank you so much for looking after it.'

Diana walked to the back of the pub to take the other window table, leaving Max to pay for the drinks.

'I nearly had that for myself, too,' said the barmaid, looking a little wistfully towards Diana as she draped the scarf around her neck and examined her reflection in the window. 'Two weeks and more it's been sitting here under the bar. I was surprised no one had come back in for something that pricey. I suppose if you're rich enough to own something like that, you can afford to be careless. If you wanted to add a tip, by the way, what with me being so helpful and not having sold that by now, it's on the screen now for you.'

Max sighed and added a tenner, and carried the Guinness and lime and soda across to the window table. Diana was examining the end of the scarf in one hand and her phone in the other. Silent, she handed him the phone and used her free hand to drink down about half the Guinness. Max winced: drinking something as fizzy as lime and soda that quickly wasn't going to be easy and his partner was clearly in a hurry.

Then he looked at the phone. It was the original picture he'd seen of Miranda Cley, the one they'd used to persuade Eliot Oakcroft that he wanted to meet the young woman in the first place. And Miranda Cley was looking coolly out at him beneath her expensive haircut and above the top of a loosely tied purple Hermès scarf.

'Miranda's scarf,' he breathed.

'Left here very shortly before we first came into the place,' said Diana. 'I don't think it was Patrick Alderton who was wearing it.'

'She was here,' said Max. 'She was here before Alderton and before us.'

'And I think we know what she was doing.'

'She killed her own dad.'

'Well, look what he did to her mum.'

'We still have to prove she wasn't in London.'

'We can talk Adrian into making a few more checks on that alibi, can't we?' said Diana. 'But it's easy enough, isn't it? She got someone to provide her with a ticket stub and a programme.' The other half of the Guinness disappeared in a swallow, and Max decided he could live without three-quarters of his lime and soda as they made to leave the pub to call on Miranda Cley.

'Hold on a second,' said Max as they reached the door. He walked back into the pub and over to a table at the back by a window. The three loud blokes who'd been drinking Cabernet Sauvignon the first time they'd been here were drinking Cabernet Sauvignon again and making a fair bit of noise about it. Max felt Diana's curiosity as she caught him up just as he reached the table.

'Excuse me,' he said, and three faces the colour of stewed tea turned towards him. Well, two faces. The other one had been sneaking looks Diana's way ever since they'd entered the pub, and was taking its opportunity now to goggle at her openly. 'Forgive me for interrupting, but aren't you Roger St George?'

The man nearest them rose to his full height. Plum-coloured V-neck jumper swelling over a domed belly above brown corduroys and brogues, a checked open-necked shirt beneath it, and a tweed cap on his head. Since his full height was about five foot two, Max didn't feel tremendously threatened. 'Lord St George to you, matey,' the man said. 'Have we been introduced?'

'I work for Eliot Oakcroft,' said Max.

'Good God,' said the man, taking a step back and spoiling the effect by nearly falling over his chair. 'Oakie,' he said to his two companions. 'Prize idiot's camped himself on me for the weekend. I hope,' he added, turning back to Max, 'Oakcroft isn't expecting me to find quarters for his servants as well.'

Max gently inserted himself between Roger St George

and the unexploded but now ticking bomb that was Diana Burton. 'Wouldn't dream of it, My Lord,' he said. 'And they tell me Fincham Hall's about as comfortable as a seventeenth-century boarding school anyway. I just wanted to know if you know where Eliot is.'

'Damn your impertinence,' said St George. 'And damn your master's too.' He turned again to his two companions. 'Oakcroft. Announces he's coming to spend the weekend, won't be put off.'

'But we're shooting this weekend,' said one of the other drinkers. 'And one of the essential prerequisites of a successful shooting party is the absence of Eliot Oakcroft.'

'Drives up to the Hall this morning, soon as he sets foot inside the place, informs me he'll be out all day for a practice shoot with some totty he's pulled, God alone knows how he found her – she must be blind and mentally defective. And off he spools into the woods, merry as a lark.'

'Oakcroft's gone shooting?' said St George's companion. 'Fellow doesn't know a stock from a breech. Accident waiting to happen.'

'The girl looked likely enough,' said St George. 'Handled her gun like a pro. No idea what she sees in a fellow like Oakie.'

'Good-looking chap, Oakie,' said the other, drunker companion.

'Does he mean Eliot?' said Diana, shocked to her core.

'Well, look at the rest of them,' said Max. 'It's all relative. Did Mr Oakcroft say who this woman is?'

'The Cley woman, the one he got out of prison,' said St George, stifling a belch. 'I expect she's been inside long enough to give even Oakcroft a chance.'

'It can't be Rebecca Cley, Max,' said Diana. 'She's in London launching her charity today.'

'Miranda, then,' said Max. 'We need to go. Where, exactly, were they going for this private shooting practice?'

'Fincham Woods,' said St George. 'Drive past the Hall and there's a car park. My clay pigeon range is behind it. Find Miss MacPherson and find out if Oakcroft's managed to blow his own foot off yet.' St George slumped back into his seat to join the brays of laughter that greeted this shaft of Wildean wit.

Max and Diana were at the door as St George yelled after them, 'And if you find your blasted master, you can tell him to stop treating my home as if it were an hotel. If he's in after midnight, tell him, there's a garden shed he can sleep in.'

'Why on earth would Eliot be seeing Miranda Cley?' asked Max as his speedometer hit fifty on the narrow country road.

'Yesterday, when Miranda and Rebecca were leaving Westminster, Eliot mentioned Fincham and the pub and Miranda said the pub was horrible.'

'So what? It is horrible.'

'But how does someone like Miranda Cley know that?' said Diana. 'Finishing school and tailored suits and vintage wines, Miranda Cley knows all about. Crappy pubs in back-of-beyond villages, she does not. I saw her face as she said it, realising that she'd just told us she'd been to that pub, knew where it was, knew how grim it is. She's going to kill him. She thinks he's on to her.'

'She can't think Eliot's figured all that out. She's met him.'

'He was the one who told her where Charlie was, Max. He's the only one who knows she knew where to find him.'

'Apart from us,' said Max.

'We can't prove it, though, can we?'

'And that's why you went looking for her scarf there,' said Max.

'The penny drops,' said Diana. 'I really am worth a pay rise, you know.'

'Assuming we've still got a boss to give you one,' said Max, the speedometer hitting sixty. 'Get on the phone to Inspector Adrian to get himself out to Fincham Hall as fast as he can.'

'Already texted him,' said Diana, smugly. 'The local cop's on the way, and Bernie's in his car, too.'

'Call Eliot, then. Tell him to get out of there. And tell him not to eat or drink anything.'

Diana hit the number on her phone, and her brow wrinkled. 'He's turned it off.'

'Shit,' said Max. Eliot Oakcroft's phone was never switched off. What if the Prime Minister called to offer him a Cabinet job? Or the BBC to ask him onto *Question Time*? Or maybe *Pointless Celebrities*? 'He sleeps with his phone on. If his phone's off, he hasn't got it any more.'

The Bentley's speedometer reached eighty-six as it turned onto the A47, cutting through the purpling of a still Norfolk sky.

The car park, as advertised, was a mile or so up the lane behind Fincham Hall. Eliot's silver Volvo was neatly parked next to a Land Rover with a trailer that looked as if it might have been driven through every puddle in the United Kingdom. Max parked the Bentley in next to it, and he and Diana set off down a narrow track, lined with hedges, leading out of the back of the car park. Halfway down the lane lay the corpses of two sky-blue clay pigeons, neatly bisected.

'You don't think Eliot did that?' said Diana.

'I think Miranda might be able to shoot,' said Max, grimly.

As they emerged from the hedges into an open field, a middle-aged woman in a blue cardigan, binoculars round her neck, tweed skirt and sensible brogues marched towards them, preceded by a fat golden Labrador.

'Are you aware that this is private property?' she announced, as if calling home the cows across the sands of Dee. 'If it's the public footpath you're wanting, you'll have to reverse and follow the public signage we had installed at quite considerable expense.'

'Would you be Miss MacPherson?' said Max, dropping to his haunches to welcome the Labrador's approach. 'His Lordship told us we'd find you here.'

'Did he, indeed,' said the woman. Max could see little

lines of disapproval around her mouth, but her eyes were twinkling sharply, her silver hair tied back in a neat bun. 'He does seem to be sending me all sorts this afternoon, doesn't he?'

'We're looking for Eliot Oakcroft,' said Diana. 'Have you seen him?'

'If he's the middle-aged gentleman with the girl young enough to be his daughter, then I've seen quite enough of him to last me a lifetime. You'll find them out there in the woods. Going for a walk he called it. I'd have rescued the poor girl if she didn't look more than capable of handling herself.'

'I think you might have misread that situation,' said Diana.

'Apparently, the gentleman,' said Miss MacPherson, and although she was far too genteel to wag her fingers in the air, Max could hear the inverted commas around 'gentleman', 'is going to be shooting with His Lordship and his friends tomorrow. There's little enough risk to the grouse, I'll grant you, but may the Lord have mercy on all their souls.'

'Did Eliot try the clay pigeons?' said Max.

'Not as much as they tried him,' said Miss MacPherson. 'Forty-five of them, I put up for him, not a one did he hit. The girl can handle a gun, mind you. I only put up a dozen for her, and every one of them right down the middle. Actually, just to get it over with, when he was firing at his forty-five, she sneakily popped off a wee shot behind him, and winged it for him. Fair away with himself he was. He's probably still telling her now he's finally got his eye in.'

'Does she have a gun with her now?' said Max.

'That she does,' said Miss MacPherson. 'She said she might shoot a rabbit or two as she walked. Your man Mr Oakcroft wanted a gun as well, but I wasn't letting him loose with a working weapon and live ammunition.'

'So she's armed and he's not.'

'As long as she's the sense not to let him have it,' said Miss MacPherson.

'Oh, I think she might let him have it,' said Diana. 'How far ahead of us are they?'

'If you follow up that way, you should come across them sooner or later. Here, have my binoculars to help you search for them.'

'Thanks,' said Max, taking the binoculars. A quick look told him how powerful they were, but a scan of the woods found no sign of a middle-aged Member of Parliament and a youthful murderer in sight.

'I'll be away home for my tea, then, if you wouldn't mind bringing back the binoculars and the gun with you when you're done.' Miss MacPherson marched away across the field, the Labrador padding placidly alongside her.

'It makes you wonder, doesn't it,' said Diana as she and Max headed up the track towards the woods Miss MacPherson had pointed out. 'Here we are trying to save Eliot Oakcroft so that he can carry on being an MP, when there are women like Miss MacPherson the world over who'd do a better job if they did it one day a week.'

'We need to find him,' said Max.

They climbed the track and found themselves on a narrow path between the trees, carpeted with pine needles and acorns. On another day, Max would, with pleasure, have breathed the pine scent and drunk in the dappled light creeping between the leaves to cast patches of shadow and luminescence on the path in front of them. A path which, he realised with a sinking heart, was about to diverge into two, one heading further uphill, the other dropping down into a shady glade. He stopped at the T-junction, irresolute, but Diana turned without stopping for the downhill run.

'It could be either way,' said Max.

'Have you ever tried to make Eliot walk upstairs or uphill?' said Diana.

'Fair point,' said Max, following her down towards the glade.

'We could try phoning him,' said Diana after a few moments.

'You said his phone was off.'

'I seem to recall you telling me he carried a BlackBerry, a Nokia and a pager. I doubt Miranda's body-searched him.'

'I'm hoping you don't use the word "body" again,' said Max with a shiver. 'And I don't think we should call. We might startle Miranda.'

'She's going to do more than startle Eliot,' said Diana, and Max shivered again. They walked on a few hundred yards, then reached a little clearing, blue sky above and a ring of trees for 360 degrees around them.

'Look,' Diana said, and Max saw that she was pointing

towards the far edge of the glade. A quick focus of the binoculars and Max saw that Eliot was chattering happily to Miranda as he led her back into the woods. They might have been a father and daughter out for a country stroll. Well, a slightly mismatched father and daughter, since Eliot's tweed jacket and cavalry twills gleamed as ceaselessly as anything that had just come out of the Ede & Ravenscroft suit carrier. And Miranda's tailored hunting coat and black jeans tucked into Hunters looked, by contrast, like she'd been born to wear them. Except for the rifle negligently resting on her hip and pointing straight at Eliot's back.

'She looks like she's ready,' said Max, handing binoculars to Diana.

'She'll want to get further away from him,' said Diana. 'She'll want it to look like an accident.'

'She tripped and the gun went off,' said Max. 'All the more believable if she's right next to him when it happens.'

'Phone him,' said Diana. 'Phone him now before they vanish again.'

Max dialled Eliot's BlackBerry on his phone. The insistent beep just carried across the glade's silence, and he could see Eliot jump and Miranda drop the gun's barrel to the ground as he turned towards her and began to pat his pockets. He could also see Miranda take the BlackBerry from Eliot and put it into her own jacket pocket as Eliot looked shocked and asked for it back.

'Come on,' said Diana, and led Max as she skirted the edge of the glade towards the arguing couple. So far as Max could make out, Eliot wanted to take his call, and Miranda was persuading him there was no need for that sort of thing when they were out together alone in the woods. Miranda had her head on one side, swishing her hair at Eliot, whose argument was running out of steam as he began to resemble a mongoose bewildered by a snake. Diana and Max had made up about two hundred metres on them by the time Miranda led Eliot back into the trees and out of sight another three hundred metres or so ahead. As soon as they were out of sight, Diana sprinted out of the tree cover and into the open, taking the most direct line across the glade. Max, unbuttoning his waistcoat, puffed behind her.

When they reached the path back into the trees, there was no sight of Eliot Oakcroft and Miranda Cley, but they could hear voices ahead, even if not make out what was being said. They followed, quickly now, heedless of whether Miranda might hear them coming.

And then came a shot, a cry of pain and distress. The echo of the shot rang around the glade, impossibly loud.

'Eliot!' yelled Max, and barrelled through a clump of low-hanging trees into a small clearing. Eliot was lying on the ground flat on his face, and Miranda was standing six feet away pointing the gun at him, a look of fury contorting her face.

'Well, that was lucky,' said Eliot, rolling over and massaging his ankle. 'If I hadn't taken a tumble, you might have hit me.'

Miranda raised the gun to her shoulder and pointed

it straight at Eliot and pulled the trigger. An empty click, and a bellow of frustration from her as she lowered the gun again, broke it and began fumbling in her pocket.

'Steady on, old girl,' said Eliot. 'I mean those things can do a lot of harm if you horse about with them like that.'

Miranda glared at Max and Diana, suddenly aware that they were charging towards her. 'I think you've shot your bolt,' said Max as Miranda's eyes flickered round the glade looking for a means of escape. 'And I think it's time you gave yourself up.'

'I tripped, you see,' said Eliot, 'went my length over that branch there, and blow me if Miranda didn't pull the trigger in her surprise. I think I may have a nasty contusion.'

'Do shut up, Eliot,' said Diana. 'We're a bit busy for the moment, and we'll be with you shortly.'

'I beg your pardon,' said Eliot. 'Any more of that sort of impertinence out of you and I'll be firing you.'

'Remind me why we're risking our lives to save him, will you, Max?' said Diana. Miranda, distracted, had broken the rifle and was fumbling for cartridges but dropping them on the forest floor. She screamed in frustration, then snapped the barrel back into the stock and began swinging her gun like a club.

'You can't get all three of us,' said Max. 'Give it up, Miranda.'

'Damn you!' said Miranda, swinging it at him, and missing by inches. As she stumbled past him, Diana hit her with a perfect rugby tackle around her waist and slid down her legs to knock her to the ground. And with Max ready to grab her arms and hold her down, the tussle was over as soon as it had begun.

'Steady on,' said Eliot, looking down at his two staff members lying on the prone and struggling body of the cursing woman he'd lately been walking through the woods. 'No call for all this rough stuff, is there. I mean the woman's a bit of a bore, but a lady's still a lady.'

'A bit of a bore!' screamed Miranda. 'You're calling me a bit of a bore? You?'

'She would walk on and on for hours maundering on about trees and rabbits,' said Eliot cheerfully to Max. 'I was all for getting back to the Hall for a spot of champers and a scone or two after my triumph with the clay pigeons. You should have seen me, Maxwell, dead-eyed Dick they'll call me when they see how I took that pigeon right out of the air.'

'I'm sure they will, Eliot,' said Max, 'but just for the moment, do you think you could sit on Miranda's legs while Diana calls Inspector Adrian and tells him where we are.'

'Right,' said Eliot, sitting on Miranda's legs as requested. 'And he'll be able to get some transport in here to get me back to the Hall, will he? Old St George must be wondering where I am by now.'

'Oh, good Lord, no,' said Tony Wenhamville, 'I was appallingly paid as a judge. This place was the fruits of my years at the bar.'

Max, Diana and Ronni were standing in the picture

window of Tony's penthouse apartment looking out over the River Thames. To the right, this side of the river, Lambeth Palace housed the Archbishop of Canterbury and sat in its little ring of trees and brick walls. Across the river further down, the House of Lords end of the Palace of Westminster faced them, fully lit, the white towers of Westminster Abbey visible from this angle off to its left.

'Worked in a bar myself before I got into Eliot's team,' said Diana. 'Must have done better than you 'cos my flat's well north of the river.'

'Point taken, Miss Burton,' said Tony, refilling Diana's glass with a bottle he'd discreetly covered with a tea towel when he'd taken it from the silver ice bucket on the table of his dining room. 'But I really did take an enormous pay cut when I became a judge, you know. Thought I should give something back.'

Max happened to know that judges of the Court of Appeal got about £250,000 a year and a concomitant pension when they retired. But having had a father who was a highly paid QC (as they then were), he also knew that a barrister in private practice could consider a quarter of a million pocket change. Tony Wenhamville, he also knew, was well aware that he was serving his best champagne to two parliamentary researchers and a journalist, even if he also knew that Max and Ronni had been left enough in property, shares and cash not to have to worry overmuch about what their salary packet contained. Max sipped his champagne contentedly, wondering how it was that Tony and Diana had formed an entirely unlikely bond, and realising that Tony would be happy to play the casual toff to her working-class hero all night if he let them.

'I suppose we really should have invited Eliot along to this,' he said. 'After all, he did sort of catch the killer in the end.'

'I fear dear Eliot is down in the constituency this evening,' said Tony, handing Max a plate of blinis with smoked salmon and sour cream. 'No doubt explaining to Mrs Oakcroft precisely what he was doing wandering around the St George estate with a woman young enough to date his elder son.'

'Have you met Lavender Oakcroft?' asked Ronni, with a small shudder.

'That pleasure has been vouchsafed me,' said Tony. 'The boys, I'll grant you, aren't bad chaps, but, then, their acquaintance with their parents appears to have ended when their prep schools first claimed them for their own.'

The four of them stepped out onto the balcony. Only one wispy white cloud in the blue sky. In the distance to the right, the London Eye turned its leisurely course. 'You can,' said Tony, 'if you lean out a bit and squint, just glimpse Eliot's London apartment block over there to the left.'

Max, looking at the sheer drop from this fourteenth-storey flat, decided leaning out a bit wasn't for him. Ronni, braver, and at her height less likely to tip over the balcony edge, gave it a go. If she could see Dolphin Square, she probably didn't know it.

'Have you been chez Eliot?' asked Max.

‘Chez Eliot?’ asked Diana. ‘Have we given up English entirely now?’

‘Dear me, no,’ said Tony. ‘That entire block is full of Members of the House of Commons. I hardly think it’s suitable for human habitation.’

‘To absent friends, then,’ said Max, raising his glass.

‘To Eliot Oakcroft, and all who sail in him,’ said Tony Wenhamville.

They stepped back into the dining room and took their places at table. Tony had arranged for a light supper to celebrate the end of the case. It stood on covered platters on a hostess trolley of the sort Max thought had last been seen on television game shows of the 1990s. His dad and mum had had one, he recalled; he wondered if Ronni, younger, remembered the same. It might have been the activity of the past few weeks, it might have been the exhilaration of having solved the case, it probably was three glasses of Tony’s spectacular champagne, but he felt a gigantic warmth for the old man, and for his sister, and for Diana. And he felt incredibly tired, as if he might just fall face down into the lamb with dauphinoise potatoes and spring greens that Tony had just placed in front of him.

‘I gather you travel east away, Ronni,’ said Tony.

‘I do,’ said Ronni. ‘Elections in Kazakhstan. Three weeks over there checking how well they’re conducted.’

‘I wish you good fortune. Perhaps they may elect representatives as fine as our own.’

‘At least they do elect them, Lord Wenhamville.’

‘Touché,’ said Tony, thoroughly enjoying himself. ‘Bring on the revolution. But until that happy day, let us drink and be merry. Would you be kind enough to do the honours with the wine, Max?’ And Max filled four glasses with a ruby-red liquid he knew would be as good as he’d ever tasted.

‘Tony,’ said Diana, sipping it, ‘I hate you.’

‘Not good, my dear?’

‘I won’t be able to drink Lidl’s Romanian Pinot Noir again, and I really like it and it’s £4.50 the litre.’

‘Send me a bottle and I’ll try it myself,’ said Tony. ‘Sounds like a bargain.’

‘Can’t send you a bottle,’ said Diana, ‘it comes in boxes or bags.’

They ate for a moment in silence. Whoever it was who was catering for Tony Wenhamville (Max suspected a silent cook out there in the kitchen) was a master of their art. Max marvelled at the food. The wine was as good as wine could be. The view from the window was unsurpassable. And, so, he had to spoil it.

‘It feels a bit much doing this when Rebecca Cley’s where she is,’ he said. ‘The husband she loved is dead. The daughter she loves killed him and is going to jail. We did the right thing, and we left her entirely devastated.’

‘And she’s stuck with running a charity with Eliot,’ said Diana.

‘Ah,’ said Tony, ‘that at least has been spared her. I met her yesterday and advised her to cancel that idea. She accepted, and will, in four or five months, quietly launch a new venture to spare women in prison the worst of their ordeals. She's a good woman and has accepted a donation to get things going, once the dust has settled.'

'A donation from who?' asked Diana.

'From whom, dear girl, do learn some grammar,' said Tony. 'From me.'

Diana got up and hugged the old man. 'And no Eliot involvement?' she asked.

'Three months from now Eliot will have forgotten her name,' said Tony. 'Now, if you wouldn't mind disentangling yourself from me – I think you may be embarrassing my guests, and I would not wish them to fail to enjoy every mouthful of this quite excellent meal.'

For a day and a bit, the sensational news of how Eliot Oakcroft MP had risked death to uncover a murderer had led every broadcast and headline. Eliot himself had been interviewed and sound-bitten on every major news outlet. But then two daytime presenters had an on-air bust-up and a minor member of the Royal Family was pictured rolling his eyes at a pensioner and normal news service was resumed. For Eliot himself, though, the afterglow of fame flickered long and lastingly. After all, if a chap had seen through the machinations of a would-be triple murderer and himself faced her down over the barrel of a gun – the word 'unloaded' had been banned from the Oakcroft office – then heroism deserved its full reward. Surely it was only a matter of time before Cabinet preferment beckoned.

And then, the weekend over, six days after Miranda Cley's arrest, came the moment when Estella Chamberlain quietly made that possible. Max and Diana were already in the office when news broke on the 8 a.m. *Today* programme that Estella had unexpectedly resigned from the Government to take care of her desperately ill mother. A friendly exchange of letters between Estella and the Prime Minister suggested both that she had been the finest minister since parliamentary democracy was invented and that she might return to front-line politics in due course. *Woman's Hour* planned to run a special on how women like Estella embodied self-sacrifice in face of the patriarchy. Max had to turn the radio off when a party grandee suggested that Estella was a great loss to front-line politics, one of the finest minds of her generation and a potential future Prime Minister.

It was but ten minutes before Eliot Oakcroft MP arrived in the office in a state of some excitement. If Max hadn't known his boss better, he'd have said Eliot had run up the stairs, and possibly run all the way from the one-bedroom flat the nation rented for him in Dolphin Square. Whatever he'd done and however he'd made his way to Westminster, his nostrils were flaring, his cheeks ablaze.

'It's under way,' he said. 'The reshuffle's under way.'

'It's a mini-shuffle, Eliot,' said Diana. 'They've already done the sensible thing and bumped Robison up from Minister of State to replace Estella Chamberlain. No wider departmental or Cabinet changes expected.'

'But they need a new Minister of State at Law and Order,

then,' said Eliot, a little of his energy draining from him.

'Nope,' said remorseless Diana. 'Ellen Bryman's been promoted from Under-Secretary to replace Robison.'

'Ellen Bryman,' said Eliot. Max was sure there was a box of Kleenex in the office somewhere and thought Eliot might need to blow his nose shortly. 'Ellen Bryman,' he repeated. 'Well, yes, women, need to promote more of them into senior ministerial, jolly good sign, pulse of the nation . . . But that means there's still the Under-Secretary post to fill, isn't there?'

A spectral, sepulchral figure had loomed in the doorway behind Eliot. For a second Max wondered if it was carrying a scythe, then realised it was Matthew Jobson MP, Eliot's next-door neighbour in this office building. The masque of death in a pale grey three-piece suit.

'Have you heard the news, Eliot?' Jobson said, and he might as well have been announcing that no such undertaking had been received from Germany and that Britain was therefore in a state of war. From down the corridor, Max could hear the sound of cheering, and a little bang that sounded very much like the popping of a champagne cork. 'They've made Alex Rattray Under-Secretary of State at the Ministry of Law and Order.'

'Alexander Rattray,' said Eliot, looking like a man on a plane to Monte Carlo who's just been told it's diverting to Luton.

'Good man, of course, Rattray,' said Jobson, almost ungritting his teeth. 'Rising star.'

'Popular in the party,' said Eliot, pulling himself together. 'A very wise choice.'

'Came into Parliament later than you, didn't he?' said Jobson.

'I've been here fifteen years. He's been here six. Younger than you, isn't he?'

'He's thirty-six, I'm forty-two,' said Jobson. 'I suppose we ought to, you know, pop next door, congratulate the fellow.'

'Of course,' said Eliot. 'Congratulate him. We ought. We must. We shall.'

'Mind if I take a pew for a few moments first?' said Jobson, sitting in Diana's desk chair. 'One likes to think through what one's going to say on these occasions.'

'Be my guest,' said Eliot, gazing out of the window at the inexorable tick and perpetual tock on the face of Big Ben across the way.

Max and Diana slipped quietly out of the office to leave two stricken, silent men to contemplate the lone and level sands of their shattered dreams stretching far away.

David Weir comes from Edinburgh and was a newspaper reporter, feature writer and film critic in Scotland and England for a decade before getting a job for 'a couple of years' at the House of Commons. Fast forward a few decades and he has worked in all its procedural offices and managed Select Committees including Treasury, Home Affairs and Standards. As he steps away from his parliamentary role, David is now at liberty to draw upon the experience of a ring-side seat in the Chamber of the House of Commons and the back-stairs knowledge of an invisible servant. *The Honourable Member for Murder* is his first novel.

Eliot Oakcroft returns
(along with Maxwell Murray and Diana Burton) in

A MOTION FOR MURDER

One of the few things Eliot Oakcroft MP knows is the secret of political survival: hire competent people and take the credit yourself. Luckily, Maxwell Murray and Diana Burton keep his office running with only occasional homicidal thoughts. Then Eliot is manoeuvred into taking on intern Robin Leishman, nephew of the formidable constituency chairwoman Dame Barbara Chard. Robin is ambitious, energetic – and utterly intolerable. Max and Diana soon find themselves wondering which of them will kill him first. So, it's a surprise when someone beats them to it.

Robin is found dead during a weekend in Eliot's idyllic constituency of Middlebury-Mid and suspicion falls on a local eccentric with a grudge. But Max and Diana aren't convinced. Robin had offended almost everyone he met – and in politics, murder is rarely the only thing people are trying to cover up.